THE LANDLORD

ALSO BY BRANDON MASSEY

THE LANDLORD

BRANDON MASSEY

DARK CORNER PUBLISHING

Published by Dark Corner Publishing

ISBN: 979-8-9854216-6-8

Cover design by Mark Thomas/Coverness.com

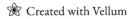 Created with Vellum

BEFORE

They'll be here soon.

As still as a wooden post, Sandra Carver stood at the bedroom window and watched the road, waiting for the prospective tenants to arrive.

She was a tall, gaunt woman who might have been any age between fifty-five and seventy-five. Lank, snow-white hair framed her narrow face and trailed to her shoulders. She wore a long, shapeless black dress and black leather flats.

Thin lips pressed together, she clasped her hands, as if in prayer.

She supposed she was offering a prayer to any god who might care. She needed a win. She needed these arriving prospects—any suitable prospect that day, actually—to sign a lease.

But there were standards, too. Exacting standards. Not anyone could rent this fine property and dwell in these luxurious rooms.

The tenants must be special. We must insist upon certain qualities —as we have very high expectations.

Would the family arriving this morning qualify?

A white Jeep Grand Cherokee turned onto the block. Butterflies took flight in her stomach. She had asked the wife what sort of vehicle they were driving, and this was the one.

They had arrived.

She turned away from the window and looked at herself in the mirror hanging on the nearby wall. She practiced her smile: show teeth, but not too many, or else you appear predatory. Smiling was difficult for her—when she smiled at children, they often cringed, and sometimes they snickered she resembled a wicked witch who feasted on babies.

She abhorred children. But her smile was ready.

She smoothed the front of her dress and went to meet her new prospects.

1

_____

"It's too good to be true," Cameron Woodson said.

It was a bright Saturday morning in September. Cam had entered the upscale Smyrna neighborhood—the ornate sign at the entrance read _Hidden Meadows_, which reminded him of a brand of salad dressing—and turned onto the tree-lined block that led to the rental house. When he saw the two-story home in the cul-de-sac, he said the first words that popped into his mind: _It's too good to be true._

His wife, Desiree—her friends called her "Dez"—sat in the passenger seat. Their three-year-old daughter, Ava, giggled from her car seat in the back row and bounced a teddy bear on her lap.

"It's a lovely home and neighborhood, isn't it?" Dez grinned at him, her eyes glittering like shiny pennies.

Dez was thirty-five, with smooth russet skin and curly, dark auburn hair. After six years of marriage, Cam still thought she was as beautiful as the day they had first met.

He was also thirty-five, and in his own opinion, an average-looking guy, five foot nine, with oak-brown skin and hair he maintained in a plain, low, and dark style. Sometimes, he wondered why

Dez had exchanged numbers with him on that day of their fateful meeting. As one of his college buddies had told him at their wedding, "You most definitely married *up*, brother."

"I've already made my decision, babe," Dez said. "We're taking the house."

He pulled closer. The house sat on about a half-acre of trimmed grass, framed by mature elms and maples. Colorful azaleas bracketed the front windows.

Although they had passed by a couple of other residences in the neighborhood with the same elevation—such cookie-cutter subdivisions were common in metro Atlanta—this one looked better than any of them. It featured sky-blue siding with red trim, and whoever owned the property had ensured that not a single detail was out of place.

"How did you find out about this place again?" Cam asked.

"Browsing online, of course. But it all checks out, babe. I researched the landlord's company on the Better Business Bureau website, too. They've got a perfect A+ rating."

"This house looks like something from a magazine."

"I knew you would love it," Dez said.

"Let me see inside first. And let me remind you: it's still above our budget."

"Boo to your budget."

Cam let the remark pass, but he felt his stomach clench. These days, every decision he made was based on their monthly budget. God knows, he wasn't pulling gigs as an Uber driver and part-time handyman because he wanted to meet new people.

A black Cadillac sedan, sleek as a shark, occupied the driveway, which ended at a two-car garage. A white panel van stood alongside the curb in front of the house.

"Miss Carver said to park in the driveway," Dez said.

Cam swung into the space behind the van. The bumper bore a flag sticker of some northern European nation—Sweden, perhaps. He avoided parking in the driveway because it felt like a trick to lure him into a sense of ownership: *pull on up, friend—imagine living here, come inside, and sign your life away!*

Dez made a *tsk-tsk* sound but made no further comment. He got out of his twelve-year-old Jeep and inhaled a deep breath.

The neighborhood was only ten minutes away from their Marietta apartment, but it felt as if they were in a different universe, one that he wasn't sure was hospitable to someone on his income level.

Yeah, too good to be true, he thought. He had seen the airbrushed photos on the real estate website. The house was huge: it boasted five bedrooms *and* a finished basement that was furnished like an apartment.

"There must be something wrong with it," he said. "Mutant sewer rats dwelling in the walls or something."

"There you go with that writer's imagination of yours." Dez rolled her eyes. She opened the passenger door and unbuckled Ava from her car seat.

In the past several years, Cam had published five thriller novels with a New York publisher, but he'd been penning wild tales since he was a teenager. His imagination never shut down.

"We'll find cockroaches as big as field mice," Cam said.

"You're so silly." Dez lifted Ava out of the vehicle. "Isn't Daddy silly, sweetheart?"

"Silly Daddy." Ava grinned at Cam, her face so much like his own that Dez often referred to their daughter as "Cam's Mini-Me."

"Neighbors from hell," Cam said.

He heard a grinding noise behind him and turned. At the house next door, an elderly man attempted to haul a trash bin away from the curb, with little success.

Cam approached him. "I can help you with that, mister."

"Certainly, young man." The neighbor chuckled and dusted off his hands on his jeans. "Want some advice? Don't get old."

Cam rolled the trash bin away from the curb and steered it along the driveway.

"Park it beside the garage, thanks." The man studied Cam as he shuffled alongside him. "Are you buying the house next door?"

Buying? Cam almost laughed. With his credit score, he'd be fortunate to put a dollhouse on credit.

"We're here to rent it, possibly." Cam maneuvered the garbage can onto a bare spot of grass beside the garage.

"Another renter, eh?" A dark cloud seemed to pass across the older man's gaze. "Good luck with that, then. Thanks for lending a hand."

"Don't mention it." Cam wanted to inquire further about the man's odd remark, but he spotted Dez on the edge of the driveway, waiting for him. "See you around."

But the neighbor was already heading back into his house. Cam met Dez and Ava in the driveway.

"What was he talking about?" she asked.

"He thanked me for helping him out." Cam shrugged, seeing no purpose in relaying the neighbor's curious remark. "Let's head on in."

He held Ava's hand as Dez led the way to the entrance and pressed the doorbell. Cam heard melodious chimes echo throughout the house.

"Fancy," he said. "They don't have doorbells at our apartment."

Dez smiled at him.

The front door opened. A tall, slender woman stood on the threshold; Cam placed her age at approximately sixty. She had shoulder-length white hair, penetrating eyes set in a narrow face, and a long neck. She reminded him of a bird of prey. Wearing a shapeless black dress and plain black flats, she looked to Cam as if she had recently attended a funeral.

"Good morning, Miss Carver," Dez said. "We're the Woodson family."

"I know who you are." Miss Carver tapped a silver watch on her slender wrist. "You're seven minutes late."

Cam glanced at Dez, who met his gaze at that same moment.

After six years of marriage, certain thoughts passed between them as if by telepathy. *Is this woman serious?*

"Sorry," Cam said. "Blame it on me. I lent a helping hand to a neighbor."

"You're here now." Miss Carver offered what looked like a practiced smile, because the expression failed to reach her piercing eyes. "Come along, then. I'll show you the property."

2

———

"Y ou're fortunate to have found this home," Miss Carver said. With a dramatic sweeping gesture, she beckoned them into the entry hall, their footsteps echoing off the gleaming hardwood floor. An ornate, sparkling chandelier hung above them.

"Nice," Cam said, and meant it.

"This rental is an absolute steal, and our landlord expects it to move quickly," Miss Carver said. "I must disclose that we've got several prospects arriving after you today."

Cam didn't like the high-pressure sales pitch, but he supposed the rental agent was only doing her job. Dez didn't appear concerned, her attention riveted on the interior.

"I absolutely adore this staircase," Dez said. The staircase swept upstairs in a gentle spiral, and Cam had to admit it was impressive. Dez turned to him, beaming. "And look at all the open space, babe! This is the kind of floor plan I've always wanted."

Ava took off running across the living room, weaving between chairs and tables, and Miss Carver looked at his daughter as if the child were a field mouse that had slipped inside the house. Cam chased down Ava and scooped her into his arms.

The place was fully furnished with contemporary pieces straight out of a Rooms to Go showroom, and it featured plenty of space—it had far more square footage than any residence he had ever lived in. He and Dez rented a two-bedroom apartment, and before he met her, Cam had shared a two-bedroom with a roommate. He'd grown up with his late mother and younger sister in an apartment in College Park. Living in a house would be a novel experience.

But he could get used to it. The big living room at the front of the house looked like a perfect space for an office. He'd never had a large area set aside for his writing business, and it was something he often fantasized about.

Remember the budget, man, he reminded himself.

"The home was constructed thirteen years ago," Miss Carver said. "The prior owner kept it in good condition, but when our landlord acquired it for his portfolio, he ordered additional improvements. See the kitchen?"

She strolled along the hallway, not waiting for them to follow.

Cam passed by a doorway that led into a two-story family room, a vast space with seating flanking a big fireplace. It was stunning.

He caught up with Dez, who had already entered the kitchen.

"Oh my goodness." Dez turned around in a circle, admiring the shiny new appliances, the cabinetry, the quartzite countertops. The kitchen boasted an immense island with a farmhouse sink. "It looks even bigger than it does in the photos."

"Sure does." Cam opened the refrigerator. It contained only bottled water, but he could imagine tossing a six-pack of his favorite adult beverage in there.

"Gas range." Miss Carver indicated the stainless-steel oven. "I imagine as apartment-dwellers you've been accustomed to those dreadful electric ovens."

"I love cooking on gas," Dez said. "It's what my parents have."

The French doors on the far side of the room opened onto a

broad wooden deck. Cam saw a massive playset standing in the middle of the grassy yard. Ava saw it, too, and pointed.

"We'll get to that, Pumpkin," Cam said. "Mommy and Daddy need to see the rest of the inside first."

"I'll set you free to explore further." Miss Carver smiled; the expression looked like a grimace. "The bedrooms are upstairs. Let me know if you have questions." She added: "I've got to prepare for my next appointment."

"It comes with the furniture?" Cam asked.

"What you see is what you get. As I mentioned, Mr. Woodson, it's an absolute steal—*if* you qualify."

If you qualify. He didn't like the sound of that at all. He glanced at Dez, and his wife gave him a hopeful smile.

They returned to the staircase. Ava raced up the stairs ahead of them. Dez reached for Cam's hand, and they ascended the steps together.

"What do you think so far?" she asked.

"There's gotta be a catch, babe. It's too perfect for the price."

"There's no catch, Mr. Glass Half Empty. It's priced to move. If we're interested, we'll need to move on it today."

"Can I finish looking around first?"

The upper level was as impressive as the rest of the house. A catwalk with a fancy wrought-iron rail spanned the width of the second floor and offered a view of the family room below.

They wandered into the master suite. It included a seating area, a gigantic bathroom with an enclosed shower and tub and dual vanities, and a walk-in closet as large as the bedroom in Cam's old apartment.

"I don't have enough clothes to fill this space," Cam said.

"I do." Dez grinned. "I could totally fill up this closet."

There were three additional bedrooms upstairs. Ava had claimed one as her own: she bounded onto the bed with her shoes on, and Cam glanced over his shoulder, worried Miss Carver would appear and cast a disapproving look.

Dez tried to open the closet of the room that Ava had selected.

"It's locked." She tugged at the door.

Cam noted a keypad lock mechanism affixed to the door. A PIN code for a closet? That was odd.

"We'll get the code if we decide to move in," he said.

"I want to see the basement."

They went back downstairs. They found Miss Carver in the kitchen, her attention focused on documents gathered in a folder.

She looked up. "Do you have any questions, Woodson family?"

"Still looking." Cam indicated a doorway on the edge of the kitchen. "Is this for the basement?"

"Naturally." She favored them with her grimace-smile.

A short wooden staircase led to the lower level. The basement boasted a large, furnished living area and a fully equipped kitchenette. It had a nice-sized bedroom, too.

"We could create a playroom for Ava down here," Dez said.

"Or a man cave." Cam winked at her.

He followed Dez around a corner, and Dez stopped so suddenly that Cam almost ran into her.

"Sorry," she said to the man ahead of them. "We'll stay out of your way, mister. Come on, babe—this gentleman's working."

Dez doubled back to the main area, but Cam didn't follow. The bear-sized man crouched on the laminate floor was so intently focused on whatever work he was performing on the wall that he didn't look in their direction. He wore a blue T-shirt with an oval sweat stain darkening the back, tattered jeans, and work boots. He smelled of cigarettes and sour sweat; earbuds were nestled in his ears, which explained why he hadn't noticed their approach.

A collection of tools and materials surrounded him. Cam assumed he was repairing drywall.

Cam was about to leave, too, when the man swung around to face him. Stubble peppered his cheeks, his face pebbled with perspiration. But his blue eyes were bright.

"You are new tenants?" the man asked, speaking in a heavy accent Cam couldn't place. He pulled out the earbuds.

It's the guy who parked the panel van out front, Cam remembered. The Swedish flag bumper sticker dude.

"We haven't decided yet," Cam said. "We're only looking."

"I am Thor." He stuck out a massive paw of a hand, his fingers smeared with dust. "I am handyman for Baron Properties."

"Cam Woodson." They shook hands.

Thor leaned sideways and glanced over Cam's shoulder. "Nice family, Cam."

"Thanks. Hey, what are you fixing there?" Cam stepped closer. "Is that blood on the wall?"

Thor's gaze met his, but the big man didn't answer the question. Cam tried to edge around him to get a better look at what he thought he had seen, and Thor shifted to block his view with a firm shake of his head.

"Your wife calls for you. Do not keep a beautiful woman waiting."

Indeed, Dez had called him, saying that she wanted to go see the backyard. Cam met her and Ava at the staircase.

"The handyman is cleaning blood off the wall," Cam said.

"Seriously? I doubt it was blood, Mr. Thriller Writer." Dez giggled. "Your daughter is dying to go outside and get on the playset. Let's head back upstairs and go see the backyard."

It was *blood,* Cam thought, the idea settling like a stone in his stomach. *I know what I saw.*

But why would such a lovely home have bloodstains on the walls?

3

———

"Have you made your decision?" Miss Carver asked.

Cam stood in the backyard with Dez and Ava. He pushed Ava on the playset swing, his daughter squealing with glee and screaming, "Higher, Daddy, higher!" When Miss Carver strode outside onto the wooden deck attached to the house, she reminded Cam of a teacher announcing the end of recess.

"Can you give us five minutes, please?" Cam asked. "We need to have a quick family meeting."

"I've got new prospects coming very soon." Miss Carver glanced at her watch. "Meet me in the kitchen."

Cam turned to his wife. He recognized the optimistic gleam in her eyes and didn't need to ask what she wanted to do.

"It's above our budget," he said. "But you knew that already."

"It's a dream rental. A steal, like Miss Carver said."

Cam surveyed the rambling, fenced-in yard, the fence painted eggshell white. The wide wooden deck included patio furniture and even a Big Green Egg barbecue grill. He had always wanted an Egg— his best friend, Victor, had one—but he'd never had the space to accommodate it. Or lately, the money.

We could throw some great parties here, he thought. Their apartment was so cramped that hosting a gathering of decent size was impossible. With a space like this, instead of going to Vic's place for parties, they could come there.

And maybe, just maybe, he wouldn't feel anymore as if his life had stalled at the tender age of thirty-five.

Cam had worked as a full-time writer for the past few years, leaving behind the teaching job he had held since graduating from college. When most people found out he was a published novelist, they assumed he was rich. He was about as far from rich as the earth was from Pluto.

And lately, things had been tighter than ever—his publisher had rejected his latest proposal along with every other house in New York, and none of his books in print sold well enough to generate royalties. His agent had lined up a couple of short-term, writer-for-hire assignments, but to generate more consistent cash flow he had joined the gig economy and started driving for Uber and doing handyman work (mostly furniture assembly) through TaskRabbit, Wayfair, and similar apps. Dez, a middle school teacher, was the primary breadwinner these days, and while she supported his writing ambitions, and believed he would get through this rough patch, he felt obligated to bring in whatever extra money he could while planning the next phase of his writing career.

Ava continued to laugh as he pushed her. His little girl was happy; his wife was watching him with shining eyes. Could he say no to them?

Dez stepped closer. He stopped pushing the swing, slid his hands around her waist, and pulled her to him.

"It's a perfect place to have another baby." She kissed him. "Add to our growing family."

"Uh-huh."

She kissed him again, nibbled his lower lip.

"You're awfully persuasive," he said.

"I'm not afraid to use my feminine wiles." She patted his butt.

"Don't stress over the budget. It's only eighty dollars above what we'd be paying if we renewed our lease. We can make it work."

"Our budget's already stretched to the breaking point."

"We'll figure it out. I want this, Cam. For us. We *need* this."

Unlike Cam, Dez had grown up in a single-family house; her well-to-do parents owned a McMansion in East Cobb. As she always told him, she wanted to live somewhere without walls so thin you could hear your neighbor flushing the toilet. She aspired to a home of their own, and he couldn't fault her for that—he wanted the same thing for them, someday.

But securing a mortgage loan was out of the question. With sky-high interest rates and his credit issues, buying a place wasn't in their immediate future. A rental property, especially one such as this, seemed like a viable alternative. A tangible step toward their dream.

"They're going to run a credit check on us," Cam said. "What if we're denied?"

"I already told Miss Carver we might have problems. She said they could probably work with us."

"If we qualify, like she pointed out."

"We need to give it a shot, babe."

Dez clasped his hand and beckoned toward the house.

Trying to ignore his knotted stomach, Cam followed his wife and daughter inside.

4

W hen they returned inside the house, they found Miss
Carver standing near the kitchen counter. She
smoothed her dress and donned her artificial smile like
someone popping on a hat.

"Ah, there you are, Woodson family. Are you ready to discuss the
future?"

"Uh, sure," Cam said.

"Excellent," Miss Carver said. "Let's adjoin to the dining room
and we'll discuss our next steps."

In the dining room, at the long cherrywood table, Cam and Dez
sat on one side, Cam bouncing Ava on his knee to keep her occupied,
while Miss Carver settled at the head of the table like a judge
presiding over a case. She removed an iPad from a slim black leather
bag and swept her gaze from Cam to Dez as if taking the measure of
them.

Cam noticed a fat housefly had landed atop the woman's head. It
circled about the stringy strands of white as if deliberating whether
to settle in and create a nest. Miss Carver seemed oblivious to the
insect.

"You have a fly in your hair," Cam said.

"Excuse me?" Miss Carver frowned at him.

"There's a fly on top of your head." Dez indicated her own head, tapping.

"Let's focus, Woodson family," Miss Carver said. "Do you wish to move forward with a lease application?"

Cam looked at Dez, and she rolled her eyes as if to say, *Well, we tried to tell her.*

The housefly buzzed away, for which Cam was grateful, or else he wouldn't have been able to "focus" as Miss Carver had chided him to do.

"Yes, we want to move forward," he said. "We love the place."

"Very good. I will be honest: we've a *rigorous* application process. Only the most qualified tenants may rent our esteemed properties."

He shifted in the chair, feeling a sickening fluttering in his stomach.

"But before we proceed to the formal application, I'd like to chat." Miss Carver steepled her spindly fingers and leaned forward, elongating her ostrich neck. "Tell me about yourselves."

Cam had never been good at fielding open-ended questions. For a moment, he drew a total blank.

Dez cleared her throat. "We've been married for six years."

"*Happily* married," Cam said, and Dez gave him an encouraging nod. "She's the love of my life."

"Ditto," Dez said.

"How sweet." Miss Carver offered her fake smile. "How did you meet?"

"Mutual friends introduced us," Dez said.

"Now, that's what I like to hear! Yes!" Miss Carver smacked the table with the palm of her hand. "Good friends taking it upon themselves to make a match! None of this smartphone app debauchery you hear about nowadays. Kindling or Tumbleweed or whatever the heck it's called."

"I think it's called Tinder," Dez said in a small voice.

"Hah! I call it trash! I'm an old-fashioned lady. I respect tradition and family values." Miss Carver clucked her tongue. "Hmph. Sadly, we've lost respect for those practices. We call them obsolete!"

"Times have changed, I guess," Cam said.

"What do you do for a living, Mr. Woodson?" She cocked her head, her gaze drilling into him.

"I'm a freelance writer." He heard the pride in his voice and hoped that didn't mark him as a braggart. "I write books."

He was expecting Miss Carver to be impressed, but she blinked, her eyes clouded.

"Books?" she asked. "Like textbooks?"

"Novels," he said.

"Novels?" She blinked again.

"*Fiction*. Stories." *Clearly, she's not much of a reader.*

"Make-believe tales?" Her lips crinkled.

"Thrillers," he said, resisting the urge to shout at her. "Have you ever heard of James Patterson? I write books in the same genre."

"I see." She folded her wiry arms across her narrow chest. "I've never heard of Jack Patterson, but I must inquire if you plan to conduct this fanciful business of yours in the residence?"

He didn't bother correcting her misstatement of the author's name; he was so put off by her tone: she said "this fanciful business of yours" as if he spent his time daydreaming.

Before he could answer, Dez grabbed his hand beneath the table and shot him a warning look that he could read as clearly as a stop sign. *Don't screw this up.*

"Why do you ask?" Cam said.

"Why do I ask?" Miss Carver straightened in the chair and stretched her neck. "Our landlord has a strict policy against work-from-home enterprises. We've had awful experiences in the past with tenants abusing this privilege, and now, we take a hard, hard line against it. It's a deal breaker, Mr. Woodson."

"A deal breaker," he said, the words like sharp rocks on his tongue. "Sitting alone in a room and typing quietly on a computer is a deal breaker."

Miss Carver only stared at him.

This woman is for real.

"May I ask why?" he said. "I don't know about your prior tenants, but I promise you, there's nothing disruptive about me writing at home."

"It sounds as though this item may be nonnegotiable for you as well, Mr. Woodson." Miss Carver checked her watch. "Are we finished here?"

"Are you serious?" he asked. "That's it, then?"

"Cam can write outside the house," Dez said. She fired a desperate look at him. "Can't you, babe? You can go to a café and work?"

He had no intention of leaving the house every time he wanted to work on a story, but he didn't dare allow this opportunity to slip away. Dez would never forgive him if he did.

"Sure, I do my best work at Starbucks, anyway." Cam tried to smile. "There are too many distractions at home."

"That's settled then." Miss Carver's rigid jaw relaxed. "There's another matter of importance we must cover: we have a no-party clause in our lease agreement. Social gatherings require prior approval from our landlord. Is that a concern?"

"We're not college students," Dez said.

"It is not our landlord's intent to dictate your lives. Our landlord has implemented these policies to ensure the safety of our rental properties, tenants, and communities."

"Right," Cam said. "No keggers, then."

Miss Carver delved into more questions. She wanted to know about Dez's profession (schoolteacher); why they wanted to leave their current rental (hefty rent increase); and then she asked if they intended to have more children.

Isn't that personal? Cam was going to reply, but Dez beat him to the punch.

"We'd love to have another child, God willing." She rested her hand on Cam's thigh.

"Indeed. Young, growing families please our landlord. It's a win-win for all parties."

Ava was getting antsy on Cam's lap. He took out his iPhone, found a *Cocomelon* video he had saved on the Netflix app, and dropped the phone into her eager hands. She hopped off his lap and clambered onto an adjacent chair, her attention fixed on the screen.

Miss Carver watched this interaction with arched eyebrows.

"I only want to keep her entertained while we finish this," he said. "It's not as though we park her in front of screens all day long."

"We'd never do that," Dez said.

"I see." Miss Carver paused. "Are you a religious family?"

"We're Christians," Dez said.

"To be clear, we don't go to church *every* Sunday," Cam said. "Is there a church attendance clause in the lease?"

He was being facetious and probably needed to shut his mouth, but the comment appeared lost on Miss Carver.

"We cannot dictate your morality, but we expect a certain standard of conduct," Miss Carver said. "We do not wish to receive notification of disturbances, calls to local authorities, that sort of thing."

"We're no-drama people," Dez said. "Aren't we, babe?"

"Absolutely," he said. "I keep my drama in my stories."

"I'm pleased to hear it." Miss Carver tapped the iPad's screen with a long black stylus and angled the tablet toward them. "Now, it's time for the credit check."

"We love those," Cam said, and he didn't know why he said it. These days, a credit check for him was like a root canal.

It took a few minutes for him and Dez to enter their personal information into the online credit application. He slid the tablet back to Miss Carver.

"Here we go," she said. "The moment of truth."

"Can I have a bottle of water?" he asked.

"Nervous, are you? Help yourself, Mr. Woodson."

Cam went to the refrigerator. Standing at the island, he chugged an entire bottle of water in a few gulps. He still felt as though he were going to vomit.

"Approved by the skin of your teeth!" Miss Carver declared with a clap.

Dez gave him the thumbs-up sign. Cam allowed himself to relax. He didn't know how they'd leaped over that credit hurdle, but he felt like dancing.

As he returned to the dining room, Miss Carver said: "Next, there's the matter of the up-front payment to secure your rental."

"First and last month's rent, right?" Cam eased back into his chair. "That's the standard."

"In your case, Woodson family, we must require *three* months' rent *and* the security deposit, which is an additional month of rent."

"What?" Cam almost shot out of the chair.

"Yes. That is the landlord's policy when leasing to tenants with, shall we say, challenging credit histories." Her eyes twinkled.

"See?" Cam glared at Dez. "I *knew* there was a catch. That's what —over five thousand dollars?"

"It's okay." Dez dropped her purse onto the table, unzipped it. "We have it."

"We do?" he asked.

"We don't accept personal checks, ever," Miss Carver said. "Cashier's check or money order only. That applies to regular rent payments as well—we prefer automatic bank drafts. Our landlord cannot tolerate the inconvenience of returned checks."

"Do you accept cash?" Dez removed an envelope from her purse, thick with dollar bills.

Cam couldn't believe it. Where had she gotten all that money?

"We are always pleased to accept cash." Miss Carver flexed her fingers like a child waiting for Halloween candy. "Gimme, gimme."

Dez counted out the payment and slid the envelope across the table to Miss Carver. When Dez caught Cam gaping at her, she said, "I wanted to be prepared for anything."

She got the money from her parents, he realized. Specifically, her dad. Lovely. He would never hear the end of it from her father.

"My folks," Dez said, echoing his train of thought. She found his hand underneath the table, squeezed. "I should have told you."

"You just did." Cam slid his hand out of her grasp. "Thanks for keeping me in the loop, babe. Appreciate it."

"I'm sorry, Cam."

Cam noticed Miss Carver watching this exchange between them with a bemused expression. He had no interest in arguing with Dez in front of a stranger. He could take this up later with his wife.

"Anyway, what's next?" Cam asked the woman.

"With that matter behind us, let's have you fine people sign the lease," Miss Carver said. "Please take your time and read it carefully." Her lips twisted. "You might be signing your lives away."

Using the iPad and stylus again, they reviewed the electronic lease document, which looked standard, in Cam's experience. Although the woman had pressed him about working from home and other matters, he didn't see any language about those items specified in the lease.

After they reviewed each page of the document, they initialed the requisite sections and signed their names in others. Miss Carver promised she would email the executed agreement to them shortly.

Cam noticed a lamp fixture attached to the wall in the dining room was crooked. He got up and inspected it and found a couple of screws had popped free from the mount. Now that they were approved, he might as well fix it himself. He kept a multi-tool in his pocket and used the screwdriver attachment to tighten the screws.

"Ah, aren't you the handy one?" Miss Carver said, a calculating glint in her eyes. "You say you are a writer, but perhaps your true calling is home repair, Mr. Woodson. There's always work available for one skilled with his hands."

"I didn't pile up student loan debt so I could repair lights, but I've always been good at fixing things," Cam said. "I had to be, where I grew up."

"And where did you grow up, Mr. Woodson?" Miss Carver asked.

"College Park," he said. "Me and my mom and my sister."

"Where was your father?" she asked.

"Is that important?" he said. "He wasn't around."

Miss Carver waited for him to continue, but he refused to elaborate. She had pried into their personal lives enough already for one day.

"When would you like to move in?" She directed her question to Dez.

"Next month," Dez said. "Our lease on the apartment is up at the end of the month."

"The first of October it is," Miss Carver said. "All of this is contingent on a background check, but I am not concerned about you, Woodson family. I've no doubt you will be *lovely* tenants." She clasped her hands and grinned, and to Cam, her expression looked like a mixture of relief and excitement. "This is thrilling."

Dez rose from her chair, came to Cam, and kissed him.

"Thank you," she whispered, and it was suddenly all worth it to see the happiness in her eyes.

A moment later, Ava started crying.

5

S aturday, October 1st
    On the morning of move-in day, Cam found Thor's
    battered white van parked in the rental's driveway.

"Gonna have to move it, man," Cam said.

Two days ago, Cam had rented a U-Haul truck to transport their items from the apartment; his cousin helped him load it up yesterday afternoon. Although the rental house was already furnished, he needed a big truck to hold all their stuff, as he planned to store excess things in the basement and avoid leasing a storage unit.

He checked the side mirror and saw Dez following the U-Haul in her white Honda Accord. He motioned to her that he was stopping and brought the truck to a halt in the middle of the cul-de-sac.

He got out and hurried to the house's front door. It opened as he was about to try the knob.

Thor emerged carrying a toolbox. Sweat trickled down his face and drenched his shirt, as if he'd stepped out of a sauna.

He also had a fresh black eye, a dark purple smudge.

"I am leaving now," Thor said. "Enjoy the house. You have the code?"

Cam was so distracted by the man's bruised eye that he didn't follow what Thor had asked him.

"Huh?"

"Code for the door." Thor pointed at the keypad beneath the knob.

"We're good, thanks." Cam tried to avoid gawking at the man's injury. "Is everything all set for us to move in?"

"Yeah." Thor grunted. "If you need something, call the lady." He clapped Cam's shoulder and shuffled past him. He tossed his toolbox into the van and backed out of the driveway. He honked at Dez as she parked her Honda at the curb.

Cam went to her car. She lowered her window.

"Is everything okay?" she asked.

"He had a black eye," Cam said.

"Oh?" She frowned. "I wonder what happened."

"Someone slugged him. Maybe he pissed off a tenant."

"I hope not." Her face wrinkled at the suggestion. "What was he doing here today?"

"Final touch-ups, maybe? Anyway, I'll back the truck into the driveway."

"I'll direct you."

He waved her off. "I'm good. You can head on inside."

"Are you sure?"

"I'm not blind, babe. It'll be easy."

While Dez fished a small box out of her car's trunk and lugged it inside, Cam returned to the U-Haul. He swung the truck around at what he thought was a good angle and started backing in.

Behind him, he heard something crunch: the ugly sound of an impact.

Shit. What was that?

He climbed out and looked. He had nailed the rental's mailbox. It leaned sideways like the Tower of Pisa.

I wonder if I can fix that.

As he studied the damage, Dez came outside.

"I don't think it was like that a few minutes ago," she said.

"Ha ha, very funny. I can fix it when we're all done here."

"If you had let me direct you . . ." she muttered, and returned to her car to get more stuff. Cam gave backing in another try and this time managed to deposit the truck in the driveway without causing further damage.

He met Dez at the back of her vehicle. "I'll help you bring in the rest of the stuff here, and then we can start on the truck."

He grabbed a box of what looked like kitchen items and carried it inside. As he wandered down the hallway, he thought: *We did it. We're really moving in here. Our first house.*

It would be wonderful to raise his daughter in such a lovely, spacious home. Dez's mom was watching Ava that day so he and Dez could focus on moving, but he looked forward to seeing the look on his little girl's face when she raced inside, and he told her it was all theirs.

It felt as though he had moved into a new chapter of his life, a promising one.

And he couldn't wait to set up his writing space in the living room. He was convinced that a fresh, open environment would boost his creativity. These days, he needed any edge he could get.

In the kitchen, he found a large gift basket adorned with a red ribbon standing on the island countertop. An assortment of items spilled out of it.

"Babe?" Cam called Dez. "Did you see this?"

"I hadn't been in here yet." She entered the kitchen carrying a box. "Is that for us?"

"Indeed, it is." An envelope lay alongside the basket, the inscription on the front stating: *Woodson Family.*

Cam tore it open and found a simple greeting card.

Enjoy your new home.

It was signed, "Your Landlord."

"Nice of them," Cam said. "Let's see what goodies they gave us."

He and Dez picked through the miscellaneous things heaped inside. There were pieces of fresh produce such as apples and mangoes and papayas; a pack of Hershey's kisses; a small teddy bear, presumably meant for Ava; a can of mixed nuts.

"What's this?" Dez dug a small plastic tube out of the basket. "Lubricant?"

"This must be a gag." Cam laughed.

Dez dug out a pocket-sized book. "And this? What the heck?"

Cam read the title: *One Shot: How to Get Pregnant on Your First Try.*

"If that's a joke, it's not funny," Dez said. "It's inappropriate."

"You *did* tell Miss Carver we were planning to have more children."

"And look: a box of condoms, too. But it's empty." She opened the container and dropped it onto the counter.

"Our landlord obviously has a twisted sense of humor," Cam said. "But it is kind of strange."

"A home pregnancy test kit?" Dez showed him the package. "Not amusing at all. I should complain."

The doorbell chimed.

"Guests already?" Cam asked. "Maybe the neighbors are welcoming us to the neighborhood."

But when Dez opened the front door, Cam saw her father standing outside, his ever-present glower already in place.

"What idiot hit the mailbox?" William Graham asked. "Was that you, Woodson?"

This, Cam thought, *is going to be a long day.*

6

Upon finding his father-in-law at the front door, Cam exhaled and mentally counted to ten.

"Hey, Daddy." Dez stepped forward and kissed her father's cheek.

"Good morning, William," Cam said. To Dez, he said, "Babe, you didn't tell me your dad was coming to help."

William reminded Cam of a bulkier, balder version of the actor Keith David. William was built like an ex-football player gone to seed. He wore a Tuskegee University T-shirt, a back brace, sweatpants, and sneakers. He had slipped on weight-lifting gloves, too. A white headband encircled his shiny head.

Although William had earned his fortune as the founder of a local chain of tire supply stores, he was renowned in the community for his youth football coaching exploits, having coached several children who had progressed to NFL careers. He preferred to be addressed as "Coach," a term that Cam found ludicrous and avoided using whenever addressing the man. That didn't stop William from talking to Cam as if he were a fledgling member of his Pop Warner squad.

"I had no choice but to help, Woodson," William said. "You were too cheap to hire professional movers."

Here we go.

"My cousin is on his way," Cam said. "He'll be helping."

"Where is he?" William turned around. "Is he here yet?"

"He'll be here soon." Cam had asked his cousin to meet him at the house at nine. It was already nine thirty, and he wasn't responding to text messages, either.

"Instead of standing around jawing, let's get to it." William clapped his hands. "I'm ready to rock and roll!"

Cam frowned at Dez, but she only shrugged as if to say, *I can't do anything about it.* But Cam had concerns. William was in his late sixties and at least fifty pounds overweight, and Cam knew (William didn't realize he knew) that his father-in-law suffered from a heart ailment. What if the older guy had a stroke while lifting a piece of furniture?

"Are you sure, Daddy?" Dez asked. "Like Cam said, his cousin is on the way."

William waved off his daughter's words.

"What are you waiting for, Woodson?" William adjusted the back brace, his pendulous belly straining against the belt. He marched toward the U-Haul's rear door. "Pop open this puppy."

"If you insist," Cam said.

"Last week at the gym, I benched two hundred and seventy pounds." William balled his meaty fists on his waist, spreading his legs as if ready to perform a dead lift. "How much can you bench, son?"

"Unlike at the gym, there's no one here to spot you."

"Open the truck now. Shit, young buck, did you know I paid my way through Tuskegee by moving furniture on the weekends? I was a *machine.*"

"That was a long time ago," Cam said under his breath.

"What was that?" William gave him a sharp look.

I tried, Cam thought. He unlatched the roll-up door and lifted it.

William grabbed the rope handle to unfurl the loading ramp from its storage slot in the bumper and snatched it out, a clamorous sound.

"I'll leave you men to it." Dez headed back inside the house.

They climbed inside the truck. A large, upholstered chair stood at the edge of the cargo area. Cam seized the back of it, while William squatted and grabbed the bottom.

"Be careful," Cam said. "Do you want me to take that side?"

"Worry about your side, son," William said. "And when are you going to pay me back? You wouldn't be moving into this house if it wasn't for my generosity. I'll do anything for my baby girl, you know."

"I never asked for the money. That was your daughter's idea."

"Are you the man of the house or not? What's your plan to make me whole?"

Cam gritted his teeth. "I'll have to get back to you on that."

They lifted the chair. It wobbled between them.

"Hold it with authority, son," William said. "Working at a desk all day has made you soft as butter."

That was how things progressed for the next hour: William barking orders at Cam and criticizing him at each turn. Over the years, Cam had learned to tune out the cantankerous man, but sometimes the relentless verbal assaults raised his blood pressure.

Come on, son! You lift like a girl!

We'll be here until midnight if you don't speed it up!

Step aside and let me do it, Woodson!

As they hauled a table around the house, intending to take it through the side entrance to the basement, William yelped.

"Dammit! My back!"

William dropped the table. Cam narrowly avoided the table leg landing on his foot.

Wincing, William shuffle-stumbled to the side of the house. He smacked his palm against the wall as if the house itself had hurt him.

"Goddamn pinched nerve acting up again! It feels like it leapt up and bit me!"

"Are you okay?" Cam asked.

"Do I look okay?" Sweat streamed down William's face, his forehead creasing as he massaged his back. "If you were holding up your side like you should have been, this wouldn't have happened."

Whatever, man.

"Maybe you should take it easy for the rest of the day," Cam said. "My cousin is five minutes away. He texted me."

Muttering, William brushed past him. A couple of minutes later, Dez hurried around the side of the house.

"What happened out here? Daddy says you dropped the table, and he got hurt."

Cam's face burned. "That's not what happened at all."

"How'd he hurt himself then?" She put her hands on her waist.

"He's not fit to move furniture, Dez. I don't know why you asked him to help."

"He invited himself." She rested her hand on his shoulder. "I'm sorry, babe. I know he's tough. This was supposed to be a happy day."

Yeah, it was supposed to be, but the day went off the rails in a hurry.

"Please give him some Aleve and an ice pack and keep him away," Cam said. "We don't need his help. He's given us plenty of assistance already, as he pointedly reminded me."

Her eyes clouded. "Was Daddy talking about the money he loaned us?"

"He demanded to know when I'll pay him back." Cam dragged his hand down his sweaty face. "It was a mistake to get the money from him. We had other options."

"Like what?" Her jaws clenched. "What long list of *other options* did we have on the table? Were you going to maybe sell some stock shares you never told me about, hmm?"

"You should have talked to me first, before you asked him."

"I'm sorry for going behind your back. I shouldn't have done that. But we didn't have any other choice."

"We have some savings," he said, and regretted it.

"Our savings? The last time I checked, Cam, we had about fifteen hundred dollars in that account. Still wouldn't have been enough to move us in. Or did you deposit several thousand dollars without telling me?"

He couldn't meet her gaze. They both knew that if her dad hadn't stepped in to lend a hand, they would still be living in the apartment.

"Forget about it," he said. "Let's make today a happy day, right?" His phone buzzed. "All right, my cousin's here. I'm getting back to work."

7

On a Saturday afternoon a week after they moved into the rental property, Dez and Cam invited their closest friends to the house for a low-key gathering.

Finally, Dez thought, *we can host our friends without bumping into each other in a cramped space.* She was excited to show off the place, even though it was only a rental.

In the short time they had lived there, Dez had taken several steps to make it feel more like their home. Hanging their artwork and pictures on the walls (without using nails) and setting up other framed photos on end tables. Adding the abundance of fresh-cut flowers and potted plants she had always wanted to keep in the apartment but had lacked space to accommodate. Moving some of the supplied furniture to the basement and bringing out their own chairs and tables and lamps and other accent pieces and reconfiguring the rooms. She had ambitions of painting, too, but hadn't gotten around to it yet and figured they might need approval from Miss Carver, anyway.

"This is lovely, girl," Ebony said as Dez took her upstairs. "It's such a big, super-cute place. I'm happy for you guys."

Ebony Royal was Dez's best girlfriend; they had met while teaching seventh grade at Cooper Middle School. Ebony's husband, Victor, was also tight with Cam. All of them, in fact, either still worked or used to work in the school system. Ebony and Vic introduced Dez to Cam eight years ago at a Super Bowl party. The rest was history.

The men socialized outside on the deck, drinking beer, and doing whatever else guys did whenever they gathered around a simmering backyard grill. The kids—Ebony's twin sons and Ava—clambered on the playset.

Although Dez and Ebony were the same age, she was already living the life Dez wanted for herself. Ebony had twins (age four), and after their birth, she left her teaching job to be a stay-at-home mom. Naturally, they lived in a beautiful house that they owned.

Dez didn't envy her friend—Ebony was a sweetheart and deserved the good life she was living—but she wanted it for herself, too. Although she and Cam had a happy marriage, the present financial struggles put a damper on things. He was pursuing his career as a full-time writer, but unless you were a bestseller, extremely prolific, or had a long backlist of royalty-earning books, things could be difficult. He assured her he was working hard to increase his income, and she supported him one hundred percent . . . but when Ebony and Vic pulled into their driveway that afternoon sporting a new Lincoln SUV, it was tough not to feel a twinge of envy.

Our time will come, Dez assured herself. Moving into the rental was a major step forward for them. Although she'd borrowed money from Daddy to get them in the door, she could already see the positive impact living there had on Cam and even Ava. More smiles. More laughter. The additional space had brought a fresh outlook for all of them. Could a new baby and transition to life as a stay-at-home mom be next?

She was optimistic. She had been raised in a traditional, old-school family, her father the primary earner and her mother (also a teacher) staying home with her and her brothers until all of them reached school age. Cam knew that she wanted the kind of lifestyle her parents had provided, and though his own background was vastly different, he and Dez were on the same page with what they desired for their own family.

"You guys have been here only a week?" Ebony asked as they strolled down the carpeted hallway.

"We moved in last Saturday."

"It looks like you've been here for months. Everything is in place. Wow."

"It came furnished, but we've used a lot of our own things," Dez said. "You know I had to add my special Desiree flair. Check out Ava's bedroom." Dez opened the door.

Ebony slipped inside, Dez following behind her. Dez had spent a fair amount of time in Ava's room, organizing the toys and books and her growing collection of teddy bears and dolls.

"She's such a girly-girl," Ebony said, beaming. "I want a girl so bad."

Dez knew that was perhaps one aspect that Ebony envied about *her* life: having a daughter.

"She's so much like me it's crazy sometimes," Dez said. "She loves playing dress-up in my clothes and having me do different things to her hair."

"Future Ms. Glamorous, like her mommy. What's the closet space like?"

Ebony tried to open the closet door. It didn't budge.

"Why is there a keypad thingy on it?" Ebony pointed at the lock pad.

"It's kind of weird. We've put in a call with the property manager to get the code. For now, I've got Ava's clothes in a different bedroom."

"I think I heard something in there," Ebony said.

"In the closet?" Dez edged forward to the door.

Ebony's brow wrinkled. "It was a clicking sound, like a clock. I could be imagining things. But it sounded like it came from inside the closet."

Dez pressed her ear to the cool door.

"I don't hear anything," Dez said.

"This must have gone straight to my head." Ebony swirled her wineglass. The chardonnay Dez had poured for her was gone.

"Let me show you the master suite," Dez said.

When Ebony followed her into the master, she gasped. "Okay, this is way bigger than ours, girl. Good Lord."

I know, Dez thought.

"How much is the rent on this place?" Ebony asked. "If you don't mind me asking."

Dez told her the amount and Ebony could only laugh. "Wow, what a steal. Is there a catch?"

"Cam said the same thing. The first words out of his mouth were, '*It's too good to be true.*' She mimicked her husband's tone.

"Our mortgage is way more and we've got way less space than you guys. I'm jealous now."

"Right place, right time, girlfriend," Dez said.

As she turned to show off the en suite, she glanced out the bedroom's front window and noticed a black Cadillac sedan crawling past their house. The car looked familiar.

Miss Carver, she thought. *Wasn't she driving a car like that when we first visited?*

The sedan paused for a beat at the driveway, and then pulled away, and Dez dismissed her initial thought as silly. There were thousands of similar-looking Cadillacs. It could be anyone.

But why did she suspect, if only for a second, that Miss Carver was spying on them?

8

"How's the writing going?" Vic asked Cam. "Have you been inspired by the new crib, man?"

Vic Royal and Cam stood outdoors on the deck, each of them sipping beers and Cam using tongs to work the hot dogs and burgers simmering on the grill (including a plant-based brat for Dez, part of her recent foray into a new fad diet). Farther out in the yard, the kids romped on the playset and chased each other around, laughing and shouting.

Considering Vic's question, Cam downed a hearty slug of beer. His friends at his house, good food on his grill, a cold beer in his hand, and happy children in the yard—what more could a guy ask for? He could freeze that moment for posterity.

"The writing is going fantastically well," Cam said.

"Fantastically well? Whoa, I've never heard you say that before."

"This past week I wrote a hundred pages." Cam sipped more beer. "That's a record for me, man."

"You wrote a hundred pages in one week?" Vic asked. "Damn."

Cam bobbed his head. "Did I tell you that, according to our lease, I'm not supposed to be working from home?"

"Bruh, that's crazy. Do they know you're a writer?"

"The landlord doesn't give a shit. They have a *strict* policy against work-from-home businesses, they say." Cam sipped his beer, burped, and smirked. "I said I wouldn't do it. I lied."

"That's straight garbage, man."

"I was going to say whatever I had to say to make sure Dez got this place—happy wife, happy life, as they say." Cam flipped over the burgers and moved them away from the hottest section of the grates. "Since we moved in, like I said, I've been smoking."

"The new place is stroking the muse, huh?" Victor studied him, drank beer. "Do you have a new contract yet?"

"I'm self-publishing this new one, Vic."

"I don't think you mentioned that before. But you have an agent, an editor. Shit, you flew to New York to meet those folks earlier this year, right?"

"Don't remind me." Cam moved a couple of the hot dogs. "I *was* in a good mood."

But the memory surfaced like a toothache: a red-eye flight to New York, his last-ditch effort to sell a proposal for a new thriller series to his publisher after his agent had failed to gain traction. His editor had promised to take him out to lunch to hear Cam's pitch, but when Cam arrived with a fresh haircut and wearing his best suit, lunch turned out to be lukewarm coffee and a stale bagel in a cramped conference room in the publisher's office. The meeting was painfully brief—like a mercy killing, Cam would later think, because the editor had zero interest in his project. *We're moving in a new direction, Cam. Maybe you should, too.*

Cam's first five novels hadn't set the world on fire, garnering tepid reviews and modest sales, but the memory stung.

"I'm going to prove them wrong," Cam said. "I'll self-publish it and sell a hefty number of copies, and they'll be begging for me to come back."

"Hmm." Sipping beer, Victor rocked back and forth on his heels. "But you've never self-published anything before."

"It's not complicated. I know how to write, and I can pay someone to edit the manuscripts and design my covers. Then I'll have to run some ads to get the word out."

"I'm not in the business but it sounds complicated to me, Cam. Expensive, too."

"Vic, I've studied over a dozen books on the subject and joined several Facebook groups for indie writers. It's legit. Some of these indie writers are hauling in seven figures."

"A year?" Vic gaped. "How?"

"They write a lot of books. Many of them publish a book every month."

"That sounds like they're hacks, doesn't it?"

"They're not getting titles reviewed in the *New York Times,* but they're making a good living. Sign me up for that, man."

"You've been writing for years, and you've published, what? Five novels? Now you're going to write a book every month?"

"It's not like I have anything else to do." Cam set his beer on a patio table, a tad too forcefully. "I can do this."

"Why don't you come back to teaching?" Vic asked in a soft tone. "You were a good teacher, Cam. We need solid brothers like you in the classroom, setting a positive example. And you remember the perks: time off in the summers, plenty of vacation during the school year, a decent pension. You could still write your pulp fiction on the side."

Vic used to be a teacher—that was how Cam had first made his acquaintance—but he had soon left behind those ranks to join the administrative side. These days, he was a bigwig in the Fulton County School District and reported directly to the superintendent. He had offered Cam a job in the school system on more than one occasion, but lately, it had been coming up more often.

"I can get you back in," Vic said. "We're desperate for experienced teachers."

"Is Dez talking to you guys about this?" Cam asked.

"About what?"

"Did she ask you to offer me a job?"

His brown face reddening, Vic drained the rest of his beer. "I'm offering as a friend. I know things have been hard for you guys."

"I don't need any charity."

"I get it. I'm the sole earner in my house. Dez is working, but I know you've got a lot of pressure on you, too, driving for Uber and all that on the side."

"Vic, there's no way in hell I'm going back to teaching with my tail tucked between my legs. No way, man. I might as well advertise my failure on a billboard."

"Dammit, Cam." Vic's eyes lit up like solar flares. "You're so *stubborn*. Look, sometimes to get to where you need to be, you need to do some things you might not want to do for a little while."

"Appreciate the wisdom, Dr. Phil. But I'm good."

"Whatever, I'm going to get another beer," Vic said. "Do you want one?"

"I'll get it myself. I'm so *stubborn* like that."

Mumbling, Vic headed back inside. Cam toyed with the hot dogs and burgers, his friend's words ringing like discordant bells in his mind. *Why don't you come back to teaching?*

Was Vic out of his mind? For over a decade, Cam had worked his tail off to land a publishing contract so he could *quit* teaching. Why would he go back to it to face rowdy students, bureaucratic red tape, and apathetic parents?

I'll show him, Cam thought. *I don't need his help, or anyone's help. I can make it on my own.*

A child's scream pierced the afternoon.

9

Ava had screamed.

No matter how many other screaming children were nearby, Cam would have recognized his daughter's cries.

He whirled, the beer sloshing in his grasp. Ava rolled on the grass near the playset. She swatted at her arm and wailed.

Oh, God, something stung her, Cam thought, his heart feeling as if it had exploded into his throat.

The twins stood frozen, eyes huge. This wasn't the scream of a fellow child having fun. This was a howl of terror.

Vic barreled onto the deck outside as Cam raced across the yard. He reached Ava. She log-rolled on the ground like someone on fire trying to extinguish the flames.

"Daddy's here, baby. Daddy's here now." He bent to pick her up. "What happened? What is it?"

She howled. Snot, grass, and dirt smeared her face. As he plucked her off the ground, she squirmed in his arms.

He found the angry red welt on her left bicep underneath the cuff of her shirt.

"Where did it come from?" he asked the twins. "Did you see what stung her?"

One boy pointed at the slide.

"It came from over there. It came out of a hole in the ground."

By then, Vic, Ebony, and Dez had reached them. Vic and Ebony swept their boys away from the commotion as if whatever had happened to Ava was contagious. Dez reached for Ava, and Cam let her take the girl.

"She's stung," he said. "Let's hope to God she's not allergic."

"We have an EpiPen if you need it," Ebony said. "We've got to have them for the twins' peanut allergy."

Dez hurried back inside the house, Cam following behind her. They examined Ava's arm and checked the rest of her body. The sting looked bad, but she hadn't suffered any allergic reactions. Now that she was inside, her crying had tapered off into sniffles.

"Keep an eye on her," he said to Dez. "I'm going to deal with these wasps, or whatever the hell is out there."

Vic followed him outside, like two men going off to war. From several feet away, Cam got on his knees and studied the ground underneath the slide. He noticed insects buzzing around the shadowed space. Some going out, some coming in. How had he missed this earlier?

"I'm lighting them up," he said.

"What?" Vic asked.

Cam pointed at the hive. "Lighter fluid and a match will wipe them out."

"Bruh, pour some vinegar into the nest."

Cam stomped to the deck. He snatched the bottle of lighter fluid off the table and grabbed his box of long-handled matches.

"I don't think that's a good idea," Vic said.

"You're full of advice, today, aren't you, Dr. Phil?" Cam said.

"Will you stop calling me that?"

Cam returned to the playset. He located the approximate area of the nest again and sprayed a silvery stream of lighter fluid into the hole. A couple of hornets swirled out of the ground like fighter jets on the prowl.

Cam struck a match and tossed it toward the nest. The saturated grass ignited with a mighty *whuff*! The surge of heat knocked him back on his heels.

"That's how you do it," he said to Vic. "They won't be terrorizing my little girl again."

The flames burned, licking the slide's metal underbelly—and then the fire spread. Acrid white smoke bloomed from the ground like a miniature mushroom cloud.

Cam gagged. He looked for something to douse the flames.

But Vic was ahead of him. His friend found the garden hose at the back of the house.

"Go switch on the water, Cam. I'll clean up your mess."

Cam thought of telling him off, decided to drop it. He raced to the faucet attached to the house and twisted it on. Vic sprayed the water over the cooking grass, and the flames died. Tendrils of smoke curled through the air, and the stench of scorched earth turned Cam's stomach.

"Thanks," Cam said.

"I think the food is burning, too. Do you smell it?"

Seriously? It's going to be that kind of day?

Just as he'd feared, Vic was right. Fire had blackened the burgers and hot dogs beyond recognition.

10

"That was a day to remember," Dez said to Cam.

Freshly showered, Dez strolled out of the bathroom and toward the bed. She wore a silk nightie—one that she knew was Cam's favorite—and had applied a scented body lotion that he liked, too.

Their friends had left hours ago, and they had put down Ava for bed, Dez giving her a bath and Cam reading from Ava's favorite book. They had the rest of the night to themselves, for which Dez was grateful. She loved entertaining and obviously loved her baby, but these days, she and Cam rarely had the opportunity to enjoy each other's company in peace.

Cam sat up in bed reading on his Kindle by the light of a bedside lamp. He looked up at her as she crawled into the bed next to him.

"It was a little too eventful for my taste," he said. "I'm only glad Ava's okay."

"She'll be fine, babe. It was traumatic for her—hell, for us, too—but she's going to be all right."

They had wound up ordering pizzas because the scorched food was inedible. It hadn't been the plan, but Dez thought it turned out fine, anyway—the kids loved pizza, and Vic and Ebony didn't mind. When you were parents of young children, you learned how to roll with the punches.

She cuddled next to Cam.

"What're you reading?" she asked him.

"Something about publishing. Book marketing stuff."

"Always working, hmm?"

"When I'm not setting off blazes in the backyard, yeah."

"Don't beat yourself up about that. You reacted to a scary situation. At least the nest is gone now."

"At least."

She touched his leg. He wore boxers and a T-shirt. She leaned into him, let him feel her leg pressed against his.

He set down the Kindle on the nightstand and took off his glasses.

"Want to switch off the lamp, too?" she asked.

He obliged. They lay together in the darkened room, the only sounds the hum of the A/C, a breeze sifting through the eaves, and their hushed breaths. It was much quieter than their old apartment, in which the walls seemed so thin that Dez would hear various noises throughout the night from their neighbors. Until they had moved into the rental, Dez didn't realize how much she missed living in a single-family home.

"I feel like a total fuckup sometimes," Cam said, breaking the stillness.

Dez only listened. She ran her fingers across his chest, feeling his heart throb beneath his shirt.

"It's just that I want so much for us," he said, his voice thick with emotion. "I didn't expect things to turn out like this."

She knew what he meant; he wasn't talking about setting off a fire in the backyard or burning dinner. He was talking about the one thing that frustrated him, obsessed him: *money.*

Or, more recently, the lack of it.

As far as Dez was concerned, anyone who said money didn't

matter had never struggled. While money alone couldn't guarantee happiness, it could certainly provide stability and peace of mind. When you had plenty of it, you never thought about it. But when you lacked it, it seemed to be *all* you could think about.

She believed Cam felt the sting of their financial circumstances more intensely than she did. She was working, after all, earning a respectable salary in her chosen profession. But the only money Cam contributed lately came mostly from gig work that she knew he hated: driving for Uber and assembling furniture.

He could go back to teaching, but that was a last resort, and if that was the step he took, she wanted him to make that decision on his own. He was too proud to accept such a suggestion from her, and would see it as a sign that she had lost faith in his ability to deliver on his promises. He was like her father in that regard, an ambitious man who believed in his own vision. One lesson her mother had taught her about strong-willed men: while you could subtly influence them, never try to overtly bend them to your will. It would lead only to strife in the relationship.

"You're doing the best you can," Dez said. "And I'm here with you every step of the way."

"I know you want to have another baby, stay home, and raise the kids. I'd love for you to be able to do that for as long as you want, to not have to work if you don't want to."

"I'll work as long as necessary to support our family, babe. I enjoy teaching, most days." She chuckled.

"But I see how you look at Ebony." He shifted to face her, their noses almost touching. His breath smelled of peppermint mouthwash.

"We'll get there in our own time." She trailed her index finger underneath his chin, kissed him on the lips. "Your new book will be a hit. We'll have another baby. If circumstances look good, I'll take a leave from teaching. It'll all work out."

"Your confidence amazes me. Sometimes, I think you believe in me more than I believe in myself."

She kissed him again. She slid her hand down to his boxers, felt his growing erection, and fondled it.

"I believe in *us*," she said.

They made love—a slow, tender love making, and Cam, always a considerate lover, knew her buttons well, took the time to give her pleasure, too. When they climaxed, a rare simultaneous orgasm, they were looking deep into each other's eyes, and she saw his soul, as corny as it sounded, and it made her feel good.

We're meant for each other, Dez thought. No matter how bad things got sometimes, it would all work out for the best in the end.

They lay together, basking in the afterglow of their intimacy. Cam trailed his fingers through her hair.

"I'm going to go downstairs and work," he said. "I feel inspired. Do you mind?"

She kissed him. "Do your thing, boo."

Cam muttered something about proving the doubters wrong, but Dez barely heard it. A soft smile on her face, she drifted off to sleep.

A short while later, she awoke to people arguing.

11

Inspiration had struck Cam. He was as eager to get in front of his laptop and start pouring out the words as a man who felt the urgent need to urinate.

He had set up his office space in what might have otherwise been the formal living room at the front of the house, arranging his things on a simple wooden desk he had gotten from Goodwill. He booted up his computer and slipped on his headphones. After finding a binaural beats track on YouTube, he plunged into the draft of his current novel.

He had high aspirations for this book. It was to be the first installment in a new thriller series, but it wasn't the same project he had tried—and failed—to sell to his editor (well, prior editor). It was a fresh take on a popular trend in the genre, drew from some of his personal experiences and interests, and he felt more in tune with the main character than he had ever felt with any of his other work. Although he'd told Vic that he planned to publish it independently, in the back of his mind he was thinking that when he was done, he might float this over to his agent and see if they got any nibbles from New York.

But first, he needed to finish it. You couldn't self-publish three chapters and an outline. At this stage in his career, he needed to have a finished manuscript. A completed book would give him options.

When he looked up from the screen a few minutes later, he found someone standing in the doorway: a tall, dark figure.

He shouted.

Miss Carver, the property manager / rental agent, stepped out of the shadowed hallway and into the room.

Cam tore off the headphones.

"What the hell are you doing here?" He glanced at the laptop, saw the clock. "It's ten o'clock at night!"

Miss Carver gave him a fake smile. She wore the same black funeral dress she had been wearing when they first met her.

"The landlord reserves the right to visit the property at any time, with reasonable advance notice," she said.

"Are you kidding me?" He erupted from his chair. "You didn't give us any notice!"

"I called you, Mr. Woodson. I left a message."

Cam grabbed his iPhone. He had put the phone in "Do Not Disturb" mode while he was writing. He saw the silenced notification that he had received a voice mail message about twenty minutes ago.

"What do you want?" he asked.

"What are you doing, Mr. Woodson?" She stepped around the desk and glanced at the computer screen. "Are you working?"

"I'm writing my book—" he said, and then he caught himself. *Shit.*

"Writing your book, eh?" Miss Carver's eyes brightened like a wolf's that had invaded a chicken coop. "We discussed this, did we not? We talked about our landlord's strict policy against working from home."

Cam slammed shut the lid of his laptop, but it was too late. He was busted. What did that mean, anyway? Were they going to take him to jail? Evict him from the house? This was ridiculous, anyway.

"It's unreasonable," he said. "I'm not doing anything disruptive."

"The landlord's expectations are plainly stated in your lease."

He heard Dez pounding downstairs. Gathering her house robe around her, Dez charged into the room, her pupils dilated.

"I thought I heard your voice," she said to Miss Carver. "Why are *you* here? Is something wrong?"

Miss Carver swept her gaze from Dez to Cam. She seemed unable to suppress a nasty grin.

"You've had quite an eventful day, Woodson family," she said. "We had reports of several incidents."

"What?" Dez and Cam said, in unison.

"A party." Miss Carver ticked off the items one by one on her long, skeletal fingers. "A fire."

"We didn't have a party." Dez came around to Cam's side of the desk. "We had our best friends over, two adults and their twin boys."

"Parties must be approved in advance by our landlord," Miss Carver said. "The lease was quite clear on this item. We discussed it in detail, at signing."

Dez glanced at Cam. It was not often that Cam found his wife at a loss for words, but her jaw literally had dropped.

"Then, there's the matter of the fire," Miss Carver said. "Destruction of property."

"Who reported us?" Cam asked. "I didn't talk to any neighbors. I didn't see anyone."

"You assured us that you were a 'no drama' family, as you called it," Miss Carver said. "But here, only one week into your lease, I've identified multiple infractions."

"This is bullshit," Cam said.

"We never received the executed lease," Dez said. "You were supposed to email it to us. You never did!"

Miss Carver lifted the black leather briefcase she was carrying and unzipped it. "I anticipated this response, Woodson family."

She withdrew a thick sheaf of papers held together by a paper clip and dropped it onto Cam's desk. It was a heavy sound, like a judge's gavel striking wood.

"Our landlord took the liberty of highlighting certain relevant sections," Miss Carver said. "There are two copies, one for each of you to read at your convenience."

Cam picked up the sheaf of papers and thumbed through it. It was as thick as one of his book manuscripts. Was this for real?

"I suggest that you become *intimately* acquainted with the terms of our legally binding agreement." Miss Carver's eyes gleamed, and Cam had the sudden idea that this woman knew he and Dez had recently had sex, that she could smell it in the air or something. He felt sick.

"Can you please leave?" Dez asked, her eyes like darts. It was about as angry as Cam had ever seen her, but she still maintained a polite tone. "*Now.*"

"Of course," Miss Carver said. She stepped toward the doorway, paused. "Remember: No working from home. No parties without prior approval. No more incidents. You've been warned, Woodson family."

"Get the hell out of here," Cam said.

Smiling her death's head grin, Miss Carver strode to the front door and let herself out.

Cam and Dez looked at each other, both of them wondering if all of that had actually happened.

12

―――――――

By unspoken agreement, Cam and Dez went into the kitchen and spread the copies of the rental lease on the island. Cam read one copy; Dez studied the other.

Cam was still so stunned by what had happened that he could barely focus on the contract. Looking up from his laptop and seeing that crazy woman standing like a wraith in the doorway was the stuff of nightmares, and the memory would linger for a while.

What are you doing, Mr. Woodson? Are you working?

"Babe?" Dez asked. She sounded as if the wind had been knocked out of her. "We've got a serious problem. Have you started reading this?"

Cam shuddered, squinted at the papers lying in front of him. As Miss Carver had stated, certain passages had been highlighted in yellow marker.

He reviewed the first one.

Restriction against work from home businesses, including freelance writing.

He felt as if the floor had dropped from beneath his feet.

"This isn't what we signed," Dez said. "We read the lease, every page, on Miss Carver's iPad. It was standard material." She pointed at the thick stack of pages as if they emitted a foul odor. "We didn't sign *this*."

"They actually put 'freelance writing' in this lease," Cam said. "Like they want it to be totally clear that this is all about me. Unbelievable."

"They can't do this," Dez said. "This is fraud. We didn't sign this!"

"But can we prove that?" Cam asked. He flipped through the pages. "They've got our initials on here, our signatures."

"Oh my God," Dez said, putting her hand to her mouth. "Listen to this: 'After a verbal or written warning is issued for the first violation, a penalty will be assessed for further incidents. Penalty is equivalent to one month's rent, payable within five business days of the incident. Nonrefundable.'"

Cam found another highlighted passage. "Look at this, what it says here about inspections: 'Landlord and authorized agent can inspect the property at any hour, provided reasonable advance notice is supplied.'" He turned to Dez. "She called me twenty minutes before she showed up inside the house. Twenty minutes. Is that 'reasonable'?"

"It's vague," Dez said, shaking her head. "Way too vague."

"'Penalty for disruptive activities,'" Cam said, reading from another highlighted section. "Again, we're fined one month's rent."

"Here's the 'no party' clause on page thirty-six." Dez indicated the section with her manicured finger. "'No party without prior approval.' It doesn't say what qualifies as a party. There's no minimum number of guests specified."

Cam shuffled to the refrigerator. He couldn't tolerate reading any more. He got the last beer out of the fridge, twisted the cap off, and took a long gulp.

Dez continued to review the lease. "It's almost sixty pages of legalese. I've never seen anything like this in my life. Have you?"

"No, and it's one hundred percent bullshit," Cam said. "Like you said, it's fraud. But I don't know how we prove it. Do you?"

Dez shook her head, covering her face with her hands.

Cam drank more beer. "I can't live like this."

"What are you talking about?"

"I love the house, but can you live like this, babe? Can you live under all these outrageous restrictions they added in, and this crazy-ass woman able to walk in whenever she wants?"

"Are you saying we should break the lease?" she asked.

"That's exactly what I'm saying. Break this fraudulent lease and go move in somewhere normal."

She beckoned him over to her, tapped her finger under another highlighted passage. He read it from over her shoulder.

Early termination of the lease agreement requires payment in full of all remaining months. Security deposit is forfeited.

"By my math, that would be over twelve thousand dollars," Dez said. "That's the only way we can break the lease. We'll have to pay them. We don't have that much money sitting around, nowhere close to it."

His legs suddenly weak, and not because of the extra beer, Cam found the nearest chair and sank into it.

13

Two days later, on Monday, Cam and Dez had a new course of action: they needed to determine if the lease was legal.

"Maybe we can't prove they deceived us into signing it," Cam said. "But if the lease itself is illegal, we can break it and see their asses in court."

Dez seemed doubtful but she was willing to see it through. Cam assured her he would take care of everything.

That morning, he dropped off Ava at the day care that she attended a couple of days a week. Then, he headed to the local Barnes & Noble that apparently would need to be one of his official workspaces, at least for a while.

At a table on the second floor of the bookstore, he met a couple of members of an informal writing group—a forty-something guy with Abe Lincoln sideburns and a bespectacled older lady wearing a pink warm-up suit. Both were full-time writers. The woman penned romance novels, and the guy wrote romance, too, under a female pen name, yet he claimed he yearned to write men's adventure fiction.

"We haven't seen you here in a spell, bud," the guy said. He barked a laugh. "I thought you might have left our sorry ranks and gotten yourself a real job."

"It's not as though I have a choice," Cam said.

He could have risked working from the house, but the idea made him nervous. Miss Carver and her precious landlord could have set up spy cams in the residence. If someone had told him a month ago that such a thing was feasible, he would have laughed. Now, he wasn't so sure.

What neighbor had reported on the backyard debacle? That was a splinter in Dez's thoughts, too. She believed Miss Carver had driven by the house on that Saturday and spotted Vic and Ebony's SUV parked in the driveway. She had thought she was being paranoid at first, but now she believed Miss Carver had been watching them all along.

"I'd put nothing past that woman at this point," Cam had said. "She's enjoying putting us through the wringer."

While at the bookstore, he searched the "Fiction" section for one of his novels. He located a single sad copy sitting spine out at the bottom of the bookcase. He put it on a higher shelf and positioned it front cover out.

He needed to get some work done, but he couldn't focus. Until they settled this matter of the lease, he would be unable to get the words flowing again.

"I'm no attorney," Vic said, after Cam emailed him the lease (Miss Carver had finally emailed it to them, also), "but it looks like you guys are screwed. Have you thought of talking to a lawyer?"

Talking to a lawyer was Cam's top priority for the day. Over the weekend, he had messaged several real estate attorneys in metro Atlanta, described his predicament, and asked for an emergency consultation. One attorney had responded last night and agreed to a one-hour consult for three hundred dollars.

Three hundred bucks for one hour! Cam wanted to scream. Clearly, he had entered the wrong profession.

He withdrew the money from their dwindling savings account.

The last remnants of the final installment payment of his publishing contract sat in that account, and he hoarded it zealously. Once that money was gone—a day fast approaching—they would be totally wiped out, living upside down, their monthly expenses greater than their income. When that day arrived, some critical things would need to be slashed from their budget, and they might be eating tuna casserole most nights.

His consultation with the attorney was scheduled for four o'clock that afternoon, via Zoom. Cam had sent the lease to the lawyer that morning, and he was hopeful that the attorney would find some clause in the agreement that would invalidate the rental contract and free them.

He had decided to take the call in his Jeep, on his iPhone, while parked in the rental's driveway. Before the call commenced, he tested the connection. The camera showed his face, and he didn't like what he saw: stress lines stenciled on his forehead and dark hollows beneath his eyes. He hadn't gotten much sleep in the past couple nights.

The attorney opened the call at precisely four o'clock. He was a silver-haired man with a bronzed, leathery face, dressed in a blue, button-down shirt with a sunflower-yellow bow tie. A gigantic oak bookcase packed with books served as his background. His name was Hal Greenberg.

"Good afternoon, Mr. Woodson," Greenberg said. "I hear you've got yourself a sticky lease situation."

"That's right," Cam said.

"Walk me through the details, please," Greenberg said. "Do me a favor and start from the very beginning, when you first toured the property."

Cam narrated his entire experience. The lawyer occasionally made notes on a legal pad as Cam spoke, and asked a few brief, clarifying questions, but for the most part he allowed Cam to talk.

"And here we are," Cam said, wrapping up his narrative. "My wife and I don't want to live under these ridiculous rules, but we don't have twelve grand to walk away from the lease. They did a bait and switch on us with the lease, and we wanted to find out if the contract is even legal and what options we've got."

"Got it, got it." Greenberg pursed his lips. "Mr. Woodson, I reviewed the lease agreement you sent me this morning, and I won't beat around the bush here: the contract is one hundred percent legal and will stand in a court of law."

Cam slumped in the driver's seat. "I was afraid you'd say that."

"You're convinced that the electronic version you signed is different than the finalized document they provided, but if you have no evidence of that, it's a moot point."

"Do you have any *good* news?" Cam asked.

"Mr. Woodson, lease laws vary by state," Greenberg said. "Here in Georgia, landlords wield tremendous power, more than any other state in the union. Most folks don't understand that until they find themselves in a pickle like you're in. A Georgia landlord is forbidden to do only a few things, such as evict without notice, and discriminate."

"Right." Cam sighed. He had done some research on Google earlier and the lawyer's remarks confirmed his findings. "They can ban me from working in the house, and everything else."

"As unreasonable as it may seem, yes," Greenberg said. "This is why I advise clients to have an attorney review a lease before signing."

"We didn't have time to do that. But like I said, we read every single page and it all looked standard. My wife's a stickler for reading contracts, things like that."

"From my perspective, Mr. Woodson, you've two options at this point." Greenberg lifted two fingers to the camera. "Number one: break the lease. It's going to cost you, but that's one way out of it."

"We don't have twelve thousand dollars, like I said. It's not an option."

"That takes us to door number two, friend: grin and bear it." The lawyer smiled, showing off porcelain veneers.

"You mean live under these draconian rules?" Cam said.

"It's a twelve-month lease in a nice home, not a sentence in a state prison. Have you ever done something you didn't want to do for a year or so? Like hold a crappy job? When I was in law school at Emory, I worked part-time in a gas station, and let me tell you, son, that job positively sucked. But I put in my time and here I am now. I look back on the experience and laugh."

"There's got to be something else we can do," Cam said. "Do you have any other ideas?"

"Well." Greenberg laced his hands behind his head and leaned back in his chair, lips puckered. After a beat, he said, "Tell me: Have you ever spoken to the landlord personally?"

"We've only dealt with his property manager. I've never talked to the landlord. I've no idea who it is."

"It's a long shot," Greenberg said. "But if you can get a meeting with the landlord, you could try to convince him to loosen the reins on your family. Get him to put an amendment on the lease that allows you more freedom."

"Now that's an excellent idea." Cam straightened in the seat.

"I'd suggest that if you get that amendment, you send it to me first to review it." Greenberg grinned again, showing off that expensive dental work.

After Cam concluded the call with Greenberg, Dez pulled into the driveway. He got out of the Jeep, pulled Ava out of the car seat, and told Dez what he had learned.

"That is a legitimate idea," Dez said. "Are you going to call Miss Carver to set up the meeting?"

"Miss Carver?" He scoffed. "Hell, no. I'm done dealing with Miss Carver. I'm going to the source. Tomorrow morning, I'm going to meet the landlord myself."

14

But that night, Cam dreamed about Miss Carver. No matter what room of the house he entered, the woman was already there, grinning at him like a jack-o-lantern and advising him of what was acceptable behavior, per their lease. *It's not allowed for you to wear shoes in this room, Mr. Woodson—you'll damage the carpet. Oh, how dare you drink more than one alcoholic beverage per day! That is a violation of your lease. No, no, no, you may not play a video game in this fine rental—such unseemly activities have been known to lead to incidents . . .*

Cam woke with a shudder. It was already morning—six o'clock, according to his iPhone. He heard rain tapping against the window at a steady cadence and groaned. Everyone who lived in metro Atlanta knew that whenever you had to drive in the rain, the time to reach your destination doubled.

Dez was already up. He found her in the family room downstairs, working through a Pilates video. She bounced off the mat as he entered.

"Morning," she said. "Did you sleep okay? Your eyes are red."

"I slept like hell. Miss Carver invaded my dreams."

Dez wrinkled her nose. "Are you still going to the city? It's nasty out."

"Wouldn't miss it for the world. I'm looking forward to ambushing them in their office."

He set off for the city around eight o'clock, and the drive was every bit as slow and frustrating as he had known it would be. He followed Google Maps to the high-rise in Midtown Atlanta and veered into the building's parking garage.

From studying the lease and then doing some online research, he had learned that Baron Properties had office space on the four-teenth floor of this skyscraper. He crawled through the dank parking garage, searching for an open spot, going higher and higher.

He spied an open slot next to a dirty white van, but he would have slammed on the brakes, anyway.

The bumper sticker bore a Swedish flag.

Was Thor here, too? Cam wondered.

He swung his SUV into the spot. He had taken care to dress a little nicer than he usually did on weekdays: he wore a collared shirt, khakis, and loafers. He had dabbed on some cologne, too.

He grabbed the manila folder that held the printed lease from the passenger seat and got out. The parking garage smelled of exhaust fumes and oil.

Curious, he stepped to the passenger window of the van and looked inside.

It was like peering inside a homeless man's crate in an alley: he saw piles of clothing and bottles of soda and crumpled bags from fast-food restaurants. It literally looked as if Thor lived inside the van.

He detected motion in the deep shadows inside the vehicle and stepped back. Thor emerged from the murk, blinking and groggy.

Cam was so shocked that he nearly tripped over his own feet in his haste to get back. But Thor had noticed him. His eyes widened.

Thor opened the door. A dank odor issued from inside, nearly making Cam gag.

"Cam Woodson," Thor said in his accented English. "Why are you here?"

I ought to be asking you the same question, Cam thought. *Are you living in your van at company headquarters?*

"Do you need help with the house?" Thor climbed out of the van. He wore only a soiled T-shirt and sagging jeans. He was barefoot. But his black eye was mostly healed.

"Are you okay, man?" Cam asked. "Are you *living* in that van?"

Thor laughed as if the question was absurd. He reached behind him and retrieved a pack of cigarettes.

"Why are you here?" Thor asked again.

"I'm here to see the landlord. I need to discuss some business."

Thor's eyes went as large as saucers. He paused in the process of lighting a smoke.

"You have a summon?" Thor asked.

"No, I—"

"You cannot speak to landlord without a summon," Thor said. "No. It cannot happen."

"You mean I have to make an appointment?" Cam asked.

"You need a summon. An invitation."

Was he serious? An invitation? But Thor's face was solemn as he took a draw on his cigarette and exhaled a plume of smoke.

"I'm here now," Cam said. "I'm going in there to talk. Fourteenth floor, right?"

Cam turned, and Thor shifted to block his path.

"Please," Thor said. "Do not go in."

"Dude, you need to relax. It's cool. I'm going in there to talk about my lease."

Thor put his heavy hand on Cam's shoulder. Cam stepped aside.

"Chill out, man, seriously," Cam said. "I'll be fine."

Thor grunted, but backed off. Cam walked to the elevator and glanced over his shoulder, and Thor watched him as if Cam were headed to the electric chair.

15

In short order, Cam navigated the building's lobby and found the next set of elevators that led to the offices upstairs.

The car chimed as it arrived on the fourteenth floor.

Cam was the only passenger. He stepped into a long, carpeted hallway, the corridor illuminated with pale fluorescent light.

He was looking for suite 1408. There were other doors along the hall marked by the suite number, but he could not see through them; they were solid wood and bore no windows. There were no signs to direct him, either.

At the end of the corridor, he looked both ways, and then turned left.

"There we go," he said.

Ahead, a door at the end of the hallway had a small sign upon it, plain black text on a white card: 1408. No company name. Like the other doors, it was all wood set in a windowless wall.

He was convinced he would find the door locked, his journey to this place for naught, but the lever opened when he twisted.

Let's do this. His heart drummed, Thor's bizarre warning echoing in his mind.

He entered a small, well-lit waiting area. A single oak desk stood in front of him, unoccupied; behind it, there was another door set in the wall. There were no windows to allow him to see what lay beyond the doorway.

Four hard plastic chairs stood in the reception area, and one of them was occupied. A dark-haired young woman huddled over her phone. She hadn't looked at Cam when he had entered.

He heard a sniffling sound, saw her shoulders tremble.

Was she sobbing?

"Miss, are you okay?" Cam asked.

The woman lifted her head. She looked Hispanic. Tears tracked down her cheeks, and her eyes were bloodshot. But she only shook her head at his inquiry.

What was going on here? Was she a tenant like he was?

Cam approached the front desk. He didn't see a bell, a computer, or a telephone. The surface was completely bare.

He turned to the woman again. "Is anyone here? Is this the office for Baron Properties?"

The woman wiped her eyes with the heel of her hand, sniffled. But she frowned at him. He wasn't sure she understood his questions.

"Do I need to go knock on that door over there?" he asked.

As he posed the question, the door opened. Miss Carver emerged, wearing a triumphant grin.

Oh shit. Not her again.

He felt as if he were back in last night's dream, finding clones of this woman wherever he turned.

"This is a surprise," Miss Carver said. "May I help you, Mr. Woodson?"

"I'm here to speak to the landlord," Cam said.

"Oh?" Her thin eyebrows arched. "Is there an issue with the property?"

"You guys tricked us," Cam said. He raised the bulging manilla folder that contained the printed rental agreement. "This lease you gave us isn't the one we read and signed. You committed fraud."

Miss Carver rested her hands on the desk and watched him, her eyes as empty as a mannequin's. Did she understand what he meant? Or did she not give a damn because she knew he couldn't prove their trickery?

"I talked to a lawyer," Cam said. "I need to speak to the landlord. Directly."

"I am the landlord's authorized agent, Mr. Woodson. If you have a matter to discuss, you discuss it with me."

"Is he here?" Cam asked.

"He?" Miss Carver's lips twisted. "How do you know the landlord is not a *she*, Mr. Woodson?"

"He, she, it—whatever. Can I talk to the landlord or not?"

"What is this concerning?"

"It's about the lease. I want to discuss modifying the terms."

Miss Carver threw back her head and laughed. Her mouth opened so wide that he could see her small, sharp teeth and the pinkish back of her throat.

"Why is that so funny?" he asked.

"Oh my dear, dear Mr. Woodson," she said, her laughter subsiding. "There is no modification of the lease agreement available to you, little man."

Little man? What?

"That's not what my attorney said," Cam said. "He said I could possibly get an amendment."

"You haven't earned an amendment, Mr. Woodson."

"Excuse me?" Cold sweat pebbled his forehead. This woman was working his nerves like no one he had ever met in his life. "How can I *earn* an amendment?"

"Furthermore, if you wish to break your lease, you will face a severe financial penalty. I doubt that you and your lovely wife could endure such a financial burden."

"I know that. I read the thousand-page contract."

"Good." Miss Carver clasped her hands in front of her. "Are we done here?"

"Wait, you said it's possible to earn an amendment. What does that mean? Can I talk to the landlord about this?"

"Do I need to contact building security, Mr. Woodson?" Miss Carver slipped her phone out of her pocket like a magician.

Cam's head felt as if it would implode. He clenched his clammy hands into fists, the folder damp in his grasp.

Be cool, man. You don't need her calling security.

Still, this was nuts. None of this had gone according to plan.

"I'm going to ask one more time," Cam said. "Are you telling me there is no way whatsoever for me to talk to the landlord about my lease?"

Miss Carver's face was like a closed fist.

"Go home, Mr. Woodson. If the landlord requires you, you will be contacted."

16

Late that afternoon, after Dez finished her day at school, she went to her parents' house to pick up Ava.

Her parents lived in East Cobb, in the same palatial home that Dez and her older brothers had grown up in. Both her parents had retired; three days a week, her mother watched Ava to give them relief from exorbitant day care expenses. Since her mother was a former kindergarten teacher, the arrangement worked out perfectly.

"Hey, Mom," Dez said when she entered the always-spotless house. "Where's my little girl? Oh, there she is!"

Ava raced across the family room and bounded against Dez. Dez swept her daughter up into her arms and planted kisses on her soft cheeks.

Mom came toward them. Her mother was a well-kept woman, in her late sixties, but with her trim figure and gleaming brown skin, she could have passed for fifteen years younger.

"We've been working on our letters today," Mom said. "She's doing such a great job, sweetheart. By the time kindergarten starts, she'll be well ahead of grade level."

"That's what we like to hear. Hey, where's Daddy?"

"Down in his dungeon, as usual," Mom said.

Dez put down her daughter and took the short staircase into the den. Wearing a headset, her father paced the carpet. It sounded as if he were arguing with someone—probably his financial advisor, because she heard terms tossed around like "rate of return" and "leverage" and "margin call."

She waved at him. She was relieved that he was occupied. Lately, he had been going in hard on her husband. Daddy moved gingerly around the den, favoring the injured side of his back. His doctor said he had aggravated an injury from several years ago and Daddy blamed Cam for it all.

He blamed Cam for everything.

Back upstairs, Dez gathered Ava's things and chatted about school with her mother. She was on the verge of leaving when Daddy surfaced from downstairs.

"How's that husband of yours doing?" Daddy asked. He said the words as if referring to a troublesome pest, like a raccoon that kept tearing through your trash.

"Hey, Daddy." Dez stepped to him and kissed his cheek. "My husband is doing quite well. He's working hard."

"Do you know who I saw yesterday?" Daddy asked. "Doctor Lamont Price. He stopped by to visit his folks. Driving a big, new Mercedes sedan. That boy was crazy about you, peanut."

Lamont was literally the boy next door. He and Dez had never dated—he wasn't her type at all—but he had graduated from Morehouse School of Medicine and now worked as an internist.

"You could have hooked up with him, way back when," Daddy said. "Imagine how different things would be, eh?"

"Come on, Daddy. Didn't Cam give you a beautiful grandchild?"

Daddy grumbled.

"How's the situation with the lease?" Mom asked.

Via telephone, Dez had filled them in on the basics: the deception Miss Carver had pulled on them (that they couldn't prove) and the overly restrictive rental agreement and their efforts, fruitless so far, to wend themselves out of it. She wondered how Cam's visit to the landlord's office had gone that day. Since she hadn't heard from him, she doubted it had gone well.

"I love the house," Dez said. "If it turns out that we've got to stay, we'll make the best of it. We can't afford to break the lease."

"But if you ever do leave, our door is always open to you and the baby," Daddy said. He puckered his lips as if tasting a sour fruit. "You could stick that husband of yours with the rental."

"Like I said, I love the house. I'm mentally prepared to stick it out."

And we may not have a choice, Dez thought.

17

"That's it, then," Cam declared to Dez that evening as they stood around the kitchen island. He had detailed the outcome of his visit to the landlord's office. "I'm fresh out of ideas. Unless we get a sudden windfall, we'll have to gut it out here."

"We gave it a go," Dez said. She poured him another glass of chardonnay, her other hand resting on his shoulder. She gave his shoulder a reassuring squeeze. "It's going to be okay. We love the place, so we'll do our best to follow their rules. It's only a year."

Later that night, sleep eluded Cam. He kept seeing Miss Carver smirking as she announced he had no way out. And what had she meant about "earning an amendment"? He had never heard of such a thing, but she had refused to elaborate.

Eventually, Cam drifted off to sleep.

Sometime later, the sound of music awakened him.

18

_____

As Cam bolted upright in bed, he noticed Dez was awake, too, her face illuminated in the dim light filtering from the hallway into the bedroom.

"Do you hear that?" he asked. "Tell me it's not my overactive imagination."

"It's coming from downstairs. Could it be the TV?"

"I turned it off before I came upstairs."

His iPhone read 2:18. He peeled away the blanket and swung his legs over the side of the bed.

"I'll go check it out," he said.

He wore boxers and a T-shirt, his usual sleep gear. He checked in on Ava to confirm she was okay, still asleep, and then he padded downstairs, the steps cool underneath his bare feet.

As he descended the steps, the music grew louder. He recognized the song: "Baby Got Back." It was a huge hip-hop hit from the nineties.

When he reached the lower level, he knew the music wasn't coming from the TV. It came, quite clearly, from the basement.

He hadn't gone into the basement in several days, but there was a television down there, too. Perhaps Dez had left it on and forgotten about it. She was turning the space into a play area for Ava.

He opened the basement door. The music's volume increased. Lights burned down there, too. He saw the glow from his vantage point at the top of the staircase.

Someone's down there. A chill settled over him.

"Hello?" he said. He felt like an idiot. But how else did you greet a home invader? He had never been in such a situation. "Is anyone down there?"

No response, but the music was so loud that whoever might have occupied the basement probably didn't hear him.

Cam looked around, spotted the knife block sitting on the kitchen counter, and crossed the distance and pulled out the chef's blade. As he returned to the doorway, Dez rounded the corner, entering the hall.

"Do you think someone's down there?" she asked.

"Maybe." The knife handle felt like an icicle in his clammy grip.

"A home invader playing Sir Mix-a-Lot?" Frowning, she looked at the doorway. "I've got my phone. Let's go look."

"I'll go first," he said.

He descended the steps, emerged into the light.

On the other side of the main area, a young Black woman removed clothing from a gigantic suitcase that lay on the sofa. Then she raised her smartphone at a selfie angle, tossed her long, dark hair over her shoulder, and posed for a photo.

Am I dreaming? Cam thought.

After she snapped her selfie, she noticed him. She punched a button on her phone to mute the music.

"Hey there," she said. "You guys must be my housemates. I'm Lola."

19

You guys must be my housemates. I'm Lola.

Cam couldn't have been any more shocked if the woman had materialized from the ether like a spirit. He almost believed that he was still dreaming, that he slumbered in his bed upstairs, immersed in fantasyland.

Dez had arrived in the basement, too. Standing beside him, she bared her teeth like a feral cat at the woman.

"Who the hell are you?" Dez asked. "And why are you in our house?"

"Oh, an Uber dropped me off. I let myself in through the side door over there." Lola smiled, as if none of this was the least bit surprising to her. She crossed the space between them, strutting like a fashion model on a runway.

Good Lord, she's fine, Cam thought. He hated that the idea came to him while Dez was standing next to him, but there it was. Lola looked to be in her mid-twenties. She wore a white crop-top and green tie-waist shorts, and she was barefoot. She wore makeup that looked as if it had taken hours to apply. In fact, everything about her —from her long hair to her hazel eyes to her smooth, tawny beige skin to her smile, and of course, her shapely body—seemed designed for maximum visual impact.

Lola extended her hand to him. He lowered the knife, feeling like a fool for bringing it. Lola's delicate hand felt soft as velvet in his grasp.

"Cam Woodson," he said.

She gave his hand a firm squeeze, her gaze locked on his. Her perfume engulfed him like a cloud. He felt dizzy.

"It's a pleasure to meet you, Cam," Lola said. She turned to Dez.

"You can address me as Mrs. Woodson," Dez said, but she didn't extend her hand. "You haven't told me what you're doing here."

"I must've awakened you guys, hmm?" Lola asked. She had a syrupy southern accent, probably came from Mississippi or Alabama, Cam thought. "I didn't realize the music was so loud. My goodness, I'm so sorry. I'm a night owl and it drives people crazy sometimes."

"If you don't tell me what you're doing here in ten seconds, I'm calling the police," Dez said, finger poised over her phone.

Lola only smiled her glittery smile. Her teeth were so bright that Cam figured she must have gotten them whitened.

"Oh, you can talk to Miss Carver about that, honey." She wriggled her dainty hand as if this were an insignificant matter, her long, manicured nails glistening. "I've been renting places from them since I moved here from Mobile."

"It could be in our lease." Cam looked at Dez. "I spotted a passage in there about subletting."

"*We* are not allowed to sublet," Dez said. "I don't remember anything about the *landlord* subletting a place that we're in."

"Excuse me, honey." Lola edged past Cam, and Cam stepped backward and crashed into a lamp. It tumbled to the rug but didn't break.

"Sorry," Cam said.

"Don't worry about that, sugar." Lola laid a warm hand on his forearm, her touch electric against his skin. She dipped to retrieve the lamp from the floor, moving as gracefully as a ballet dancer, and Cam got a glimpse of cleavage that he didn't need to see.

Cam heard Dez make a noise of disapproval.

"This is a lot to swallow." Dez pressed her hand to her temple, wincing. "We didn't expect to have a roommate."

"I won't be bothering y'all." Lola grinned. "I'll be down here in the basement, just little old me. I won't crank up my music again like that. You won't know I'm here most days. I work a lot."

"What kind of work do you do?" Cam asked.

Lola was about to answer when Dez interrupted.

"Listen, it's late," Dez said. "We have to work tomorrow. We'll be talking to Miss Carver in the morning. Please don't touch our stuff, and keep the music down—*way down*. We have a child sleeping upstairs. Can you do that, Lola?"

"Of course." Lola clasped her hands. "Pleasure meeting y'all. Sorry again about the music."

Dez spun on her heel and marched to the staircase. Cam glanced at Lola, shrugged, and followed his wife.

But before he left, Lola winked at him.

20

Dez was fuming. As soon as they got back to the first floor and shut the basement door, she whirled on Cam.

Cam took a step back. His wife looked ready to eviscerate someone with her bare hands.

"Can you believe this shit?" Dez asked. "They moved someone into the basement! Without telling us or asking us!"

"I'm going to make a prediction." Cam returned the chef's knife to the storage block. "I predict that when we talk to Miss Carver, she's going to explain that our landlord reserves the right to put more tenants in a property."

"My God." Groaning, Dez covered her face in her hands and leaned against the counter. "This is a nightmare."

"It could be a lot worse. What if instead of one woman we had a family of six down there?"

"Aren't you upset about this?" She put her hands on her hips. "Oh, I know what it is. You think she's hot. I saw how you knocked over that lamp. You always get clumsy around pretty women."

"No, I don't." But heat flushed his face.

"Whatever, I'm calling Miss Carver in the morning. She's going to need to tell me exactly what is going on here."

"I dunno, babe. Like the lawyer told me, landlords in Georgia have crazy power. They can do almost anything they want."

"Regardless, I'm calling her." She started to leave the kitchen, turned. "Are you coming back to bed? Or are you hoping to chat with our new hoochie mama housemate?"

"That's harsh, Dez."

"Like she didn't realize that blasting music in the middle of the night would wake us up. Please."

"She apologized. She seemed genuinely sorry."

"Right." Dez rolled her eyes. "Everything about her is as fake as a three-dollar bill—including her hair."

Dez charged off down the hallway. Cam glanced toward the basement, hoping their new housemate hadn't heard his wife's tirade (*why do I care?*), and then he followed his wife to bed.

21

"Mmmm. That coffee sure smells good, honey."

That morning around nine o'clock, Cam stood at the kitchen counter in front of his coffee machine waiting on a pod to be transformed into espresso, when he heard the young woman's Alabama twang. He looked over his shoulder and saw Lola peeking around the corner of the basement doorway.

He had been preparing to leave the house to visit a local café and work on his book. Although the work from home restriction was absurd, that morning, he welcomed it.

Being at home knowing Lola was in the basement was distracting.

Dez had left with Ava over an hour ago. Before leaving, she had issued a stern warning to Cam: *Keep our bedroom doors locked. Don't leave out anything valuable. We don't know a thing about this Lola character. I don't trust her, and neither should you.*

Cam figured the young lady was harmless, if a bit naive perhaps, but he didn't want to get on his wife's bad side. He had locked up everything and his last step before leaving the house was to fill his thermos with coffee.

But Lola's sudden appearance knocked him off balance.

He cleared his throat. "Hey, good morning. Do you want a cup?"

"Would that be cool?" She stepped into the kitchen. "I've got only an old, busted machine and I'm totally out of K-cups." She raised her hand. "I'm an addict, I admit it."

He laughed. "It's cool. I've got plenty to share." He gestured toward a display rack beside the machine, which held an assortment of over a dozen pods.

"Aww, you're such a sweetie." She sauntered toward him. As it had last night, her perfume or body lotion or whatever sweet fragrance she wore engulfed him.

He had to try hard to avoid checking her out. She wore a pink halter top that displayed abundant cleavage and left her sculpted midriff exposed, and high-cut green shorts so tight they might have been shrink-wrapped to her body.

Why didn't anything like this ever happen to me when I was single? he wondered, and banished the thought.

"Are you sure it's okay?" she asked. "I promise I won't make this a habit."

"No worries at all. It's my pleasure."

"This is a super nice machine." Lola ran a lacquered nail along the shiny LED panel. "Like something you'd see in a Starbucks."

"It was the one nice gift I bought for myself when I landed my first book deal."

"Wait." She batted her long lashes. "You're a writer?"

"Five novels to my name so far. I doubt you've heard of any of them."

"This is amazing!" Her eyes shimmered. "I've never met a *real* writer, wow. Can I see your books?"

After she selected a pod and the machine brewed her a cup, Cam led her into his office area (well, former office area). A small bookcase held every edition of his novels: hardcovers, paperbacks, one German edition.

"This is so cool." She sipped delicately from her mug and ran her finger along the back cover of one of his novels. "It's got your photo —it really is you. You're better looking in person, though."

Is she flirting with me? Me with my plain looks and my glasses and my dad bod? No. She's only being nice because I gave her a cup of coffee.

"Last night, you said you work a lot," he said. "What do you do?"

"Do you promise not to laugh?" She leaned against the doorway and crossed her legs.

"Promise."

"I'm a social media influencer."

"I've never met a *real* social media influencer." He grinned.

"You promised not to make fun of me," she said, but she laughed.

"Exactly what do you influence? I'm serious. How does that work?"

"I promote mostly lingerie, bikinis, cute shoes, stuff like that." She shrugged. "Brands send me things to wear, and I try them on and post pictures of myself. I get paid for each post depending on how many people see it. Whatever."

"I bet you're earning a fortune," he said.

She giggled. "Not quite, but I do okay. Are you on Instagram?"

"No," he lied.

"Oh, I was gonna give you my handle and then you could look for yourself if you were curious. It's BamaLola69."

"Social media is a huge time sink for me," he said. "I stopped using it so I could spend more time on my writing." He made a dramatic show of checking his phone. "Speaking of which, I need to head out."

"I didn't mean to keep you; I need to get going, too," she said. "Thanks again for the delicious coffee and the convo, Cammy."

Cammy? That's a new one.

Lola sashayed out of the room, humming the melody from "Baby Got Back."

Watching her go, Cam exhaled.

As soon as she closed the basement door, he opened the Instagram app on his phone and typed in her handle. Her profile surfaced immediately. She had over a hundred thousand followers, and from one glance at her photo feed he could see why.

Cam, my man, you really do not *need to be looking at this.*

His phone buzzed. He was so shocked he nearly fumbled the phone, and when he looked to see who had called he was convinced it would be Dez, aware of his ogling photos of another woman via a wifely sixth sense.

But the number came from Baron Properties. Was it Miss Carver again, warning him that she was thirty seconds away from conducting a home inspection?

"Hello?" Cam said.

"Good morning, Mr. Woodson!" It was a man's booming baritone voice, unfamiliar to Cam.

But in the pit of his stomach, Cam knew the caller's identity as surely as he knew his own name.

"This is your landlord."

22

When Dez got a break at school that morning, between classes, she went outside to her car so she could have privacy and called Miss Carver.

She was going to get to the bottom of this new housemate situation. The mere thought of some strange young woman living downstairs infuriated her. The nerve of the landlord to install another tenant in the house without disclosing from the beginning that they planned to do it! Who did something like that?

Cam's response to the situation grated on her, too. He seemed to dismiss it as a minor annoyance. *We weren't going to do anything important with the basement, anyway, babe. It's way more space than we need.*

I was going to create a playroom for Ava down there, she reminded him.

Ava has plenty of space in her bedroom. She doesn't need an entirely separate room for her toys.

Although Cam would never admit it to her, Dez was convinced that he didn't mind having Lola there because he found the young woman attractive. She was eye candy—there was no question about that—but the principle of her tenancy was like a splinter in Dez's finger.

She had no idea whether Miss Carver would answer or if she'd need to leave a message, but when Dez called the number on her smartphone, Miss Carver picked up after the first ring.

"Good morning, Mrs. Woodson," Miss Carver said.

Dez could hear the amusement in the woman's tone. Like this was all a big damn joke. Her stomach clenched.

"How're you getting along with your new housemate?" Miss Carver asked.

"I reviewed the lease," Dez said. "There's nothing that says the landlord can't install a new tenant, but we obviously weren't expecting this, Miss Carver. You know that."

"Lola's a lovely young lady. You warn that husband of yours to behave himself." Miss Carver chuckled.

"I don't want her there!" Dez said. She hadn't meant to yell but the words exploded out of her. "You never said someone else would be renting out the house!"

"You never asked," Miss Carver said.

Dez felt a migraine coming on. Wincing, she put her hand to her throbbing temple. From time to time, she suffered epic headaches that made her want to crawl into a bed and black out every light in the room. Usually, financial stresses conjured those migraines, but this rental situation was becoming so crazy that it was no surprise it was inducing physical pain.

She closed her eyes for a beat, drew a couple of deep breaths.

"Mrs. Woodson?" Miss Carver asked.

Dez opened her eyes.

"We had plans for the basement," Dez said. "I was going to build a playroom for my daughter."

"Man plans; God laughs," Miss Carver said. "You've over four thousand square feet of living space, not including the basement, Mrs. Woodson. Surely you can figure out a solution to provide a recreational area for your child."

She was getting nowhere with this woman. But her breathing was so rapid that she had fogged up the windows in her car.

"Advance notice would have been appreciated," Dez said. "From day one. Before we signed the shady lease."

"Fair enough. If we decide to lease space to other tenants at the rental, I'll let you know about it."

Dez squeezed the phone so tightly her knuckles popped. "Wait, you're going to put more people in the house?"

"It's at the landlord's discretion, Mrs. Woodson. I suggest you review your local occupancy codes. From what I recall, the landlord can add up to two tenants per bedroom."

Is this woman insane?

"Two tenants per bedroom," Dez repeated. "We have five bedrooms, not factoring in the basement. At least seven more people could be added."

"You must be a math teacher, Mrs. Woodson. That was some rather rapid mental arithmetic you demonstrated." She laughed.

Dez hung up on her. She was so angry she couldn't summon any more words.

And now, she had a migraine for the ages.

23

A few minutes after one o'clock in the afternoon, Cam arrived at the house in Norcross. Thor was already there, as the landlord had promised. His van stood in front of the garage.

Cam pulled into the driveway beside the van. During the drive there, he had reflected on his surreal discussion with the landlord earlier that morning.

"I've been told that you're a man with a useful skill set," the landlord had said. "Mr. Woodson, in my profession, I value men such as yourself."

"You mean my writing?" Cam asked.

"You've quite a knack for working with your hands, I've been told."

Cam had no idea what he was talking about, and then he remembered the day they had signed the lease. He had done some minor repair to a light fixture in the dining room and Miss Carver had seemed impressed. *Ah, aren't you the handy one? You say you are a writer, but perhaps your true calling is home repair, Mr. Woodson. There's always work available for one skilled with his hands . . .*

The woman must have passed along her observation to the landlord.

"Oh," Cam said. "I actually wanted to talk to you about our lease, sir."

Cam didn't know why he addressed the landlord as "sir," yet it felt appropriate. He had no idea what the man looked like, but his writer's imagination had conjured a vivid image: he would be a tall, broad-shouldered, seasoned gentleman wearing an expensive black suit, conducting himself with the authoritative demeanor of a man who moved mountains with merely a few words. Sort of like the late Sean Connery in the latter phase of his career, minus the Scottish accent. The landlord conveyed that kind of commanding presence, even over the telephone.

"We'd like to request an amendment to some of the conditions, please," Cam said. "Like my working from home and the no-party thing."

"We'll get to that, friend, in due time. I'd like to hire you for a task. A handyman job. It's right up your alley, as they say."

"But I'm a writer," Cam said.

"I'm aware that you've written a handful of books."

He spoke as if Cam were a hobbyist writer, noodling over his work in his spare time on the weekends. Cam struggled to suppress his irritation. He couldn't afford to make an enemy of this guy.

"I'm heading out to a coffee shop to work on my novel," Cam said. "I'd rather stay here at home to write, but I'm trying to follow your rules."

"I pay very well, Mr. Woodson. You would be handsomely compensated for your time."

"I'm not a handyman," Cam said, drawing out the words. "I'm a full-time writer, sir. It's . . . it's what I do."

"Your books sell poorly, Mr. Woodson. I've looked them up."

Cam had been pacing the kitchen. The cold remark made his knees lock. "Ouch."

"Your credit is in the shitter, as we both know. You barely met our credit requirements. Other landlords would not have been so flexible."

"You don't need to remind me of that. I'm working on it."

"Are you? What's your brilliant plan to revive your financial standing, Mr. Woodson?"

"I've got a new project in the works. I'm making great progress on it."

"How long until it bears fruit? Months? Years? An eternity?" The landlord chuckled.

"I have a *plan*," Cam said.

"Meanwhile, your lovely wife is the primary breadwinner. How does that feel, Mr. Woodson? To have failed so spectacularly in your chosen profession?"

Cam swallowed. He was surprised at the tears he felt welling in his eyes. No one in his life had ever talked to him like this, with such disregard for his feelings. Even William, Dez's father, didn't draw blood like this.

Cam took off his glasses, pinched the bridge of his nose. *Don't let this guy rattle you, man. He doesn't know you. Why do you care what he says?*

But the man's incisive remarks struck at the core of Cam's deepest insecurities. He *had* failed. He had failed his wife and daughter, the most important people in his life.

Most importantly, he had failed himself. His life that day was a far cry from the lifestyle to which he aspired when he wrote his first story as a teenager, showed it to his mother, and mustered the courage to declare himself a writer. Mom had been gently dismissive: *That's nice, but how are you going to provide for yourself?* He had vowed to prove her wrong. He had vowed to prove everyone wrong.

But where had that steely-eyed determination gotten him? A cold shoulder from his publisher and everyone else in New York. A shrinking bank account. Driving for Uber and putting together furniture in between working on a manuscript that no one might want anyway.

"You want to provide for your family, like any decent husband and father should," the landlord said. "I'm offering you an opportunity, Mr. Woodson, to earn good money today."

Cam should have ended the call; that was what his conscience told him. He didn't want to *work* for his landlord, in any capacity. That seemed like a violation of the entire tenant-landlord relationship.

But desperation made you do things you probably shouldn't have considered.

"I already drive for Uber and assemble furniture, sometimes," Cam said in a mumble.

The landlord scoffed. "My tasks pay much better, I assure you."

"What kind of task are you talking about, anyway?" Cam asked.

"Equip yourself with pen and paper . . ." the landlord began.

That was how Cam had wound up in Norcross that afternoon, the back of his SUV full of items he had purchased from The Home Depot and for which the landlord promised prompt reimbursement once he had completed the job. The landlord had said Thor would already be there, and Cam found some relief in finding the man's van parked at the house. Everything about the situation was so weird that he appreciated a familiar face.

He got out of the Jeep and assessed the residence. It was a two-story house, perhaps twenty years old, in decent condition. But plywood had been nailed to a couple of windows on the second floor. What was that all about?

He grabbed the plastic bags from the cargo area and carried them to the front door. The door hung open; he heard hammer blows coming from inside.

He set down the bags on the edge of the hallway. He located Thor in the kitchen, which had been gutted. The big man appeared to be hanging drywall. A small Bluetooth speaker sitting atop an Igloo cooler played country western music, the singer's twangy voice going on about hard drinking and hard living.

"Cam Woodson." Thor turned. "You are here to work, our land-lord says."

"Hey, Thor. Yeah, he hired me to replace light fixtures in the bedrooms."

"Good. Do you have the proper tools?"

"My toolbox is in the Jeep. I should be set."

Thor nodded. "If you need anything, you come to see me. But I think you will not need me. I hear you are good."

"I guess word has spread."

Cam turned to go back to his SUV, but Thor stopped him with a grunt.

"Do not explore the house," Thor said. "This is for your safety. Open only the doors I marked for you like this." He fished a yellow Post-it Note out of his shirt pocket and waved it like a flag.

"Sure."

"Very important," Thor said.

Why? Cam wanted to ask. But he didn't. He was there to complete a specific task. He needed to get started.

24

Cam returned inside the house carrying his toolbox. He picked his way through the first floor. Much of it, like the kitchen, was in the midst of a major renovation.

"Your job is upstairs." Thor pointed upward. "Do not explore."

I heard you the first time, Cam thought.

The steps groaned underneath his feet as he ascended to the upper level. He found himself in a long corridor, construction debris strewn about.

He saw three closed doors marked with yellow paper squares. He spotted another square attached to the damaged light fixture in the middle of the hallway.

One closed door, at the end of the hall, was unmarked and steeped in shadow. A large cardboard box barred entry.

I suppose that's where I'm not *supposed to look.*

He thought about the plywood nailed to the second-floor windows. Probably in that room.

Do not explore.

He got to work, starting in the nearest room, a smallish bedroom heaped with debris. He located the ladder downstairs and brought it up to the room.

He had a fair amount of experience switching out light fixtures, had done it at his in-laws' house and for a couple of friends. It took him about twenty minutes to replace the first one. When he was done, he tested it out by flicking the light switch. Brightness filled the room.

Success. He snapped a photo with his phone of the completed repair.

One down, three to go.

He had slipped in his earbuds and streamed music while he worked, up-tempo tunes that kept him focused on the task. It felt good to work with his hands, to see the fruit of his labors within minutes, as opposed to the months it often required to complete a novel. Although he'd planned to work on his book that morning, the landlord's call had knocked him off course, and he was going to fall behind the schedule he had mapped out for himself.

But it's for a good cause, he reminded himself. *I'm getting paid today for doing this work.*

He looked forward to telling Dez about it. He wondered how she had gotten along with her inquiry to Miss Carver about their new housemate—the fact that Dez hadn't called him made him suspect the conversation hadn't gone well. She didn't like sharing bad news over the phone, would undoubtedly want to discuss it that evening.

Was having Lola in the basement so terrible? She seemed like a nice young lady. He was self-aware enough to realize that the fact that she was easy on the eyes probably influenced his opinion on the matter, but couldn't it have been worse? They didn't need the basement, anyway. They had plenty of space in the rest of the house.

It took Cam a little more than an hour to replace all four light fixtures and take photos of all of them. As directed, he sent a text message to the landlord's phone number with the pics attached.

All done, Cam said in his message.

The reply came within a minute.

Excellent work, Mr. Woodson! Payment is forthcoming.

Cam typed: *What about earning that amendment? Can we discuss that now?*

In due course. Enjoy your cash reward for a job well done.

The Cash App notification on his phone chimed. Cam opened the app.

"Damn," Cam said.

Baron Properties had paid him six hundred dollars. The lights had set back Cam about two hundred; that meant he had netted four hundred dollars in profit, give or take a few bucks for travel time.

Standing in the hallway, he laughed, giddy as a child. Four hundred dollars for easy work! This was nuts. He felt as if he had participated in some wacky reality show.

He couldn't wait to tell Dez. *Guess who brought home the bacon today, babe.*

He gathered his toolbox and the trash. The shadows in the hallway had shifted as the afternoon lengthened. He glanced at the door at the end of the corridor and had a better view of the region around the cardboard box that barricaded the room.

A chill plucked his spine.

He ran the back of his hand across his mouth. He glanced over his shoulder, confirming he was still alone upstairs, and crept closer to the room.

As he suspected, a rust-colored stain on the carpet peeked from underneath the edge of the box.

Blood.

He ought to leave. Thor had warned him about exploring. The landlord had paid him, handsomely, for his work that afternoon.

Perhaps it was the writer in him, but insatiable curiosity held him like a steel pin to a magnet.

One quick look won't hurt.

As quietly as possible, he shifted aside the box. The contents rattled as he moved it, and he paused, convinced that Thor might hear, but then remembered the guy was listening to his country western tunes and probably wouldn't hear a thing.

Still, Thor might come upstairs to check on him. He needed to do this quickly.

He discovered more blood as he shifted the box aside: a full, bloody footprint.

His stomach curdled.

He reached for the doorknob, actually hoping that it was locked so he could not explore further. But it opened.

Now I've gotta look. I need to know.

The door drifted open soundlessly. Beyond, shadows ruled, the plywood slats blotting out the daylight.

He edged forward. Bracing odors hit him in the face: old blood, something rotten, and there was an undercurrent of urine, too.

It must have been the master bedroom because it seemed much larger than the other rooms, and he didn't see any hulking shapes of furniture. But the shadows were too thick for him to see details.

He raised his phone and switched on the flashlight app. He panned it around.

Oh my God.

A copious amount of blood stained the carpet. It looked as if someone had a bucketful of gore, brought it inside, and splashed it all over the floor until the can was empty. Footsteps were tracked across it; he saw handprints here and there on the walls, too.

A shred of crime scene tape from the Gwinnett County Policy Department lay in the corner, like a discarded holiday decoration.

Although he wrote stories in which bad things happened to people, wrote about murders and violence and terrible acts, he had a weak stomach for real blood. He felt his gag reflex kick in and he doubled over. The contents of his lunch surged up his throat, a sour taste filling his mouth. Cold perspiration beaded his forehead.

He had the presence of mind to take a couple of photos. The blood on the carpet and the walls and the crime scene tape. He didn't know why he took photos, but it felt important to do so.

Breathing hard, his heart banging, he finally backed out of the room and shut the door. He tried to reposition the cardboard box exactly where he had left it.

In a bathroom located between two of the bedrooms, he washed his face with cold water and rinsed out his mouth. He felt slightly better, but he couldn't shut down his thoughts.

What the hell had happened in there?

He hurried to the staircase with the trash he needed to discard, and his toolbox. Thor came around the corner and Cam was so shocked to see him he almost screamed.

"Are you done with the job?" Thor asked.

Cam swallowed. "Yep, all done. I already sent photos to the landlord."

Thor's gaze narrowed. "You did not explore?"

"You told me not to."

"Excellent." Thor clapped him on the shoulder. "I will put in a good word for you. Perhaps we will work together again, Cam Woodson."

25

When Dez arrived home with Ava that evening, the migraine headache that she had experienced earlier that day returned, triggered by the mere sight of the rental house.

I can't believe we've got to share this house with a stranger. This isn't what I wanted. How will I live like this?

Although her mother had babysat Ava that day, when Dez picked up her daughter she hadn't told Mom about the housemate predicament, and fortunately, Daddy wasn't home to interrogate her about the latest status. She couldn't explain the situation to her parents without sounding like a loon. Knowing her family, they would insist she move out of the house and into theirs, lease be damned. She couldn't do something so impulsive and irresponsible.

She had kept her mouth shut. But when she pulled into the rental's driveway, the migraine roared back, bright lights flickering in her vision. She groaned, pressed her fingers to her temples.

Pull it together, girl. When handed lemons, make lemonade.

She brought Ava inside. As Ava raced into the family room, Dez checked the house. The master bedroom door was locked, as she had requested of Cam; Ava's bedroom was secured as well.

The girl hasn't robbed us blind yet. That's a start.

But she couldn't avoid Lola. She had commandeered the basement that Dez had planned to remodel into a playroom for her daughter. They had items down there and she needed them.

After taking another pair of ibuprofen tablets for her headache, Dez knocked on the basement door, Ava at her side. No answer. She didn't know whether Lola was home since the young woman didn't own a vehicle.

Dez opened the door and rapped on the stairwell wall.

"Hello, Lola? It's Mrs. Woodson."

"Come on down, honey," Lola said, her voice distant.

When Dez reached the bottom of the staircase, she saw Lola on the other side of the room. She stood in front of an easel and held a paintbrush. She wore a maroon and white Alabama A&M sweatshirt and baggy jeans, her long hair swept back into a ponytail. She wasn't wearing any makeup or jewelry.

Her casual appearance surprised Dez. Dez had pegged Lola as one of those social media airheads who loved posing in front of their smartphones in their skimpy outfits and glam-girl makeup, sharing filtered photos with their adoring followers.

"Oh my, is that your baby girl?" Lola asked, in a high-pitched voice. She hurried around the sofa. "She is so gorgeous! Oh my goodness!"

"What do you say to a compliment, Ava?" Dez asked her daughter.

"Thank you." Ava giggled.

"Ava? Such a pretty name!" Lola kneeled so she was eye level with Ava. "Ava, my name is Lola. It's nice to meet you."

"Hi." Ava looked up at Dez, basking in the young woman's attention.

"She has your eyes," Lola said to Dez. "Have you heard that before, Mrs. Woodson?"

"What I usually hear is how she's my husband's mini-me."

"She's got your eyes for sure. And your dimples, too." Lola gave Dez a megawatt smile. "She's a doll."

"Thank you. I didn't mean to interrupt." Dez glanced toward the easel.

"Oh, no worries, honey. I hope you aren't still upset with me. Did you talk to Miss Carver?"

"She clarified the situation," Dez said. *Did she ever.*

"I'm so sorry for last night. I think we got off on the wrong foot, Mrs. Woodson. Can you please accept my apology? It's been heavy on my heart all day."

Dez found a smile for the young woman; she seemed truly apologetic. "It's fine, Lola. And please, call me Dez. I don't think I'm that much older than you are."

"Dez it is." Lola beamed at her.

"I had a box down here full of Ava's toys. I'd like to get that, please."

"I set it aside 'cause I figured you'd want it. I was gonna bring it upstairs, but I didn't wanna be traipsing around up there without asking y'all."

You might be sharper than I assumed, Dez thought.

"Lemme go get it." Lola whirled away like a ballerina. Dez crossed the room and studied the painting on the easel. It was a stunning watercolor depicting a sunrise on a beach, and a vast ocean.

"This painting is amazing," Dez said, when Lola returned lugging a cardboard box.

"Thanks, honey. It's something I threw together. Inspiration strikes sometimes."

"Did you study art in college?"

"I wanted to, 'til my folks said I needed to learn something that would give me a career." Lola rolled her eyes. "I got me a business degree from Alabama A&M, but I still like painting in my free time."

"I'd paint more, myself, if I had time. It was all I wanted to do when I was growing up."

"Is that right?" Lola's hazel eyes shimmered. "Sounds like we got something else in common then, including being housemates."

Maybe this will work out, Dez thought, as she returned upstairs carrying the box of toys. *Maybe this will work out just fine.*

26

I t was a murder-suicide.

Later that night, after Dez went to bed, Cam opened his laptop and read about the crime that had occurred at the property in Norcross where he'd performed the task for the landlord. He found the story on the *Atlanta Journal-Constitution* website, dated in early September of that year.

GWINNETT COUNTY, Ga. - Gwinnett County detectives are investigating the murder-suicide of a married couple whose bodies were found inside their Norcross rental home, Saturday evening.

The bodies of Michael Parker, 39, and his wife, Tiffany Parker, 36, were discovered by Parker's 18-year-old son around 9:30 PM. The bodies were lying in the bedroom of the house, located in the 400 block of South Sugar Hill Drive.

According to investigators, Parker shot his wife in the head, then turned the gun on himself. He apparently died of a self-inflicted wound to the head. Paramedics pronounced the couple dead at the scene.

Police believe the motive for the incident is domestic-violence related. The couple had been married for about six years.

Cam held a cold beer as he read the news story, but the chill that settled into his body was far colder than the bottle.

He swiped through the photos he had taken with his phone. So much blood. As he remembered the fetid smell of death, his insides churned.

Earlier, while eating dinner with Dez and Ava, he hadn't said anything about what he'd seen or how he'd spent most of his day. He muttered about working on his book at Starbucks (which he'd done after he completed the landlord's task, struggling to focus) and listened to Dez chat about Lola and Miss Carver. While Dez no longer thought Lola was the Whore of Babylon, Miss Carver remained the Wicked Witch of the West.

Cam used a portion of the day's earnings to pay a past-due credit card bill; he deposited the balance into their joint savings account. It felt great to contribute money to the household.

Still, he avoided discussing the landlord's assignment. He didn't quite understand his reticence to tell Dez about it. Was he ashamed, considering how the landlord had browbeaten him earlier? Or was he afraid to disclose what he'd found in the house?

One thing was clear: he regretted that he ignored Thor's warning to avoid exploring. Some things you could never *unsee*.

He read the news story again, and one phrase jumped out at him:

. . . bodies were found inside their Norcross rental home . . .

Rental home. Did the landlord own the Norcross house, too, at the time of the crime?

It was a reasonable assumption that he owned the property back then. The murder had taken place a little over a month ago.

And what about the blood on the wall Cam had seen in the basement in *this* house, when they originally toured the property? Could a homicide have taken place in this very home?

The chill sank deeper, leaked into his bone marrow.

He pushed away from the table, unable to sit still. Pacing across the living room, he ran his fingers through his hair.

His imagination raced. None of these incidents could be connected, he told himself. He didn't even know what the connection might be.

—the landlord—

"Don't be ridiculous," he said aloud.

He sat in front of the computer again and reread the news story.

Had Miss Carver visited those people late at night, too? Subjected them to an absurdly restrictive lease agreement? Banned them from working from home and holding small gatherings?

Did they drive the husband so far over the brink that he lost his mind, killed his wife and then himself?

"No way," Cam said to himself.

But his heart thundered like a bass drum.

He returned to Google and entered the address of their own rental house, along with the words "police" and "crime." The search engine returned no results.

"See? You're worried about nothing," Cam said to himself. "Keep that imagination of yours focused on fiction, man. You have nothing to worry about."

Despite his self-assurances, worry gnawed at his mind.

To refocus his attention, he yearned to open the file for his current manuscript and pound out a few pages, but caution won over. Instead of "working from home" (he gave the phrase air quotes these days) he would read something until he got drowsy and then go to bed. He had a legitimate opportunity to make inroads with the landlord, to earn an amendment, possibly. He couldn't risk jeopardizing it.

And if the landlord offered him another task, his answer was going to be *yes*.

27

C am was at a Starbucks on Friday morning, sipping homemade coffee from his thermos and writing on his laptop, when he looked up and saw Lola enter the café.

He sat up straighter in his chair.

The young woman wore chunky designer sunglasses that hid most of her face, but he recognized her immediately. She wore a white blouse and a casual red skirt that swirled around her as she strolled to the counter in that distinctive strut of hers.

He had landed a table in the far corner and wasn't sure if she noticed him—and he wasn't sure he *wanted* her to see him. He was deep into an important scene in his novel, and frankly, he found the young woman distracting. He had encountered her only twice since she had moved into the rental, and he wanted to minimize their interactions.

Pulling his Atlanta Braves baseball cap lower on his head, he sank into his chair and stared at the glowing words on the computer screen, refusing to allow himself to look in her direction. He increased the volume of the music he streamed into his headphones.

But a few minutes later, he smelled Lola's sweet fragrance.

I knew this was coming. He looked up.

Lola had removed her sunglasses, nesting them in her thick, silky hair. She gave him the full effect of her large, shimmering eyes and long eyelashes. His heart stuttered.

He muted his music.

"Hey, Cammy," Lola said. "What a coincidence, huh? Running into you here."

"Hey there. Yeah, this is one of my spots these days."

"Is anybody sitting here?" She pointed at the small table next to him.

Before he could answer, she swept closer, depositing her expensive bag and beverage onto the table.

"I promise I'm not stalking you, Cammy." She unzipped her bag and removed a slender Mac laptop, the lid festooned with colorful stickers of teddy bears. "I was literally craving a pumpkin spice latte when I woke up this morning, and you know, I still haven't gotten a new coffee machine. I think you spoiled me when you poured me a cup from that fancy gadget of yours."

"Use it whenever you want," he said, and wished he hadn't said that. He could have kicked himself.

"I couldn't impose on you like that, honey." She sipped her drink, popped open her laptop. "I gotta work on editing some photos, but hey, I get a bonus—I get to see a real author at work."

"In the flesh." He laughed.

"Will you make me a character in your next book?"

"Well . . ."

"I'm only kidding with you, sweetheart." She touched his shoulder, and the sensation lingered. "Don't mind me. Do your thing."

I'll try. Cam returned his focus to his manuscript. But in his peripheral vision, he saw Lola cross her legs, her elegantly shaped calves on full display, a gold anklet glistening on her ankle.

He gulped his coffee. *Focus, man.*

He increased the volume of the binaural beats track he streamed from YouTube. Although he had assumed Lola's presence would distract him, he dove back into his work with vigor, typing faster than he usually did, and in the back of his mind he mused maybe he wanted to impress her, show off his typing speed, let her see what a "real" author could do, as silly as it sounded, and—

—a warm liquid spilled onto his jeans.

Startled, Cam looked up. Lola's lips formed a perfect "O." He snatched off his headphones.

"I'm so sorry!" she said. He saw her beverage cup lying on her table—half of its contents now on his pants. "I'm sorry, Cammy!"

"It's okay." He slid aside his laptop, thankful she hadn't spilled the stuff onto his machine. "I'll dip into the restroom and clean myself up. Can you keep an eye on my computer?"

"Of course; again, I'm sorry!" She mopped up the spill with a wad of napkins.

When Cam returned from the restroom a few minutes later, Lola had wiped up all remnants of her mishap.

"I'm such a klutz sometimes," she said.

"No worries." He pulled his laptop toward him and keyed in the password to unlock it. He felt Lola watching him and he turned.

"Did I ruin your jeans?" she asked. "I can get you another pair— designers send me stuff all the time and I can put in a request for men's—"

"It's cool, Lola. Forget about it. These were old dad pants, anyway."

"You're too sweet. I'm gonna get you some, anyway. I think I got your size—thirty-four waist and thirty-two length?"

"How do you know that?"

"It says so right on the tag above your butt." She winked at him.

Cam swallowed. "Really, don't worry about it."

"The offer stands. Lemme know if you change your mind."

I won't change my mind. What would Dez say if she found out you gave me clothes?

He tried to resume working, but struggled to find a groove again.

About five minutes later, Lola packed her things. She wriggled her fingers at him in a goodbye wave.

He returned the wave. *Finally, she's leaving.*

He watched her saunter out of the café and get into a white Kia SUV parked at the curb, a Lyft sticker on the rear windshield. She had said she was there to edit some photos, but he estimated she had spent less than twenty minutes working, and he wondered about that, briefly.

The social media influencer lifestyle, he supposed.

He went back to work.

28

Arriving back at the rental house later that afternoon, Cam discovered the waste management company had visited. The trash and recycling bins stood at the curb, lids popped open.

He returned the first bin to its spot beside the house. As he went to grab the other one, he saw the elderly gentleman who lived next door shuffling along his driveway.

Cam waved. "Good afternoon, mister."

The man returned the wave. He grabbed his own trash can and struggled to haul it down the driveway.

"I can give you a hand with that." Cam headed toward him.

"I appreciate that, young man." He nodded toward the house. "You moved in, eh?"

"Sure did."

The man's thin lips curled. "I thought so."

Why the sour expression? Cam wondered.

"It's actually a great house," Cam said.

"Do you want my advice? Keep your family safe."

Cam paused, clutching the trash bin handle. "Excuse me?"

"I call it as I see it, chief. At my age I don't see the point of shoveling bullshit."

"Did something happen to the last renters in the house?"

"*Every* renter in that house runs into bad luck. Every one of them —and there's been plenty of 'em."

"What kind of bad luck? What happened?"

"Talk to your landlord."

The older man thanked Cam for his help and shuffled back into his house.

29

On Saturday, Cam and Dez took Ava to a birthday party their best friends hosted for their twin boys. The party took place at Air Arena, a children's indoor playcenter in Powder Springs.

Dez had been there before for other parties. The cavernous place featured a gigantic, three-story soft play castle. Dozens of shrieking children climbed, crawled, ran, and slid up and down slides and ladders and tunnels, and some more ambitious adults tried to keep up with their kids. Dez had learned better from prior visits. They set Ava loose to play with her friends, and then she and Cam met Ebony and Vic in the party room they had booked.

Cam seemed happy to be there, Dez noted. Typically, he disliked birthday parties—scream fests for kids high on sugar, he called them —but he exchanged hugs and handshakes with their friends. He had surprised Dez and purchased the birthday gift for the twins, a set of remotely controlled race cars. When Dez inquired where he had gotten the money to indulge their friends' children, he only winked at her.

It was strange, but good. She didn't press the matter further, but she made a mental note.

They had been at Air Arena for about half an hour, Dez and Ebony exchanging gossip about teacher-friends, when Cam approached her and pressed the Jeep's key fob into her palm.

"I've gotta head out," he said.

"Head out?"

"I've got a task to do."

"A task?" Was he joking? "What kind of task?"

In a whisper, Cam said, "I've been working for our landlord. He pays very well. He texted me and gave me another assignment."

That's where he got the money to buy the birthday gifts, Dez thought.

Dez slid away from Ebony, who was soaking up more of the conversation than Dez preferred. She steered Cam into a quiet corner of the room.

"What's going on?" she asked.

Cam shifted from one foot to the other like a child who needed to urinate. "Babe, I need to go now. It's gotta be done today."

"How long has this been going on?" she asked.

"Later."

"Why didn't you tell me—"

"I promise, later. I'll explain it all." He kissed her forehead. "Drive the Jeep home. I'm catching an Uber. I'll text you later on, okay? Love you."

Before she could say anything else, he turned and left. Ebony approached Dez, brown eyes wide with curiosity.

"Is everything okay, girl?" Ebony asked.

"Cam forgot to do something back at the house. It's all good."

"He said something about a job?" Ebony asked.

Dez looked away. "I could go for a slice of pizza. Is there a veggie pie over there?"

Ebony took the hint and dropped it, but Dez vowed Cam was going to give her answers, soon.

30

I have another task for you, Mr. Woodson. It must be completed today. Go to the job site you visited for the prior assignment. Thor will be there to provide further instruction.
You will be compensated handsomely for your labor, as before.

Cam read the text again as he sat in the rear row of the Uber driver's Ford Explorer. He disliked leaving Dez and Ava behind at the party, but what choice did he have? The money was too good to resist, and he didn't have time to explain the situation.

There would be time later to set Dez's mind at ease. He had to focus on the assignment ahead.

. . . the job site you visited for the prior assignment . . .

Right, The Murder House. The prospect of going back into that hellhole chilled him. But he had a job to do. The landlord was obviously renovating the place, getting it ready to either sell or rent out again. What business was it of Cam's what had happened there before? How many other homes had been the site of crimes and misdeeds that never made the news?

I'm only hired help, he decided. *I'll do my job, mind my business, and go home.*

He thought about his recent, brief interaction with his neighbor, the older man's comments about "bad luck" striking renters of their rental home and his advice to "talk to your landlord." But Cam was reluctant to broach the subject with his new benefactor. He needed the money the man was paying him, didn't want to risk pissing him off. Besides, other than the silly lease restrictions and Lola's unexpected occupancy, living there was going well for his family.

About fifty minutes later, the Uber driver dropped Cam off in front of the house. Getting out of the SUV, Cam glanced at the master bedroom's second-floor window. The plywood had been removed. Partly open venetian blinds covered the glass.

Maybe that horrific crime scene has been cleaned up.

Thor's van was parked in the driveway. Cam hurried inside. He found Thor in the entry hall sorting through a toolbox, a cigarette tucked behind his ear.

They shook hands.

"I am glad you are here," Thor said. "I told our landlord you did well before."

"What do I need to do this time? He didn't tell me."

"Much, much harder work. I hope you are ready for it."

"I like a challenge," Cam said.

Thor grunted, beckoned Cam forward. Cam followed him to a powder room located off the main hallway.

A stack of cardboard boxes stood on the floor, underneath the sink.

"You are to put down new tile in here," Thor said.

Uh-oh, Cam thought, but he tried to keep his face neutral. Inwardly, his stomach shriveled. He didn't know jack about installing tile.

"See?" Thor put his boot on the boxes. "Tile is here. I have tools and materials you will need. You can do this, Cam?"

"I'll figure it out."

"There is more," Thor said.

More? This room will take me all day.

Thor led Cam to the second floor. Cam held his breath as they arrived in the hallway, but he saw the door at the end of the hall hanging open, golden afternoon sunshine pouring into the room.

He followed Thor inside. The blood-soaked carpet had been ripped out and replaced by new carpeting, and the walls were newly painted.

Cam sighed. Thor frowned at him.

"Are you okay?" Thor asked.

I'm just relieved the murder-suicide evidence has been cleaned up, buddy.

"What do I need to do up here, anyway?" Cam asked.

Thor directed him to the en suite. A bathroom as large as the one at their own rental house awaited.

Thor pointed to a pile of familiar-looking boxes. "Install tile in here."

Wow. "Okay."

"There is more."

"More? All this needs to be done today?"

"Our landlord has a tight schedule for getting this home back on the market."

Thor guided him to one of the bedrooms that Cam had worked in the last time. Several long cardboard boxes lay in the center of the room.

"Assemble furniture," Thor said, pointing with a cigarette.

Cam looked at the boxes and saw a bookcase, a desk, a bed frame, and a chest of drawers.

"All right. Is that all?" Cam asked.

Thor laughed. "You want more?"

"I think I'm going to be here pretty late tonight."

"Yes." Thor grinned. "Tell your beautiful wife, yeah? You are a working man now." He clapped Cam's shoulder. "You are doing well, earning our landlord's trust. Bigger things are in store for you."

As long as big money is part of it, I'm all in.

"Then I'd better get to work," Cam said.

31

W hen Cam searched on YouTube for videos related to "tile a bathroom floor" and scanned the results, he realized he was in for an exceptionally long day.

Prepping the floor—which included removing the toilet. Stripping the floor. Installing screws into floor joists. Cutting the door casing. Putting in backer board. Laying out the tile. Cutting the tile. Grouting. He felt dizzy from absorbing the details of the work that lay ahead of him.

I can't do it, he thought. *It's too much. I don't know anything about tiling a floor.*

But he had already accepted the assignment. What would the landlord do if he backed out? He wouldn't pay Cam merely for traveling to the job site. If Cam bailed, he could kiss any future work goodbye.

Kneeling on the floor in the powder room, cold sweat gathering on his brow, he gazed at the stack of cardboard boxes and the dirty vinyl floor the landlord had charged him with replacing.

I'm good at this sort of thing, right? I've never done this type of job before, but I can figure it out.

I've got to figure it out. We need the money.

The stark truth of that realization struck him like a hammer blow. When you were skating along the edge of financial disaster, with a family that needed you to contribute, was there anything you would *not* do to make ends meet, short of breaking the law? Truth be told, some nights he had lain awake, unable to find sleep, and even mused about illegal activities that could raise fast cash. He had never committed a crime in his life and didn't think he ever would, but staring at dwindling bank account balances, relentless bills, and debt collection notices made you consider all kinds of things you thought you never would.

Yes, he would figure it out.

He sent Dez a text message: *Going to be here for a while. There's a lot to be done. Will text you later. Love you.* He included the residence's address.

About a minute later, Dez sent a one-word response: *Ok.*

She might as well have sent him an angry face emoji. But that was okay. After the landlord paid him for the task and he told her what he had earned, he would turn that scowl into a smile.

Removing the toilet in the powder room took forever, but once he got past that part, he felt as if he were skiing downhill on a steep slope. That didn't mean it was easy—he made mistakes and had to double back, redo things. But the truth was, he had a knack for this kind of work. It was satisfying, in fact, to work with his hands. He listened to music via his headphones and hummed along with old-school hip-hop jams as he stripped, measured, and cut.

At one point, he looked up from his labors and found Thor in the hallway outside the powder room. Thor pantomimed taking a drink.

Cam muted his music, wiped his hand across his damp forehead. "You got anything with caffeine? I need the boost, man."

"Of course." Thor grinned. "Red Bull?"

"That'll hit the spot."

By the time Cam finished tiling the powder room and had

polished off a cold can of Red Bull, Thor ordered two pizzas. But they didn't stop to mill around and drink and nibble food—Cam took an entire pizza box upstairs with him and another energy beverage and kept working. It was already six o'clock. He couldn't afford to waste any time. He had to finish everything that day.

The master bath was next. He knew what to do after tiling the smaller room. The difference was only in the dimensions.

Still, when his iPhone flashed nine o'clock, he thought it was prudent to call Dez. He was half-done in the bathroom, but he hadn't heard anything from her since her terse, one-word text.

"*What* are you doing?" she asked. "You've been gone for hours! I've already put Ava to bed!"

"I'm tiling a master bathroom," he said.

"Tiling? What?"

"It's handyman work, babe. Switching out light fixtures—that was the first task—tiling floors, going to put together some furniture when I'm done in here."

Dez was silent for a beat. "We need to have a serious discussion, Cam. You never told me you were working for our landlord."

"We'll chat when I get home. I'll be here until . . ." He glanced at the time. "Probably about midnight."

"Midnight?" She made a sound in her throat.

"I'll catch an Uber."

Thor peeked into the bathroom, gave Cam a thumbs-up, and said, "Tell the missus I said hello."

"Who the hell is *that*?" Dez asked.

"Thor. You remember Thor? The handyman?"

"I'm done." He heard her sighing. "Please text me when you're on your way back home. I don't care how late it is."

"I love you," he said. "It's all going to be worth it. I promise."

"Please get home soon," she said.

The clock ticked past eleven when Cam wrapped up the master bath. He was drenched in sweat, spattered with grout and grime, had eaten an entire large pepperoni pizza, and knocked back three Red Bulls—but he still had work to do.

He was exhausted. And invigorated.

As he hurried toward the bedroom that contained the furniture, Thor waved at him from the bottom of the staircase.

"How are you doing?" Thor asked.

"About to knock out the last thing, the furniture."

"Do you want to go home? It is late."

"I'm not done yet."

"You are a trooper. That is what I like to hear."

"What about you?" Cam asked.

"I will sleep when I die," Thor said.

Cam laughed and headed into the bedroom.

After the tiling work, putting together furniture was like taking a break. Cam sorted through the boxes and decided to assemble the bed frame first, since it was the largest item. He had grabbed his toolbox from the Jeep before he left the birthday party.

In short order, he assembled the frame. A mattress still wrapped in plastic leaned against a closet door. He might as well toss it onto the frame, he decided.

When he lifted the mattress away from the closet door, he discovered a keypad lock on the closet. Exactly like the one at his rental house.

But this closet door hung open.

32

Cam studied the closet door.

It bore the same keypad locking mechanism as Ava's closet door at their rental house. Twice, Dez had asked Miss Carver for the PIN so they could open the door, and the woman had ignored her requests.

This door hung open about an inch. Cam looked over his shoulder, confirmed that Thor wasn't nearby, and pulled the door open.

It was a fair-sized closet, with a shelf and plenty of storage beneath. It was bare.

What were you expecting to find, Cam? A treasure chest?

For good measure, he activated the flashlight app on his smartphone and panned the light beam inside. He saw a couple of dust bunnies, but nothing else.

Get back to work.

He swept the light across the shelf above him. Something winked back at him. He reached up, groping. His fingers touched something solid and wafer-thin, and he brought it into the light.

It was a DVD, sans storage case or dust jacket. A typed label had been affixed to the disc: *August 2022.*

The murder-suicide that had occurred in this house had taken place in September. One month later.

Cam swallowed.

Carefully, he tucked the disc into his back pocket.

33

Perched on a chair in the family room, the TV tuned to a Netflix show, Dez waited for Cam to get home. A flurry of questions whirled through her mind. *How did you start working for our landlord? How much is he paying you? Why didn't you tell me about this?*

It seemed inappropriate, didn't it, for a tenant to actually *work* for a landlord? Obviously, he was paying Cam—Cam sounded thrilled about the money—but something about it felt wrong to Dez. Already, the landlord and his onerous lease had restricted their activities, and they had Lola living in the basement to boot—and on top of that, Cam was working for him, too?

Although the show on Netflix was a true crime documentary, the type of program that typically consumed her interest, she couldn't focus on it. She wouldn't be able to concentrate on anything until Cam got home and gave her answers.

He had texted her at half-past midnight and said he was on his way. It was a quarter past one when she heard him open the front door.

She sprang off the chair.

"You're still up?" he asked.

If she had any doubts about the work he had said he was performing, his appearance laid them to rest. He looked like a man who had spent the past twelve hours doing difficult manual labor—shirt and pants spattered with grime, face and arms coated with dust.

"I told you I would wait up for you," she said. "What's going on, Cam?"

Cam lifted his iPhone and showed her a balance display on Cash App.

"We're three thousand dollars richer," he said. "That's what's going on, babe."

She took the phone from Cam and studied the screen.

"I don't understand this." She gave him back the phone. "Why is he paying you all this money?"

"I tiled two bathrooms, put together furniture. Hard work, babe —seriously challenging work in those bathrooms. But I did it." He showed her pics of bathroom floors. "The landlord said it looked pro-level."

"*Who* is the landlord? Have you met him?"

"I've talked to him on the phone. He's a straight shooter. You know what? He said I could soon earn an amendment to the lease, too."

Dez had hoped that talking to Cam would put her mind at ease, but the conversation was leading to only more bewildering questions.

"Why haven't you told me any of this?" she asked. "I find out these things after you suddenly leave the party today? I was worried sick about you."

"I was going to tell you." Cam looked away. "I thought you'd get upset."

"I get upset when you keep secrets from me."

"I'm supposed to be a writer, not a handyman." He turned away and went into the kitchen. He dispensed water from the tap into a tall plastic cup and drank it in several gulps. "Wow, I'm so wired. Shouldn't have had all those Red Bulls."

"Listen." Dez touched his shoulder. "I appreciate you trying to make extra money, but I'm not comfortable with you working for our landlord. It feels inappropriate."

"It's money, Dez. We need it."

"Not like this, we don't. What if you screw up one of these gigs and he gets angry? He could make things worse for all of us."

"That's not going to happen."

He wasn't listening to her. He could be like that sometimes, his mind so set on one way of doing things he was like an immovable object. His strong sense of purpose had attracted her—in his own way, he reminded her of Daddy—and it was a quality of his that she still loved, but at other moments, like right now, it drove her crazy.

"*I* need this, babe," he said, voice softening. "Let me help us. It's not fair for you to carry the entire household."

"We're in a temporary rough patch. We'll work through it. You should be writing—that's what you said you wanted to do."

"I'm still writing. Making great progress on the book. But we need money today."

"At what cost, Cam?" she asked.

Cam looked away, didn't respond. She reached for his hand.

"Come to bed with me," she said.

"Babe, I'm high on caffeine. I'll probably be up all night."

"I didn't say we have to sleep." She pulled his hand toward her waist, let his palm encircle her hip. "I missed my husband today."

He kissed her forehead.

"Let me take a quick shower and I'm there."

34

Before going upstairs, Cam dropped the DVD he had taken from the job site into his desk drawer.

He didn't have a DVD drive on his laptop, but he was sure they had a player somewhere in the house. Later, he would look for it, he promised himself.

The truth, however, was that he feared what he might find on the disc.

He hadn't seen the point of sharing the house's macabre past with Dez. It would only worry her, and besides, most homes had a history, not all the stories public knowledge. Why stir up her anxiety for no good reason?

Upstairs, he showered off the dust and grime and then slid under the bedsheets beside Dez. She was still awake, her eyes shining in the faint moonlight spilling through the window. They made love—a slow, patient lovemaking despite the late hour. Mounted above her, Cam noticed a spark of brightness in the corner of his eye.

The bedroom door hung open, light leaking in.

"Is everything okay?" Dez whispered.

"I must've left the door open."

Naked, he rolled away from her, crossed the room to the door. He peered into the hall. The corridor was empty, as it should have been. Ava's bedroom door was shut, too.

But a distinctive fragrance wafted through the cool air.

Cam closed—and locked—the door and returned to bed.

"All good?" Dez reached for him.

He responded by kissing her, and they eased back into their rhythm. Afterward, when Dez drifted into slumber in his arms, Cam slipped out of bed, tossed on shorts and a T-shirt, and padded downstairs.

He opened the basement door without knocking.

Lola danced in the middle of the carpeted area, AirPods nestled in her ears. She wore a cherry-red lace lingerie set and matching stilettos. A long mirror stood propped on the opposite wall, positioned so she could watch and film herself. Holding her smartphone aloft, she twisted in sinuous movements, head thrust back, long hair swinging, her attention focused on her reflection as she captured video for her followers.

Cam watched, heart thudding. It was as surreal as it was titillating. He felt as if he had stumbled into a peep show.

After about a minute, Lola noticed him across the room. She smiled as if she had known all along that he stood there.

"Hey, you," she said.

He cleared his throat. "Did you come upstairs to our bedroom?"

"When?" She cocked her head.

"Tonight. A little while ago."

"Why would I go up to your bedroom, Cammy?"

"I thought you were up there watching us."

"Like you were watching me just now?"

Heat warmed his face.

"Please don't do that again," he said.

"Do what again, honey?"

"Sneak upstairs and watch us. It would upset my wife."

"But it wouldn't upset you? If I did that, I mean."

Cam blushed again.

"Your writer's imagination is running away with you, Cammy. I've been down here filming for a post."

"Our door was open. I smelled your perfume in the hallway."

"I don't wear perfume. It's body cream. Chanel."

"Whatever, I smelled it. You were there. Please respect our privacy. This time, I won't tell Dez about it."

"Are you keeping secrets between us?" She grinned.

"Like I said, this time, I won't tell my wife."

"Fair enough, honey. I won't tell Dez that you came down here to watch me dance." She flicked her tongue across her lips. "Did you enjoy it, by the way?"

By "it" Cam wasn't sure if she referred to sex with his wife, or her erotic dancing. Maybe she meant both.

"I'm going to bed," he said. "Please remember what I said. I want to keep the peace between all of us."

"Goodnight, Cammy." She wriggled her fingers in a wave. "Sweet dreams."

35

About once a month, Cam, Dez, and Ava joined Dez's parents for Sunday dinner. As of late, dinner had been at her parents' house, but Cam proposed they meet at an Italian restaurant on Cobb Parkway. Cam picked a spot that he knew William favored. The man was fussy and prone to complaining throughout a meal if he disliked the food.

"You're late, Woodson," William said when Cam stepped into the waiting area, Dez and Ava in tow.

Ignoring the jibe, Cam shook his hand, William employing his usual bone-crusher handshake. They had arrived three minutes after four o'clock, after proposing to meet at four. He would not allow William to spoil his mood. He hugged Dez's mother, Nora, and kissed her cheek.

Once they settled at the table, Cam ordered a bottle of cabernet sauvignon for the table. This raised William's bushy eyebrows, but Cam offered no insight and he had warned Dez against sharing news about his new income stream.

"How's the book coming, Woodson?" William asked, as he tore

apart a buttery garlic roll. "Did I tell you that the last time I walked into a Barnes & Noble, they didn't have a single copy of any of your books on the shelves? It's like your books don't exist in their system. I can find plenty of James Patterson, but he's a bestseller. That's the difference, eh, son?"

"I've been busy," Cam said. "Also, James Patterson didn't hit the bestseller lists until he was in his mid-forties. I have time to hit my stride."

"Tell that to the creditors," William said.

"Come on, dear." Nora put a placating hand on her husband's arm. "It's Sunday. Let's not discuss business."

William grumbled. Dez offered Cam an apologetic smile, but he cleared his throat and reached into his jacket pocket.

"While we're on the subject of creditors, William," Cam said, "I have something for you."

"An IOU?" William scowled.

Cam unfolded a personal check and handed it across the table. With a grunt, William snatched the check from his fingers.

"It's a thousand dollars," Cam said. "It's a payment toward what we owe you for the rental move-in fees."

William's glare shifted from Cam to Dez.

"Is this going to bounce?" he asked Dez.

Dez pointed at Cam. "This is all Cam, Daddy. He promised to repay you. He's keeping his word."

"When will I get the rest?" William said. "You're deep in the red with me, Woodson."

"I'm working on it." Cam sipped wine, glanced at Dez. "The way things are going, I might pay you back in full sooner than you think." He tapped the menu. "By the way, dinner is on me. Order whatever you'd like."

William's eyes went wide, and for once, he didn't have a snappy comeback. Cam found Dez's hand underneath the table and squeezed it. Dez grinned at him.

Whatever the landlord asks me to do next, it's worth it, Cam thought. To silence his father-in-law, to summon a smile like that from his wife . . . he would do whatever was necessary.

36

Five days a week, Dez rose before Ava awakened to do her Pilates routine. On that Monday morning, she put on her fitness gear and rolled out her mat in the family room, and pulled up the Pilates mat workout series she streamed from her Amazon video account.

Halfway through her routine, she was performing the roll-up exercise when she saw Lola standing at the edge of the room, head cocked.

Dez's heart fluttered like a startled bird.

"Oh," Dez said. She grabbed a nearby towel and blotted perspiration from her forehead. "I didn't know you were there. Do you need something?"

"You look amazing, girl." Lola grinned. "Wow."

"Thank you. I work hard at it."

"I didn't mean to startle you. I heard bumping and wanted to make sure everything was okay."

"Sorry, I didn't realize you could hear me." Dez glanced at the floor. "I suppose this is right above your bedroom down there."

"It's fine, honey. I can sleep through anything." Giggling, Lola stepped forward. She wore only a pink tank top that ended well above her knees. "Have you ever modeled?"

It was Dez's turn to laugh. "Model? No. I try to keep myself up, but I'm not model material."

"You might be surprised. I think you could be a fitness model, seriously."

"You're sweet. Thank you."

"Can I take a selfie with you?" Lola asked. "You're inspiring. One quick pic, please?"

Smiling, Lola already had her phone out and beckoned for Dez to stand beside her. Dez got to her feet but said, "I don't want a photo of me posted on social media."

"It's only for me," Lola said. "Promise."

What the heck does it hurt? Dez thought. She stood next to the young woman, who directed her to angle her body just so. Lola snapped a series of pics.

"You are so photogenic," Lola said, scrolling through the photos. "Really, you could be an IG influencer if you wanted."

Laughing, Dez waved her off. "You're flattering me too much. I need to get back to my workout before Ava wakes up."

"Think about it. You could be a stay-at-home mom, do your posts whenever, in between maybe working on your painting and being a mommy and wifey." Lola winked. "I've got friends who do that. They make *good* money, girl. Six figures, easy."

"Is that what you do?" Dez asked. "Social media influencing?"

"Yup. If you ever wanna chat about it over lunch or something, lemme know. I can share *all* the insider secrets."

"I teach seventh grade, Lola. I could never do something . . . like that." She didn't want to insult the young woman, but the word she almost said was *frivolous*. Posting videos and pictures to social media for money? Exposing herself to leering strangers? What if the parents of her students saw her? What if her colleagues saw her?

"I'll leave you to your workout," Lola said. "Think about it.

You've got the look. You'd have a hundred thousand followers like that." She snapped her manicured fingers.

Dez resumed her exercise routine, but the young woman's words echoed in her thoughts. *Pure silliness,* Dez told herself. *The girl was only being nice. I could never do something like that. Ever.*

37

One morning that week, while Dez dressed Ava for day care, she called Cam into Ava's bedroom.

"Yeah?" Yawning, Cam shuffled through the doorway, still wearing his unofficial sleepwear: baggy boxers and a rumpled Atlanta Hawks T-shirt. Her husband, usually an early riser, had become someone who slept in on weekdays, and Dez assumed it was because of their lease's absurd restriction about working from home. Cam couldn't write until he visited a café or library (he preferred the library, which didn't have an expectation of buying a high-priced latte) and had started sleeping in.

Dez slipped a blouse over Ava's head. Ava looked past Dez and grinned at her father.

"Hey, beautiful." Cam kissed Ava's cheek. "How's Daddy's little girl? Can you say, 'good morning'?"

"Good morning," Ava said so clearly Dez could only smile. Cam had a way of bringing out the best in their daughter, which Dez chalked up to the mysterious bond between fathers and their girls.

"Did you need something, babe?" Cam asked.

"This here." She pointed at the locked closet. "This situation has gotten ridiculous. I'm keeping Ava's clothes in a separate bedroom because I can't use the closet in here!"

Something passed over Cam's eyes when he glanced at the door. It looked like fear. But why would he fear a closet?

"I thought you asked Miss Carver for the keycode," he said.

"Twice now. She's ignoring me."

"Miss Carver isn't a member of the Cam Woodson fan club, either."

"What about your new connection with the landlord?" Dez asked. "Can you ask him?"

Cam scratched his chin. "I guess so."

"That doesn't sound like a 'yes.'"

"He's probably going to refer me to Miss Carver. Whenever I communicate with the landlord, we don't talk about things like this."

"What *are* you talking about, then?" She frowned. "He's the landlord of the property we're living in. This seems like a perfect topic for discussion."

"We talk about the tasks he has for me."

"These unplanned gigs that make you leave parties and keep you away from home until midnight. Of course."

"Dez, please." Cam yawned. "It's too early for this."

"Can you please try to get the keycode from the landlord?" Turning, Dez put on Ava's shoes. "I'm ready to take the door off the hinges and replace it with a new one. We need to use the closet!"

"The lease probably has a restriction about that. Altering of property."

"What're they keeping in there, anyway?" Hands on her hips, Dez considered the door again, turned to Cam. "Why do you think they've locked it?"

"No idea." Cam glanced at the door. That unsettling look passed over his eyes again, and as if by psychic osmosis, Dez felt a quiver pass through her, too.

Does he know something that he isn't telling me? Dez wondered. *If so, what?*

But she needed to get Ava ready to leave; they had a tight schedule on weekday mornings, and every minute counted. Further questioning would have to wait.

"I'll see what I can do about it," Cam said.

38

On Wednesday night, Cam arrived at Vic's house for their monthly poker game.

Cam, Vic, and five other guys, all of them faculty from local school districts, had been playing Texas Hold 'Em together for years. Vic usually hosted; he had a lavishly appointed finished basement, with a wet bar, a projection screen television, and a fancy poker table that seated their entire group.

That night, Cam volunteered to bring the beer (much to Vic's surprise) and showed up with a twenty-four pack of Stella Artois. Another friend brought boxes of chicken wings, and someone else ordered pizzas.

"Let's get this party started," Cam said, settling into his usual chair at the table. He rubbed his hands together. "I'm ready to take *everyone's* money tonight, fellas."

Vic gave him an eyebrows-raised look. Cam hadn't shared anything with Vic about his lucrative handyman gigs, and he had no intention of discussing it, either. Let Vic and everyone else assume his books were hauling in the dough.

The truth was, for three consecutive days that week the landlord had tapped him to work at the house in Norcross. On Monday, he'd installed new faucets in the kitchen and bathrooms, and been paid two thousand dollars. On Tuesday, he added a new subway tile backsplash in the kitchen—and earned another two thousand. Earlier that same day, Wednesday, he'd done extensive interior painting, for yet another two grand.

The irony? Instead of getting behind on his book, earning good money performing time-consuming, handyman work seemed to *improve* his writing. Without financial worries hanging over him like a storm cloud, his evening writing sessions at local cafés were brief— maybe ninety minutes or so—but more productive than ever. Right before he had arrived at Vic's, he had banged out ten pages at a nearby coffee shop.

"What's the buy-in tonight?" Phil asked. He was in his fifties and taught tenth-grade science. "I say we do five bucks."

"Way too low, Phil, my boy," Cam said. "Let's do twenty."

"Cheapo Cam wants a twenty-buck buy-in?" Reynolds asked, a red-haired assistant principal with a fuzzy beard. "Did someone win the lottery lately?"

Cam slipped a crisp twenty-dollar bill out of his wallet.

"Who else is in?" Cam asked. "Dig deep, guys."

"This is supposed to be only a friendly game," Vic said. "You know our rules. This isn't the World Series of Poker."

"A twenty-dollar buy-in is a high roller game?" Cam asked. "We need to expand our horizons, fellas."

"Keep it chill, all right?" Vic said. He dropped a twenty into the buy-in box, and the other men grumbled and followed suit.

Clayton served as dealer for the first hand, and Cam got a good one. He bet aggressively, raising at every opportunity. In the end, only Cam and Vic were left with a pile of chips lying on the table between them. Cam raised again, and Vic stared at him hard, as if he could see the machinery spinning in Cam's brain.

I'm not backing down, Cam thought, as he kept his gaze locked on his friend. *This is my night. This is my time. Finally.*

Vic folded.

Laughing, Cam pulled the heap of chips toward him.

"Show your cards," Vic said.

"No way, bruh. Them ain't the rules."

"You were bluffing, asshole. Weren't you?"

Cam grinned.

For the rest of the evening, Cam played more aggressively than he ever had in his life. Adrenaline crackled through his blood. He guzzled beer and ate wings and pizza and he boasted and raised and never folded, regardless of his hand. The other guys weren't accustomed to this style of play and kept backing down, folding when confronted with Cam's continued raises.

At the end of the night, as the clock neared ten, they wrapped up the last hand, which Cam had also won. He shoved the stack of chips toward Vic.

"Cash me out," he said.

Grumbling, Vic counted out his money. Cam had won two hundred and forty dollars, his highest take ever.

"Can I chat with you for a minute?" Vic said, as the other guys were heading out.

"I need to get home to the fam," Cam said.

"It'll take only a second."

The rest of the group drifted out of the basement, leaving Cam and Vic facing each other across the poker table. Vic turned away from the door and glowered at Cam.

"What the hell was that all about, man?" Vic asked.

"It was a friendly game of poker. You're the only one mad, 'cause I took your money."

"It's not how we play. It's not how *you* play. What's going on with you?"

"You never had an issue when everyone called me Cheapo Cam and I always folded. Now I'm playing better and you're being a sore loser."

"I'm not being a sore loser. You ruined the vibe of the whole evening with your high roller bullshit. No one liked that."

"I had plenty of fun." Cam patted his pocket. "And now, I'm two hundred and forty bucks richer. Enough to buy the fam a decent steak dinner."

"If that's how you want to play, you need to find a different game."

"You're kicking me out of the club? After six, seven years?"

"I'm protecting the integrity of our group. Casual, low-stakes poker. If you want to play that way, you're in. If not . . ."

"I'm out." Cam glared at him.

Vic sipped his beer. "Your decision, bruh."

Cam's phone buzzed. It was the distinctive cash-register chime ringtone that he had assigned to the contact who lately had become the center of his universe.

"I've got to take this," Cam said.

39

H eart thudding, Cam stepped outdoors into the crisp
October night. He put the phone to his ear.

"Hello?" Cam said.

"Mr. Woodson!" It was the landlord, his distinctive baritone
sounding as energetic as if it were eight o'clock that morning and he
was sipping his first cup of coffee. "How are you this fine autumn
evening?"

"Okay, I guess." Cam didn't know what he could tell the man
without triggering some kind of violation. Was revealing that he had
played poker in a friend's house outlawed by the lease, too?

Also, he remembered Dez wanted him to ask the landlord
about unlocking the closet in Ava's bedroom. Dez had become
annoyed that despite his performing multiple tasks for the landlord
that week, he had declined to raise the question, and he had
promised that the next time he had the man on the phone, he
would ask.

But why was the landlord calling Cam at ten o'clock at night?

"Are you interested in performing another task, Mr. Woodson?"

"Tonight?"

"It's timely, and important. And, need I add, you would be handsomely compensated in the sum of five hundred dollars."

Cam swallowed. Five hundred? The landlord had never revealed the pay up front before. Why now?

"What do I need to do?" Cam asked.

"Before I reveal the details, I must confirm your agreement to perform the task, Mr. Woodson."

Dez was expecting him home within twenty minutes. But she would understand if he took on a profitable gig at a moment's notice. Was he supposed to turn down five hundred dollars? Although he had hauled in thousands of dollars that week, it wasn't as though he received a regularly scheduled paycheck like an employee. A freelance writer's life cycled through booms and busts, and he had learned that he had to grab opportunities whenever they arose.

Beggars can't be choosers.

Besides, this was only a temporary situation, he promised himself. Once he finished his manuscript—which he was on track to do very soon—he would have other, better options.

"I'll do it," Cam said. "What's the assignment?"

"Excellent. As you have proven your handyman talents quite impressively, I am shifting your responsibilities to different areas. Tonight, you must pick up a package, deliver it to the property in Norcross that you've visited previously, and then return to your home."

"That's it?" Cam asked.

"The pickup location is in Gray, Georgia, Mr. Woodson. As I calculate it from your location, it's a drive of approximately an hour and forty-five minutes."

Cam thought about it. One hour and forty-five minutes to get to Gray; a similar amount of time to drive from there to Norcross; then forty or so minutes to get home. About four hours, in total. It was already ten o'clock. He might not get to bed until sometime well after two in the morning.

It's going to be a long night.

"What's in this package?" Cam asked. "Why does it need to be delivered tonight?"

"You must not, under any circumstances, open the parcel, Mr. Woodson. If I discover that you have, you won't receive a penny. Are we clear?"

"Crystal. But why not call UPS?"

"Would you prefer that I engage another resource to complete this simple task, Mr. Woodson?"

Cam laughed, uncomfortably. "I mean, I'll take the money. It was only a question."

"I prefer to transact my most important business with individuals with whom I am well acquainted. It's a matter of principle."

"Okay, then. I'm in."

But it didn't make any sense. Sending him to pick up a mysterious package from some town he had never heard of, late at night, only to deliver it to an empty house. Why was he paying him five hundred bucks to do something so trivial?

I don't know and I don't care. It's five hundred dollars!

"Before we get into the details, can I ask a question about the rental?" Cam said. "I promised my wife I'd ask about unlocking the bedroom closet in my daughter's room. The one that has the keypad on it? Can we get the code?"

"I suggest you discuss this matter with my agent," the landlord said.

"Miss Carver? She keeps ignoring us."

"I don't traffic in these petty tenant matters, Mr. Woodson. Are you ready to get to work tonight or not? My patience runs short."

"Sorry." *I tried, Dez.*

"Now, I've more details to share about your assignment," the landlord continued. "Get a pen and paper and write down this information . . ."

Five minutes later, after he had concluded the phone call with the landlord, scribbling the rest of the information on a notepad he kept in the Jeep's glove compartment, he called Dez.

"Are you coming home now?" Dez asked.

Cam paused. "The landlord called me."

Dez didn't respond for a beat. Then: "He offered you a gig?"

"It has to be done tonight, babe."

"*Tonight?* It's past ten o'clock!"

"He's going to pay us five hundred dollars. I couldn't say no."

"What are you supposed to do for him this time? Build a garage with your bare hands?"

"It's not handyman work. I'm doing a pickup and a delivery."

"A what?"

Cam summarized the assignment the landlord had given him. Explaining the task to his wife made it sound even more bizarre to Cam. *Did I really agree to do this? I guess I'll do anything for money.*

"This is strange," she said. "Do you think it's something illegal?"

"No," he said quickly, but almost said, *I hope not.* "It's going to be fine. But I don't think I'll make it home until late."

"How late?"

"Sometime after two o'clock." The words felt like ice cubes in his mouth.

Dez sighed. "I love you, Cam. That means I trust you. I pray you know what you're doing here."

Me, too, he thought. He swallowed. "Thank you."

"But no more of these, okay? Please. I don't care about the money. This is too much."

Cam didn't say anything.

"Did you ask him about the closet?" she asked.

"He said we should talk to Miss Carver. Sounded annoyed that I asked him at all."

Another sigh. He wanted nothing more than to be home with her, lying in their bed together. He hated putting her through this situation and blamed himself for even being in a position where he felt obligated to accept these tasks. She deserved better.

But you need the money, man. Beggars can't be choosers.

"I love you," he said. "I'll text you when I'm on my way home."

40

It took two hours for Cam to reach the town of Gray, a small community located on the fringes of Macon, in Jones County. An eighteen-wheeler had overturned on I-75 South, triggering a traffic snarl that added another fifteen minutes to his drive. Cam finished his last sip of Red Bull as he exited the highway and searched the dark road for the address.

He considered himself a night owl but staying up late to play video games was a different experience than driving on a highway to a destination you had never visited in your life, in the dead of night. Despite the caffeine, his head felt stuffed with cotton. He had a newfound respect for long-haul truckers.

A mile off the interstate, he spotted a sign; tarnished gold letters against a white background: *Asgard Gardens.*

He made a right turn and rolled toward the entrance. After checking the address he had scribbled in his notebook, he drove forward.

Older models of manufactured homes occupied the trailer park, many of them in poor repair. Trash littered the sides of the road. He saw bicycles lying on weed-choked lawns, cars sitting on concrete blocks, old appliances scattered about like relics of civilization in a dystopian film. A shaggy-haired man standing on the edge of the road scrutinized Cam.

If the landlord hadn't advised him that his destination lay in a trailer park, Cam would have been convinced he'd gotten the details incorrect.

Interspersed among the run-down models, he spotted a few well-tended trailers sitting on trimmed grass and bordered with flowers and shrubs, signs of hope in an otherwise dreary environment.

He neared a double-wide trailer at the end of the gravel lane. A silver Ford F-150 sat in the driveway. The landlord had said to look for the vehicle as proof that he had reached the right place.

Cam parked behind the truck and got out. He heard a yowling cat somewhere, a barking dog. Distantly, a siren warbled.

Above, the stars were cold as chips of ice.

What the hell am I doing here at a quarter past midnight? Cam asked himself. He wished he were home in his warm bed with his wife. He had never yearned so strongly to be anywhere else.

Beggars can't be choosers . . .

He approached the trailer's door and knocked.

A man who was a dead ringer for Willie Nelson opened the door. He had salt-and-pepper hair gathered in a ponytail. He wore a black Anthrax T-shirt, ragged jeans, and Chuck Taylor Converse sneakers. A gold chain encircled his neck, a pendant of a snake consuming its own tail nestled in his furry thatch of gray chest hair. Faded tattoos mapped his neck and arms, and a cigarette glowed in the corner of his mouth. His eyes were the color of black tea that had steeped too long.

"I'm here for the package," Cam said.

It was what the landlord had ordered him to say. But speaking the words made him sound like a bad actor in a low-budget spy movie.

"Huh?" Removing his smoke from his lips, the man looked Cam up and down. "A package of what?"

Is this a joke? Did the landlord send me all the way down here to make a fool out of me?

Cam stammered. "I was told—"

"I'm shittin' you, bro." The man grinned, exposing a wide gap in his front teeth. "I know what you're here for. Got it in my truck bed over there." He gestured with his cigarette, extending his long, scrawny arm. "All wrapped up nice for you."

Cam sighed. "Funny. Thank you."

"Damn, you jumpy as a virgin at a prison rodeo. This your first time?"

"First time?"

"First time working on behalf of our *mutual friend*." The man winked.

"I've done handyman gigs for him before," Cam said.

"That's how he got you?" The man guffawed. "Handyman gigs? What'd he tell you to do? Replace a shitter or somethin'?"

"Something like that. Listen, can I use your bathroom, please?"

"Nah, ain't a good idea for you to come in here, bro. I'm in the middle of some things you don't need to see. You can drain the lizard over there in the yard." He motioned with the cigarette, chuckled, hitched up his jeans on his narrow hips. "Let's get you that package."

While Cam relieved himself on the edge of the man's lawn—his first time urinating outdoors since he was a kid—the Willie Nelson clone peeled back the cover in his pickup's flatbed.

A cardboard box stood on the flatbed, about two feet long and three feet wide. It had an Amazon logo printed on the side.

"Amazon?" Cam asked.

"I put it in a spare box I had," the man said. "Don't mean nothing."

"What's in there?" Cam looked from the package to the stranger.

"I ain't supposed to tell you that, am I?" The man sucked his teeth. "Landscaping shit."

"Like dirt or something?"

"Or something." His eyes twinkled. "Go on and grab it. You got any kids?"

"We have a three-year-old little girl, why?"

"Carry that box like you carried your newborn girlie. *Gentle.*"

The box weighed perhaps forty pounds. Cam lifted it—something shifted inside—and carried it to the back of the Jeep, opened the rear door, and deposited the box inside while the older man watched and smoked.

"Is that all, then?" Cam snapped the trunk shut.

"I'd say that's plenty. You drive straight to where you need to go and drop that off. No detours. No dickin' around. We clear?"

"I never got your name," Cam said.

The man grinned. "Ain't got yours, either. Don't want it. We're better off that way." He clapped Cam's shoulder. "Get your ass on the road. If anyone asks, you never met me."

Driving to Norcross, Cam didn't hit any traffic snarls, but it still seemed to take forever to get there. As he drove, he speculated about the stranger and his mysterious cargo.

Landscaping shit.

He was convinced the man was lying. The box had to contain some sort of contraband. Drugs, possibly. Something banned or otherwise illegal.

How did I become the landlord's mule?

He kept to the speed limit as he drove. The last thing he needed was a police officer pulling him over, asking him questions, wanting to search the Jeep—

—what's in the box, sir?—

—and Cam getting caught with something that could land him in prison. All because he wanted to earn some extra money. Dez would be *livid*.

I can't do this again, he thought. *I can do handyman tasks for the landlord, and that's it. None of this strange transporter mule bullshit.*

The clock had ticked past two in the morning when Cam finally arrived at the Norcross residence. He half-expected to find Thor's van there, but the driveway was empty.

The landlord had given him the keycode to open the garage door via the external control panel. The roll-up door clambered open, noisy in the otherwise tranquil night.

He recalled the landlord's verbal instructions he had written down: *Leave the box sitting on the eastern wall of the garage, Mr. Woodson.*

Cam was so exhausted that he needed the compass app on his smartphone to determine the correct wall. He hauled the box out of the SUV and carried it inside, noticed a spot between a lawn mower and a red plastic fuel container, and placed the package there.

Take a photo and send it to me. I must confirm that the package is fully intact.

Cam took three photos, all from different angles. He sent the photos via text message to the landlord's usual number.

The landlord didn't respond to the texted photos.

Cam turned toward his SUV, then paused on the threshold of the garage door, lips pursed. Scratching his beard-stubbled chin, he swiveled back to face the box.

I need to know what's in there, for my own peace of mind.

He had already sent the photos to the landlord. Why not open the package and confirm the contents weren't going to land him in prison for twenty years? If he didn't check and later got in deep shit, he would never forgive himself.

"To hell with it," he said to himself.

He approached the box, knelt beside it. Opening it via the topmost flaps was too obvious. He decided to turn it over. Gently, he did so, the contents shifting.

He carefully peeled away a corner of the bottom flap, just a couple of inches, so he could peek inside.

He saw a shiny bag within. It looked like . . . lawn fertilizer?

Landscaping shit.

Cam laughed. Weed-and-feed for the grass? Was that all? All the cloak-and-dagger nonsense was for this?

He felt as if the landlord had played a joke on him, had given him this ridiculous task merely to test him.

Shaking his head, he turned the box right-side up and positioned it where he had left it before. He stepped out of the garage, punched the button to lower the door.

Yawning, he crawled behind the steering wheel. He was so tired he could barely keep his eyes open, but he fired off a text message to Dez telling her that he was finally coming home.

She didn't respond. He figured she had gone to bed. He couldn't blame her—it wasn't fair for him to expect her to wait up for him while he worked into the wee hours of the morning.

But the landlord had given him one final step to complete.

When you arrive home—and only when you arrive home—call me at this number. This is essential. If you neglect this step, you will not be compensated.

Arriving home about forty minutes later—somehow, he avoided falling asleep behind the wheel—he called the number the landlord had given him before he went inside the house.

The line rang four times; then Cam heard a click, as the call was forwarded to a voice mail box.

"I dropped off the package," Cam said. He didn't know what else to say. "That should be all." *Don't ever ask me to do something stupid like this again,* he wanted to say, but he didn't.

He hung up, stared at the phone in his hand. As he climbed out of the Jeep, he heard the Cash App chime.

Eight hundred dollars—more than the landlord had promised—had arrived in his account.

Cam was so wiped out he couldn't even get excited about it.

41

On Friday afternoon, sitting alone in a study room at the library, Cam typed the last page of his manuscript and added "*The End*" at the bottom of the page.

He contemplated those final words. Reaching the end of a manuscript always felt to him like crossing the finish line in a marathon. You wanted to shout and wave your hands in the air while you also wanted to collapse in a bed for the next twenty hours.

He had written this book in record time, despite the work-from-home ban, despite the numerous job assignments the landlord had given him. He also believed—though he was a bit biased on the matter—that it was the best book he had ever written.

He had to mark this occasion. He decided he would go home, but on the way, he would pick up a nice bottle of champagne. That weekend, perhaps he could take Dez and Ava out to dinner.

He had plenty of disposable income these days, thanks to the landlord.

After he arrived home and was sliding the champagne into the refrigerator, Lola emerged from the basement.

"Hey, Cammy," she said. "What's shakin'?"

Cam turned. The young woman wore a skintight tank top and yoga pants. Did she own any clothing that didn't display her physical assets to the maximum?

"I finished my book today." He grinned.

"That's awesome!" She beamed. "What's the title?"

"*We All Fall Down*," he said. "First book in a new thriller series."

"Can I read it?"

"I need to send it to a copy editor first. But you could read it after that if you want."

"Oooh, I want." She batted her long eyelashes.

"Usually, Dez reads it first. I could let both of you read it."

"I get wifey privileges now?"

His face felt hot. "I didn't mean it like that. Maybe you shouldn't tell her."

"Another secret between us, hmm?" She giggled.

He cleared his throat. "Did you need something?"

"I wanted to borrow some honey, if that's okay. I'm about to brew a cup of tea and found I was totally out of it."

"Sure." He stepped to the bank of cabinets across the kitchen. As he did, he felt Lola draw closer to him, and when he turned around with the small bottle of honey in his hand, she was less than a foot away, on the perimeter of his personal space. She gazed at him, giving him the full effect of her big eyes and thick lashes, her alluring fragrance filling his head.

He fumbled the bottle, and it dropped to the floor.

"Oopsie," she said.

"Sorry." He bent to pick up the bottle and Lola didn't budge an inch, his head only centimeters away from her legs. He straightened. "Here you go."

"Thanks, Cammy."

Their fingers connected as he passed the bottle to her.

"Bring it back whenever you get a chance," he said. "No rush."

"You're such a sweetie. Do you have a brother?"

"Only a sister, why?"

She wetted her bottom lip with her tongue.

"I was hoping there might be more where you came from," she said.

He laughed. "There's only me."

"Too bad." She pouted. "Thanks for the honey—honey." She snickered at her play on words.

She flung her hair over her shoulder, turned, sauntered to the basement. As soon as she was out of the kitchen, Cam took a long, cold drink of water to settle his racing pulse. The young lady liked to flirt, but it was only in good fun, wasn't it? She couldn't truly be interested in him. She knew he was married, that he loved his wife.

She's only teasing me, he thought.

What disturbed him was that he liked it.

42

Soon after Dez and Ava arrived home that evening, Cam popped the cork on the champagne. He poured the bubbly into two crystal flutes and passed one to Dez.

"Nice." She accepted the glass. He noticed she was in a buoyant mood, eyes bright with good cheer, which he attributed to the end of the workweek. "What's the occasion, babe?"

"My book is . . . *done*."

"Congratulations!" She leaned forward, kissed him. "I'm so proud of you! Despite it all, huh?"

"Yup, despite every roadblock, I got it done. I'm toasting to that."

They clinked glasses, and Cam took a big slurp, but Dez didn't sip from hers.

"Not in the mood for champagne?" he asked. "I know it can be dry, but I thought you'd like this one. The guy at the liquor store recommended it."

"I have some good news, too."

"What is it? Did you get a raise?"

"Be right back." She placed the glass on the counter and went upstairs. Ava pointed at the champagne flute.

"Apple juice for you, Pumpkin," Cam said. He got a juice box out of the fridge and popped the straw in it. He clinked his flute against her juice, and she giggled and sipped daintily.

Dez returned carrying a small plastic baggie.

"I took it this morning, then again at lunch," she said.

She opened the baggie and showed him the test strip.

"Oh my God," he said. "You're pregnant?"

Nodding and grinning, she came into his arms. Ava saw them embracing and wanted in on it, too, her little arms wrapped around their legs. Cam lifted his daughter and kissed her, and then he kissed Dez.

No matter what we've been through, moments like this make it all worthwhile, Cam thought, hugging his family close. *A new book done, a new baby on the way . . . it's a new day for the Woodson family. The tide has finally turned for me, for all of us.*

43

"**D**o you have a Cash App account, Dez?"

Saturday morning, Dez prepared breakfast for Ava when Lola popped in from the basement. Dez had been whipping together the meal on autopilot, her thoughts focused on yesterday's discovery of her pregnancy and the exciting times that lay ahead for them.

"Hey, good morning." Dez set down the box of Cheerios. "Why do you ask?"

"I owe you some money and I don't have a checkbook or any cash on me. I'm a mobile pay kind of gal." She grinned.

"You've lost me, Lola. Why do you owe me money?"

"Well." Color bloomed in Lola's cheeks. "I sort of posted that pic we took the other day to my IG account."

"You did what? I said I didn't want you to post that photo! You promised!"

"I know, honey, and I'm so sorry, but guess what? We got paid, big-time. It got a *massive* number of views and likes."

Dez dropped the spoon she had picked up. "It did?"

"Yup. Like I knew it would." Lola bobbed her head. "I got an instinct for this stuff, girl. Anyway, I want to give you your cut of the post fee. It's only fair."

"I still can't believe you posted that pic after you promised you wouldn't, Lola. That's shady."

"Tell me that after I pay you. What's your account name?"

Dez grabbed her phone and opened the app. She showed the screen to Lola, who typed, her manicured fingers a blur.

"Sent," Lola said.

"A thousand dollars?" Dez gaped at the new balance in her account. "For one picture?"

"I was wearing a piece from one of my designers," Lola said. "They pay me per post. I gave you half of what I got, since so many folks loved seeing you."

A spell of vertigo hit Dez, and she had to sit down next to Ava at the kitchen table to steady herself. Laughing, Lola came over to the table, ruffled Ava's hair.

"Such a pretty little girl y'all got," Lola said. "Hey, you going to be all right, Dez? You need some water?"

"I can't believe it was so easy." Dez gaped at her phone again. "A thousand dollars!"

"I got over a hundred thousand followers, honey. Those are good numbers. But hey, like I said before, you could do this, too."

"You can't be serious, Lola."

"Sure, we'd have to build up your own following, but I know *exactly* how to do that, girl."

"I can't." Dez shook her head. "I'm a teacher."

"I ain't saying you gotta quit your job tomorrow. We could build you up over the next few months. I promise you: if you want it, this would be your *last* year of teaching."

"There's another reason I can't do this." Dez hesitated. She hadn't shared news of her pregnancy with her parents yet but felt compelled to spill the information to this young woman so she would drop this foolishness about Dez becoming a social media influencer. "I'm pregnant."

"Wow, congratulations!" Lola's lips broke into a broad grin. "You are glowing, girl. No wonder!" She clapped.

"So, there's no way I can keep posting pics, you see? Soon, I'll start showing, and—"

"Are you kidding me? People love to see pregnant ladies."

Dez fixed Lola with a stern look. "Lola, you're joking with me."

"Don't you ever get on social media? Do you see how much attention celebs get when they post baby bumps? It's massive."

"I'm not a celebrity. I'm a regular person."

"You're beautiful, Dez. Celebrities, beautiful people—the world wants to see *us*. A beautiful woman getting ready to bring life into the world is exciting." Lola rubbed her hands together, her eyes gleaming. "I could totally make this work. I'll make you a social media superstar."

Dez laughed at the young woman's excitement. It was nuts, but the prospect of making money from doing something so easy was exhilarating.

Still, doubts lingered.

"I'm not sure I could handle being in the spotlight," Dez said.

"You get used to that." Lola gave a dismissive wave, her gold bracelets jangling. "Think about it. After you have the baby, you can be a stay-at-home mommy, do posts whenever. It would be a perfect life for you and your young family."

Quietly, Dez imagined what it would be like to pursue the life she wanted, to be home for her children and Cam all the time. Like her best friend, Ebony; like her mother had been there for her and her brothers and Daddy. Despite its challenges, Dez enjoyed teaching most of the time, but she wanted a break. Was there anything wrong with that? If posting some simple photos on social media was a ticket to a carefree lifestyle, wasn't it worth it?

"Will you at least think it over?" Lola touched her shoulder. "I admit, I get something out of this, too—I'd take a little cut here and there for helping. But that's it. I love to see good folks succeed. You deserve it, girl. Think it over."

"I'll talk to Cam about it," Dez said.

44

"Lola wants to make you a social media superstar, huh?" Cam said. "I've always told you how photogenic you are, Dez."

They had gone to lunch that Saturday afternoon at The Battery, a live-work-play community located next to the Atlanta Braves stadium. There, they dined at a Tex-Mex restaurant that served excellent drinks and even better food. Cam ordered a margarita, and Dez, newly pregnant, asked for a diet Coke. Ava drank lemonade from a juice box.

It was a warm day for mid-October, punctuated by a gentle breeze. Cam had asked for a patio table so he could people-watch while they dined. It felt great to have the financial means to go out into the world, to take his family to nice places without fretting over the cost of everything.

He believed it would last. With his book done, more good fortune loomed on the horizon.

And it was right on time, too. His head still spun at the idea of Dez having another baby. If not for his recent uptick in earnings, news of the pregnancy would have triggered a panic attack, but that day, he felt confident about their capacity to care for a new child.

Dez dipped a tortilla chip in a bowl of salsa, took a small bite. "It sounds like you're okay with it, then?"

"Lola obviously knows what she's talking about. You could make serious money, babe. There's a large audience for this stuff."

"What would I tell my parents? Our friends? My colleagues?"

"Why do you have to tell them anything?" He drank his margarita. "Keep it between us."

"I don't know." She stirred her soda with the straw. "I've never done anything like this before. I'm not an attention-seeker."

"It's not porn, Dez, and you're not shakin' your moneymaker at Magic City, either."

She wrinkled her nose. "It feels inappropriate, for me, personally. But . . ."

"But what?"

"The money could be nice. If I can build it up and then, maybe, take a leave from teaching for a few years . . ."

"It's what you've always wanted to do." Cam swirled the ice cubes in his glass. "You've got the looks, that's for damn sure. Why do you think I married you?"

She tossed a tortilla chip at him.

Cam laughed. "You could post only the photos you're comfortable sharing. Keep it tasteful."

"Can you believe we're having this discussion?" Her eyes sparkled. "It's amazing how quickly things have changed since we moved into the rental."

"It started out rough, but we've come through on the other side, for sure."

"I want to sleep on this social media thing. If I still feel good about it tomorrow, I'll tell Lola I want to do it."

Driving home afterward, Cam saw Miss Carver's black Cadillac sedan parked in front of the rental house.

"Uh-oh," he said. "Cruella de Vil is on the scene."

"Lord, I wonder what she wants." Dez flipped down the sun visor and checked her reflection in the mirror. "I always feel as though she's judging me."

"Because she is."

He parked in the driveway. As he got out, Miss Carver strode toward them. She wore her customary black dress and flats, the wind tossing her stringy white hair across her long face. Her black briefcase swung from her narrow shoulders.

"Good afternoon, Woodson family," Miss Carver said. "I've got wonderful news to share."

"You do?" Cam glanced at Dez, who looked as skeptical as he did.

"You've earned amendments to your lease agreement." Miss Carver flashed her grimace-grin and fished a manilla folder out of her bag. She thrust it toward Cam.

"You may now work from home," Miss Carver said.

"Get out of town," Cam said. "Seriously?"

"You may also host gatherings—*small* gatherings," Miss Carver said. "A maximum of five guests. No prior approval is required."

Cam flipped open the folder, saw the printed pages with the words "Lease Amendment" bolded at the top, followed by several paragraphs of legalese.

"What brought about this change?" Dez asked.

"Mr. Woodson has impressed our landlord, I hear. Our landlord is just and fair when one renders loyal service."

Miss Carver glanced at Cam, a glint in her eye.

"He's worked me hard, no doubt about that." Cam tapped the folder. "I feel as though I've earned this."

"While we're getting permissions," Dez said, "can I get the code to open the closet in my daughter's bedroom, too?"

"Hmph. Enjoy the rest of your day, Woodson family." She spun on her heel and marched back to her vehicle.

"Did you see that?" Dez said. "She totally ignored me."

"Let's not push it. We've earned some breathing room, babe." He waved the sheaf of papers. "I ought to frame this."

45

---

ater that night, Cam and Dez made love, and once again, Cam noticed the bedroom door had been opened a few inches. He didn't mention this to Dez; he lay with his wife, their bodies spooned, until he heard her breathing deepen and she rolled out of his arms.

Careful not to awaken her, Cam got out of bed, slipped on a T-shirt and lounge pants. He padded into the hallway, shutting the bedroom door behind him.

The familiar fragrance had evaporated by then. He went downstairs into the kitchen, flicking on the light switch.

The basement door hung half open, light leaking upstairs from below.

Cam's mouth was dry as cotton. He filled a glass with water from the refrigerator dispenser. As he drank, he gazed at the door.

Shut the door and go upstairs, he thought. *That's the right move here.*

He placed the glass in the sink, his hand shaking.

Shut the door. Go to bed.

He switched off the kitchen light. In the darkness, the basement doorway shimmered like a portal to an alternate dimension. He crossed over to it and put his hand on the cool knob.

Shut it.

From his vantage point at the top of the staircase, he could see an end table on the basement's perimeter. A hardback copy of his first novel lay on the table.

Cam stepped through the doorway, closed the door behind him. He went down the steps.

He picked up the book. It looked like a gently used edition; it was not a copy from his personal inventory.

He didn't see Lola in the basement's main, open area, but lamps glowed. Holding the book, he went deeper into the room, saw light shining in the bedroom off the short corridor.

"Lola?" he said. He sounded froggy.

"I'm back here." Her voice came from the bedroom.

Cam edged down the hallway to the door's threshold. Inside, Lola stood in front of a floor-to-ceiling mirror. She wore pink lace panties, but no bra at all.

His heart whammed. He averted his gaze to the book in his hands.

Lola snickered. "It's okay, Cammy. Two thousand subscribers get an eyeful a few times a week."

"What're you talking about?"

"I've got a platform on *OnlyFans*, too. Good, *good* money."

Much to his chagrin, Cam was familiar with the website. It was an amateur porn portal, mostly. Vic had shown it to him.

"You were watching us again," Cam said. He kept his attention fastened on his book cover. "I warned you about sneaking upstairs to watch us."

"You came down here to spank me for being a bad girl?"

This wasn't going as he expected. He swallowed, looked up. Lola strutted toward him.

He wanted to look away, but he didn't.

"They're only boobs, honey." A smile played on her lips. She had slipped into his personal space, less than a foot away. Tapping the book cover with a lacquered fingernail, she said, "I was going to ask you to sign it for me."

"Right now?" He gulped.

"You got somewhere else you wanna be?" She put her hands on her hips, thrust her chest forward.

"I need to go back upstairs. To my wife. She won't be happy if she knew I was down here."

"I wasn't gonna tell her. Are you?"

"She won't be happy to know you've been sneaking around, either."

"Are you gonna share our little secret?" She pouted.

"This needs to stop, Lola. Whatever you're trying to do here, I need you to knock it off. I'm a happily married man."

"But here you are." She tickled the bottom of his chin with her lacquered fingernail.

Cam dropped the book. As he bent to pick it up, Lola sauntered to a small table.

"Let me get you a pen so you can put your John Hancock on my book," she said, emphasizing the "cock" in the surname.

"If I do this, will you leave me alone?" he asked.

"Is that what you want?"

She handed him a ballpoint pen. As he accepted it, her fingers closed over his. Her gaze locked on him, she guided his hand to one of her breasts, the pen slipping out of his grasp, tumbling to the carpet.

This woman had offered herself to him on a platinum platter, and if he were another kind of guy, he would have greedily accepted her. But as he had said—he *was* happily married. He loved Dez, loved Ava, loved the new life forming in his wife's belly. A tryst with Lola wasn't worth jeopardizing the blessings he had been given, and even if Dez never found out, he would know what he had done and would never forgive himself for it.

He withdrew his hand from her breast.

"I need to get upstairs," he said. "I can't do this."

Something hard flashed in Lola's eyes.

"Maybe we were wrong about you," she said.

"What're you talking about?"

She waved him away. "Go on, run back to your wifey. I've got work to do."

"Fine." Cam backed out of the room. He left the book where he found it.

But Lola's words echoed in his thoughts.

. . . we were wrong about you.

Who was she talking about?

46

S unday morning while eating breakfast, Dez announced to Cam: "I've slept on it. I'm going to accept Lola's offer."

She expected a smile from him, a *that's great* response, but when he looked up from his bacon and eggs, she saw his eyebrows furrowed.

"I don't think that's a good idea, babe," he said.

Dez's heart kicked. She set down her coffee mug so hard that Ava flinched.

"Did I imagine yesterday at lunch?" Dez asked.

"You wanted to sleep on it. I slept on it, too." His gaze touched her, flicked away as if he were afraid to meet her eyes. "I'm not comfortable with you posting photos for the public to salivate over."

"It's not porn. You said that yourself. I'd post tasteful pics only."

"Tasteful pics probably won't drive likes, follows, whatever. You've gotta be damn near naked to get attention these days." He leaned back in the chair, crossed his arms over his chest. "Think about your reputation at school, your parents."

Dez drew in a shaky breath, ran both hands through her hair. She didn't understand this about-face from him. Yesterday, he was one hundred percent in favor of the idea, and now, this morning, he was trying to talk her out of it. What was going on?

"We agreed I would keep it between us," she said.

His gaze shifted to a spot behind her.

In a low voice, he said, "Another thing. I don't think it's smart to get tangled up with our housemate on a business venture."

Dez looked over her shoulder as if Lola had entered the kitchen, but it was only the three of them, the basement door closed.

"I thought you liked her," Dez said. "I think she's cool, Cam."

His face was tight as a fist. "We need to keep boundaries. She's only a housemate." He pointed. "She's down there, living her life. We're up here, living ours."

"But you work for the landlord."

"We have a lease with the landlord. We don't have a contract with *her*. Big difference."

"I only wanted to make some extra money." Dez rose from her chair and grabbed her plate and Ava's bowl of cereal, carried the dishes to the sink. "Maybe it's too optimistic, naive, but I want to leave teaching behind by the time the new baby gets here."

"That's still in the cards, babe." Cam rose from his chair and came to her. "I have a great feeling about this new book. It's the best thing I've ever written. Once I get it out there, we'll be in a position for you to take a leave, God willing."

He seemed so convinced of his plan, as if it were all taken care of, that Dez was inclined to believe him.

"When can I read this magnum opus?" she asked.

"You know how I am. It's technically done, but I'm reading through it again, making little tweaks before I send it off to my agent."

"I thought you were going to self-publish this one?" she asked. "Cut your agent out since you were annoyed with the whole industry?"

"It's such a great book I want to give the agent a look. Just to see what happens."

"I want to read it."

"Absolutely. You will, babe." He kissed her forehead. "But please, drop this social media influencer nonsense, okay? We don't need that in our lives."

"Okay," she said, but she didn't feel good about it. She felt as if he had been less than forthcoming about his misgivings.

Admit it. You think he's hiding something. But what?

47

On Monday afternoon, as Cam drove home after working at the library all day, his literary agent returned his call.

Ironically, since the landlord had granted him permission to work from home, Cam discovered that he preferred to write outside of the house. Without the temptation to step away from his desk and binge-watch a show, boot up a video game, or nibble on junk food that would only widen his waistline, he managed to stay focused. That day, he had further polished his manuscript and started an outline for the next installment in the series.

"Cam, my man," Ethan Knight said, his voice crackling through the Jeep's speakers. "I read your synopsis. It sounds like a winner."

I knew it, Cam thought. His instincts about his work, which in the past had led him to publish five underwhelming titles, had sharpened. Bottoming out tended to have that effect. To get back into the game, you had to regroup and rediscover your strengths. He meant what he had said to Dez: the book was the best he had ever written, and he'd be cheating himself if he didn't give New York one last shot.

"Do you think Daniel will take a look?" Cam asked. Daniel was the editor of his prior titles at his old publisher. Cam had endured a discouraging meeting with the editor in Manhattan a few months ago, but he still had emotional ties to the company.

"Hmm." Ethan clucked his tongue. "Daniel's not in the game anymore."

"He was fired?" Cam asked.

"He moved out to Hollywood to work at a film agency."

"I didn't know that." To save money, Cam had canceled his subscriptions to all the industry magazines. Whatever he learned, he picked up from free email newsletters, blogs, and online writers groups.

"I don't believe this project would be a good fit for your old house anyway, Cam. All they want these days are celebrity exposés and political bios. If we move forward, we need to find a new home for you, somewhere that can handle top-notch commercial thrillers."

"If we move forward?" Cam asked.

"The last time we talked, you said you were going to self-publish, which I understand. You want more leverage with a strong sales history. It's a solid plan, but I think we should give this a shot with a few folks before you go down that road. Interested?"

"Absolutely. What do you need?"

"First three chapters. This is a killer synopsis, but can you send me a tagline, too? Something punchy. I think that'll complete the package."

"You'll have it first thing tomorrow."

Giddy, Cam turned into his neighborhood. He couldn't wait to share this news with Dez. She was upset with him because he had changed his tune about her social media influencer thing, and he wanted to assure her that this new course of action held promise. It wasn't wishful thinking.

But he could never come clean with Dez about why working with Lola was a terrible idea. *Oh, Lola? She wanted me to sleep with her the other night and I turned her down, which pissed her off. I'm sure she won't hold that against either of us, though.*

Yeah, right.

Cam turned onto the road that led to the rental house. As he cruised along the tree-shaded street, he saw a familiar-looking black Cadillac sedan heading toward him.

Miss Carver? he thought, his stomach clenching. He slowed and peered into the car as it cruised past.

It was Miss Carver, all right. He waved at her.

She didn't return the greeting.

Why had she been on their street? Had she snooped inside the house while both he and Dez were away? What was she looking for?

Unsettled, he pulled into the driveway.

48

Monday afternoon after school ended, Dez visited a nearby Publix supermarket to pick up some items for dinner. While there, she spotted her friend Ebony sorting through organic bananas in the produce department.

Ebony didn't see her; a good twenty feet separated them. From afar, her hands resting on the shopping cart handle, Dez observed her best friend.

Ebony was alone, and she must have come to the supermarket after leaving the gym. She wore an outfit straight from Lululemon: plum-colored, high-rise leggings, a gray half-hoodie, and stylish trainers. Her dark hair was pulled back into a ponytail; AirPods were nestled in her ears. She moved from fruit to cart with grace.

She looked fabulous.

A woman living her best life, Dez thought.

Dez had spent her Monday teaching social studies to several classes of boisterous seventh graders, about half of whom had zero interest in school and viewed her class as an interruption to their smartphone usage, and it required every trick at her disposal for her to keep them on task. Then she fielded emails from parents interrogating her about their children's poor grades and missing assignments. Meanwhile, another of her colleagues, a young woman who taught sixth grade, announced with a proud grin that she was starting maternity leave and wasn't certain when—or if—she would return.

How had Ebony spent her Monday? Dez didn't have to imagine what her friend had done—she knew, because Ebony enjoyed detailing her daily schedule. Prior to her fitness class at a local studio, Ebony would have visited her mother for lunch and gossip. Before that—some light housework (Ebony had a housekeeper visit weekly), puttering around in her garden, and perhaps scheduling dentist appointments for her "boys" (a term that included her husband).

As for what Ebony would do afterward: her twins attended a highly regarded private academy. She would pick them up after she completed grocery shopping. Then go home to prepare dinner for the family while Vic bragged about an upcoming promotion.

Meanwhile, Dez would have to devote a good chunk of her evening to grading assignments and working on lesson plans. The time she spent working at the school was never sufficient to get everything done.

Why not me? Why can't I have a life like Ebony?

Lola had dangled a life-changing opportunity in front of her, and Dez had a thousand dollars in her bank account as evidence of what might be. Make real money doing something easy. Leave teaching behind. Be home for her family.

Be like Ebony, who still hadn't spotted Dez.

Dez noticed other women attired like Ebony, too. Wearing tennis skirts and yoga pants and trainers and hoodies over sports bras, hair pinned back, checking smartphones for grocery lists and affirming how much time remained before they needed to pick up children. She felt as if she were the only woman in the store who held a full-time job—an absurd idea—but she couldn't dislodge it from her mind.

I want it, and I want it now. I don't want to wait for Cam's writing to pay off. I can make it happen on my own. Why shouldn't I?

It wasn't as though Cam had notified her in advance that he had started doing gigs for the landlord, had he? He didn't ask for her approval.

She regretted she had even told him about Lola's offer. She should have plunged right into it. That was what Cam would have done. How did the saying go? *It was better to beg for forgiveness than to ask for permission.*

She still didn't understand his change of heart, either, and that bugged her. He hadn't "slept on it" and awakened with a different opinion. Something had happened to trigger his worries. But what?

Regardless, she wasn't willing to let this chance slip away. This was her shot, and she needed to capitalize on it.

"Excuse me, hon," an older woman said, brushing past Dez.

Dez moved aside the shopping cart. She realized she clutched the handle so tightly her knuckles had turned milk white.

She needed to pick up produce, too. But she couldn't tolerate the prospect of interacting with Ebony then, in her current state of mind. She just couldn't.

She maneuvered her cart in the opposite direction and hurried to the other side of the store.

49

"Mr. Woodson! I have a new task for you."

It was Wednesday evening, and Cam had settled down for dinner with Dez and Ava. When his phone chimed the cash-register ringtone and he saw the landlord's number, he excused himself from the table (triggering Dez's obvious annoyance) and stepped outdoors onto the deck.

It was a clear night, with a bite in the air, but Cam's blood warmed at the promise of another profitable assignment. *Mo money, mo money, mo money.*

"What's the payout for this one?" Cam asked.

The landlord chuckled. "Straight to the point, eh? Like a veteran. You've come a long way in a short duration, Mr. Woodson. I'm impressed with your evolution."

Cam waited for the man to continue. Cold wind nipped his ears.

"For this task, you will be paid five thousand dollars."

Five thousand dollars! Damn!

His knees sagging, Cam leaned against the deck's railing. He did a quick mental calculation. Five grand would put him over the finish line for his annual earnings target, would give them the cushion they needed.

I did it.

He couldn't wait to tell Dez. He glanced inside through the French doors' windows and caught her attention; he pumped his fist like a baseball player who had smacked a home run. Her forehead wrinkled in confusion, and she gave him a tentative smile. Ava saw him, too, and she grinned and thrust her little arms in the air in a victory gesture.

Smiling at his family, Cam turned away from the window. He needed to keep his eyes on the prize. The landlord's task might be impossible, and if he couldn't do it, he wouldn't earn a penny.

"That sounds great," Cam said. "What's the task this time? I hope it's nothing weird like the last one."

"It's trash disposal, Mr. Woodson. Straightforward, but messy work. I suggest you wear clothing you don't mind soiling and bring a fresh set of clothes to wear afterward."

Hell, that's easy.

"Am I going to be cleaning one of your properties? For five grand, it's got to be a major cleanup job, right?"

"Thor will share the details with you. You will be partnered with him on this assignment."

"Cool. I like Thor."

"He requested you, in fact, Mr. Woodson. The feeling is mutual."

"Are we doing this tonight?" Cam asked, though he already knew the answer to the question.

"You must complete the task before sunrise tomorrow. I have an abundance of resources but a shortage of patience." A gentle laugh.

"I'd better get started," Cam said. "Please give me the details on where I need to go."

A few minutes later, Cam returned inside the house. Dez stood beside the counter, arms crossed over her chest, a question in her eyes.

"What's going on now?" she asked. "Let me guess, the landlord has given you a new job, and you won't come back until the weekend."

"Very funny. It's fantastic news, babe. I've got to do a job tonight, but he's paying me—he's paying *us*—five thousand dollars."

She blinked. "Five thousand?"

"Yup."

"Wow." Dez's lips formed a large "O." "What are you supposed to do?"

"It's a cleanup job," he said. "I've got to hook up with Thor— you remember Thor, the handyman—at an address in Cumming. From what I gather, it's basically cleaning up one of the landlord's properties."

"He's paying you five thousand dollars for cleaning a house? That sounds excessive."

Cam's words poured out in a torrent: "Listen, I don't ask too many questions. All I know is that every time I've done a job for the landlord, he's paid me, and he's paid me extremely well. Maybe he has money to burn, he's trying to deduct business expenses from his taxes. I don't really know—and I don't give a damn. All I know is that I'm going to go there, do whatever trash disposal is needed, and come home five grand richer. Do you see a problem with that?"

Dez turned to the sink and started rinsing dishes. "If I saw a problem with it, you would do it anyway, Cam."

"Baby, I've earned over ten thousand dollars this month!" Cam said. "This is a great thing for us. Why're you giving me attitude?"

"The money's great. I'm happy for you." She opened the dishwasher, arranged plates and silverware on the racks.

Cam wanted to scream. He didn't understand Dez's issue with what he had told her. He thought that she would be as excited as he was, but here she was acting as though she didn't understand the value of the money that they were going to be paid for a relatively simple task. Quite frankly, he didn't have time to convince her. The job needed to be done by sunrise.

"I've gotta go," he said. "We can talk about this later. I don't know how long this job is going to take, but it's got to be done before tomorrow morning, so don't wait up for me, okay?"

"I wasn't going to."

I'll use some of the money to buy her something nice, Cam thought. *That'll thaw her frosty attitude. A nice bracelet, or maybe a day at her favorite spa. I'll get her on my side.*

He kissed Dez on the forehead, went to his daughter and kissed her, too, and then he hurried to leave so he could meet Thor.

50

Cam pulled in front of the dark, two-story home and double-checked the address against what the landlord had given him.

"It's the right place," he said to himself. "Where the hell is Thor?"

The driveway was empty. Cam turned into it and let the engine idle, warm air pumping from the vents, the SUV's headlamps illuminating a garage in front of him.

Driving to Cumming had taken about forty minutes; it was half past eight. Cam had drunk a can of Red Bull during the trip, figuring he would need that and several more to get through the night.

He sent Dez a quick text: *Here at the job.* He included the address.

Ok, she responded. It was the most he could hope for.

Sighing, he tapped the steering wheel. The landlord hadn't given him the keycode to access the property; Thor had that information, he assumed. Until Thor arrived, all he could do was wait.

He didn't need to wait long. A vehicle nosed in behind him, headlights glowing.

Cam switched off the engine and climbed out, raising his hand to shield his eyes against the bright lights. A sleek black panel van had parked behind him, not Thor's usual beat-up white model.

Is this really the right address? Who is this?

"Get in, Cam!" Thor rolled down the driver's-side window. He beckoned Cam toward him. "Bring your bag!"

Cam grabbed his backpack from the Jeep and then hurried to the van's passenger side, hopped in.

Thor muted the country western music he had been playing.

"It's a frosty night, yes?" Thor grinned. In the backsplash of the greenish dashboard lights his face looked ghoulish. He wore a black sweater, pants, and gloves. His hair was slicked back, emphasizing his widow's peak.

"Freezing out." Cam shivered, despite his hoodie and sweatpants. "Is this the right address?"

"Our business is not here. This was only the pickup location."

"Where are we going?"

Thor reversed out of the driveway. "Not far. Are you ready to work?"

"I was born ready."

"That is what I like to hear. We have a messy job to do, but important."

"Trash disposal, right?"

Thor grunted in agreement. He steered the van around the darkened neighborhood, a quiet community of large homes and well-kept lawns. After he made a series of turns, he pulled in front of a house standing in a cul-de-sac.

A white Camaro occupied the driveway, and a light glowed in the front window.

"Is this the place?" Cam asked. "It looks like someone is here."

"Come." Thor switched off the van. "Follow my lead."

"Follow your lead?" Cam asked. *What is he talking about?*

Ignoring him, Thor got out of the van. Cam hesitated, then

climbed out, too. He brought his backpack with him, slinging the strap over his shoulder.

Thor marched down the walkway, Cam trailing behind him, mist puffing from his mouth. The night was quiet, the nearest home hundreds of yards away. As they neared the entrance, Cam noticed the door didn't have a keypad as he had seen on the landlord's other properties.

"Stand back," Thor said. He spread his feet into a broad stance, gaze fastened on the door.

"Huh?" Cam said, but he gave Thor a wide berth.

With one mighty kick from his boot, Thor smashed open the door.

Cam leaped backward. The door flew open so hard that it banged against the opposite wall.

Cam had only seen someone kick open a door in movies, but Thor had done it as if he spent his weekends kicking in the doors of strange houses.

"What's happening here, man?" Cam asked.

Thor flashed a predatory grin, but he didn't speak a word. He charged inside through the open doorway.

Cam trembled. He didn't know whether to follow the man or run. He looked around, didn't see any activity from the distant neighbors.

From inside, Cam heard a muffled shout. Breaking glass.

Oh shit, what's going on?

His heart had crawled into his throat. Was this a dream? An elaborate prank?

"Cam!" Thor barked at him. "Get in here!"

Cam slid into the entry hall, his feet feeling as if he were skating on an ice rink. He pivoted to the left.

He saw a furnished living room, a big-screen TV. An overturned coffee table. Thor sitting on top of a gray-haired man, the man's beet-red face mashed against the carpet. Thor pressed a stun gun against the stranger's neck. The victim quivered like a malfunctioning robot.

"Did you shut the door?" Thor said.

"What . . . what're you doing? Who is this?"

"Shut the door now!" Thor had retracted the stun weapon and fished a set of zip ties out of his pocket.

"Tell me what's going on, man!" Cam said.

Cursing, Thor shot to his feet and stormed toward Cam, shoving aside furniture. Behind him, the man lay on the floor shaking, lips working but no sound coming out.

Cam backpedaled as Thor drew near, convinced Thor might attack him, too, but the man brushed past him and slammed the door shut.

"This man, he is the trash." Thor ran a gloved hand through his hair, licked his lips. "He is a deadbeat, a former tenant of our landlord. Tonight, we are teaching him a lesson."

"No, no, no." Cam shook his head. "Fuck that, no way. I'm not doing this." He kept shaking his head. "I gotta go home. I gotta get outta here."

"Our landlord will not pay you if you do not finish the job."

"Are you insane? I said I'm not doing this!"

"What about the money that you will be paid for your work? Good money. You need the money."

"I don't need this." Cam stepped to the door and grabbed the knob. Thor seized Cam's shoulder and spun Cam toward him as easily as if Cam were a child.

"Let me go, man," Cam said.

"This is a mistake you are making. The landlord will be upset."

"I'll deal with the landlord." Cam glanced toward the room where the stranger lay paralyzed, and a fearsome thought took him. "Are you going to . . ."

"Better if you do not know. Tell no one what you have seen here." Thor released Cam's shoulder. "Go."

Cam swallowed, turned the doorknob.

"But I must warn you," Thor said.

"What?"

"The landlord is your enemy now."

51

Shivering, the chill in his bones unrelated to the frosty weather, Cam lurched away from the house like a man in a drunken stupor. He paused at the edge of the driveway and looked back over his shoulder.

Would Thor torture that man? Maim him? Kill him?

I need to do something about it. I need to stop it.

But what could he do? If he placed a call to 911 on his iPhone, it would link him to the crime. How could he explain his involvement to the police?

I thought we were going to clean up trash, Officer. I had no idea.

It was the truth, but to a jaded police officer and a prosecuting attorney and a jury, it would sound ridiculous.

Authorities would charge him as an accessory in the commission of a violent felony. Probably they would convict him, though he had never broken the law in his life. Ignorance wasn't a viable legal defense for participation in a criminal act.

He couldn't do this to Dez, Ava, the baby on the way. He had too much to lose.

I'll call the police, but not on my phone. I need to find a pay phone.

But he couldn't remember the last time he had seen a coin-operated telephone. It was an artifact of a bygone era, like VHS players, corduroy jackets, and manual typewriters.

Maybe none of it had been real. He wanted to dismiss the entire incident as theater, something like that old reality show on MTV, *Punk'd*, in which undercover actors performed outrageous practical jokes on celebrity marks.

You fell for it, Cam. It was all done in good fun, see?

But Thor's victim had been drooling, paralyzed, terror glistening in his eyes.

At the memory, Cam's heart clutched.

He should have seen the truth all along, should have realized that he was being set up for something like this. Why had the landlord paid him such enormous sums of money for assignments that rarely justified the fee? Hundreds of dollars to switch out a few light fixtures. Eight hundred more to pick up and drop off a package. Five thousand dollars promised for "trash disposal."

He was desperate for money, so he didn't want to ask those probing questions. *Beggars can't be choosers.*

But somewhere, desperation had given way to greed.

He didn't know how he could get out of this predicament, but he needed to get home. Along the way, he would look for a pay phone—a gas station was his best shot—and place an anonymous call to the police.

He snapped a pic of the residence's mailbox, which bore the street number. He resumed walking.

How could he get back to his Jeep? He hadn't memorized the various turns they'd taken to arrive at the house. He pulled up his smartphone again and entered in the original address of what Thor had called the "pickup" spot. A GPS pin on the virtual map confirmed he was five blocks away from the driveway where he had left his SUV.

He drew his hood over his head, got on the sidewalk, quickened his pace. Darkened homes drifted past like smoky figments from a dream.

At the end of the block, he glanced over his shoulder again. Hoping that the van he and Thor had arrived in was gone, vanished into the ether like a magical carriage in a fairy tale, and that none of this had ever happened.

The van hadn't moved. But the lights that had been glowing in the front window had been extinguished.

What did that mean?

I can't stay to figure it out, Cam thought. *I'm already in this way too deep. All I can do is get as far away from here as possible.*

As he resumed his walk, his phone buzzed. He knew the identity of the caller before he looked.

The landlord knows. Thor told him I bailed on the job.

Cam ignored the ringing, and after a minute, the phone stopped chiming.

Maybe he'll leave me alone.

Within a minute, a text message arrived.

Look at what you did to my property, Mr. Woodson.

The message included a link to an Atlanta news website.

Cam halted. His finger trembling, he clicked the link. A web browser opened on his phone. The page featured a local news story posted last week.

Fire Damages Norcross Home

Norcross, Ga. (Atlanta News First) - A home was heavily damaged by fire early Thursday morning in Norcross.

The Norcross Fire Department says the call came in around 2:30 a.m. Upon arrival, fire crews found heavy flames coming from a home on the 400 block of South Sugar Hill Drive.

It is not known whether there were any occupants in the residence at the time.

Fire officials say the roof collapsed. There is significant damage, but the house is not a total loss.

The cause of the fire is under investigation.

The story included a vivid photograph of a house engulfed in flames. But Cam recognized the place: it was the property where he had spent so much time working—and where he had dropped off that innocuous package.

Another text message from the landlord popped up.

I believe the local authorities would like to know what you were doing there, dropping off ammonium nitrate fertilizer . . . and then triggering an explosion with a cell phone detonator.

Arson is a felony, Mr. Woodson. You are guilty.

The lawn fertilizer—"landscaping shit," as the Willie Nelson clone had claimed—had been engineered to explode and had obviously included a cell phone trigger. Cam remembered calling the unfamiliar phone number, as instructed, when he arrived home after that errand . . .

He sank to his knees. His stomach heaved, and he couldn't hold it down. He vomited on the sidewalk, his gut convulsing painfully.

Just wanted to make some extra money. Trembling, he wiped the back of his hand across his mouth.

His phone buzzed again with another message. He read it, salty tears leaking from his eyes and trickling down his cheeks.

I own your home. I own your family. I own you, Mr. Woodson.

52

After Cam left that evening on yet another unplanned "landlord gig," Dez decided to talk to Lola again.

Dez strove to keep peace in her marriage. Doing so required compromise daily. You couldn't always do whatever you wanted, couldn't have whatever you liked whenever you felt like it. You needed to consult with your partner, take their needs and wishes into account, and arrive at a happy medium; a win-win, always preferable to one person satisfied, while the other person stewed in anger. In a strong marriage, both partners shared that approach, creating fertile ground for marital bliss to blossom.

But the opportunity Lola had presented was too tempting for Dez to ignore. Whether Cam agreed with her or not, she needed to take advantage of it.

Was it fair that he got to pursue his writing ambitions while she worked a nine-to-five job and put her own dreams on hold? She supported him in his aspirations.

It was time for him to support her. She was doing this for their family.

Dez put Ava down to bed, returned to the kitchen, opened the basement door an inch, and knocked on it.

She thought Lola was there, though she did not know the young woman's comings and goings. Earlier, she had heard muted sounds issuing from the basement and assumed that the young woman was home.

"Come on down!" Lola said.

Dez smoothed the front of her shirt and descended the staircase, butterflies fluttering in her stomach. She had never done anything like this before. When she was a teenager, she had often heard that she could have been a model. But her parents frowned upon such pursuits, advised that using your looks to earn money was unbecoming for a proper young woman. "Use your brains, not your beauty," her mother had said. "Looks fade, sweetheart."

They haven't faded yet, apparently, Dez thought. *I better take advantage of them before they do.*

"Hey there." Lola strutted toward her. The woman wore a baggy T-shirt and sweats, a sheen of perspiration glistening on her skin. She wasn't wearing any makeup, either.

Despite her lack of adornment, she was beautiful, and it gave Dez pause. *I'm nowhere near as good looking as she is. Can I really do this social media thing?*

"Just doing a little workout," Lola said. "What's up?"

"I hope I'm not bothering you," Dez said. "But I wanted to talk about the thing we discussed last time."

"Oh!" Lola grinned. "You wanna be a social media superstar, huh?"

"I've thought it over. I'm still a little uncomfortable with posting photos anyone could see, but if you think I can do this, I'm willing to try it."

"Absolutely! You wanna make that money, honey!" Lola giggled.

"I'm thinking about my family," Dez said. "Teaching is great. Some days I love it, some days I don't love it as much, but it's an important job. I'm not saying I want to quit forever, but I want to be here for my children for those early years. So why not?"

"That's right!" Lola laughed again. "Did you talk to Cammy about it?"

Dez frowned. "Cammy?"

"Cam." Lola cleared her throat. "Mr. Woodson."

"Let's keep this between us for now," Dez said.

"Of course." Lola gave her a secretive, *just-us-girls* grin. "This is wonderful news, honey. I'm so excited for you!"

"I know you're probably not ready to chat tonight, but if we can get together for lunch sometime soon, I'd love to do that. I'd like to start this as soon as possible, while I still have the nerve." Dez laughed at herself.

"I'm so glad you trusted me with this. Lemme grab my phone and check my calendar." Lola sashayed to an end table and disconnected her phone from a charging cable. She tapped and swiped the screen. "Okay, Dez, let's see. What does your schedule look like on—"

Lola's phone chimed. Her tapered eyebrows bunched.

"Is everything okay?" Dez asked.

Lola laughed, but it was a nervous sound.

"I gotta take this," she said. "It's a . . . a family matter. I'll get back to you soon about our little thing, 'kay?"

"Sure. I'll jot down my number. Text me whenever you can."

Lola gave her a tight smile. As if she didn't want Dez to overhear her conversation, she hurried to the bedroom and slammed the door.

Taking a hint, Dez scribbled her number on a nearby scrap of paper and returned upstairs, closing the door behind her. Although she had dared to voice her ambitions, she feared they may have been put on hold.

53

Back in his SUV driving through the chilly night, Cam shuddered so badly he could barely keep his hands on the steering wheel.

He wasn't sure of his destination. He needed to get home, yet he was not ready to return to the rental and face the new reality in which he found himself.

I own your home . . .

After he had been driving for perhaps ten minutes, he realized his intent: he was traveling to Norcross. He drove on Jimmy Carter Boulevard, one of the busy thoroughfares that ran through Gwinnett County.

I need to see it myself, he thought.

As the realization dawned on him, he became aware of a simpler need: getting to a restroom. The Red Bull he had guzzled earlier pressed upon his bladder like a stone.

He neared a Waffle House on his right. He swung into the parking lot, grabbed the spot near the front door.

Inside the restaurant, the aromas of grilling onions, bacon, and frying potatoes engulfed him. Hunger gnawed at his stomach. He hadn't finished eating dinner because of the landlord's summons. But as hungry as he was, his nerves were too jangled for him to sit still and eat in a diner.

On his left, a hallway led to the restrooms. As he hurried along the corridor, he noticed a public pay phone. A gray-haired man wearing a black trench coat used the telephone, hand cupped to his mouth as if were a CIA agent making a secret call.

In the small restroom, Cam relieved himself. At the sink, he washed his hands and examined his reflection in the mirror. Shadows ringed his reddened eyes, his face lined with grimy sweat.

It was the face of a man in trouble.

When he walked out of the restroom, the pay phone stood available.

He didn't have any coins in his pocket. But he probably had some spare change in his SUV. He could grab a few quarters, return inside, and place a phone call to the local police department.

As he approached the phone, the landlord's warning echoed in his mind.

I own your home. I own your family. I own you, Mr. Woodson.

If Cam summoned the police, even if he claimed to be a neighbor who had "seen something that didn't look right," the landlord would suspect Cam was responsible. The landlord had evidence that Cam had committed a crime of his own. What would the landlord do to him and his family?

Cam valued civic duty. He voted in elections, donated to charities when he had spare funds, volunteered to help the less fortunate. He liked to think of himself as a man of ethics, too, a moral being. Whatever infraction Thor's victim had committed didn't deserve physical punishment.

A police officer entered the restaurant. He greeted the staff and strode in Cam's direction.

"Excuse me, buddy," the cop said, on his way to the restroom. Cam stood aside.

I can tell him, Cam thought.

And in the next breath: *No, I can't. I've got my own problems to tackle.*

He got out of there. Back in the Jeep, he resumed his journey and arrived in the Norcross neighborhood about fifteen minutes later.

He knew his way around by then since he had visited several times, though never at that late hour. It was easy to spot: from several hundred yards away, Cam saw the crime scene tape encircling the property.

His stomach plummeted.

The house itself looked as if a missile had struck it. Just as the news article said, the roof had collapsed from the fire.

He was so shaken he almost braked in the middle of the road. But he didn't want to draw attention, and pulled in front of a nearby home, at a safe distance, and gawked.

He had worked in that house—spent blood, sweat, and tears making improvements, in good faith. Being paid well to work, and for what? Why had the landlord deceived him into destroying the property? Was he planning to pocket the insurance money? Or did he only want to prove a point to Cam?

I own you, Mr. Woodson.

His heart thundered.

Like a beetle hanging in a black widow's web, Cam was trapped.

54

When Cam arrived home, he dragged himself into the house, feeling as if he carried a sack of bricks on his back. He was hungry, but too tired to bother eating. He needed to think, but he lacked the energy to focus on a single thought. Useful thought required clarity, and clarity was the one asset that Cam lacked. He wanted to shut down his brain and pray that when he awoke tomorrow, he would have answers to his predicament.

He shuffled upstairs and entered the bedroom. Much to his surprise, Dez was awake.

He wasn't prepared to see her, though she sometimes stayed up late. Dressed in her nightgown, she sat in bed with her iPad angled on her lap, stylus in her hand as she swiped and tapped the screen.

"You're back early," she said.

She didn't smile. He knew she hadn't forgiven him for rushing out of the house earlier.

"I thought you'd be asleep by now," he said.

"I've been browsing. How did the gig go? Did you get paid?"

"They didn't need me. Thor took care of it."

"You drove all that way for nothing? They should at least compensate you for gas."

He wasn't ready to tell her what was happening. First, he needed to figure out his next step, get his thoughts in order. He couldn't dump his problems into her lap.

But she's your wife, Cam, and this affects her, too, doesn't it? The landlord said: I own your family.

He loved Dez and appreciated her counsel, but he often struggled to discuss difficult subjects with her, especially if the situation cast him in a poor light. When his writing career crashed into the rocks, he waited weeks before sharing the news with her. He kept bad news tucked away, letting it marinate in his brain while he told himself he would confide in her after he had a solution.

This situation was a disaster of epic proportions, and he hated looking like a failure to her. He had walked right into the landlord's trap.

I'll tell her when the time is right. Whenever that is.

Cam turned toward the bathroom, intending to take a shower, wash off the stink of his sour sweat, and then collapse into bed.

"Hang on." She swung her legs to the side of the mattress, stood. "I need to clear the air between us."

"I'm exhausted. Can it wait till tomorrow?"

"I don't like keeping secrets." She knotted her hands together.

Cam dragged his hand down his face. "Go ahead."

"While you were gone, I talked to Lola. I told her I'm accepting her offer."

He paused, his mind so jumbled he couldn't remember what she was talking about.

"Her offer for what?" he asked.

"The social media thing," Dez said.

"I told you that's a bad idea, Dez."

Dez balled her fists on her waist and spread her legs as if she were digging in her heels.

"It's what I want to do," she said. "You need to support me, like I support you."

"It has nothing to do with that. We need to keep our distance from her. We already talked about this."

"We talked about it, but I want to do this." Her jaws clenched. "With or without your support."

"I see what's going on here. You're trying to get back at me. That's what this is about, huh? My working for the landlord without discussing it with you first. Tit for tat, right?"

"It has nothing to do with you! I want this for our family. Can't you see that?"

"You don't believe in me anymore," he said. "You think I'm a failure."

"I never said that!"

"You don't have to say it." His voice quivered, emotion fluttering in his chest. "I see how you look at Ebony and Vic. Seething with envy. It's so obvious."

"No, no, no." Tears glistened in her eyes. "No, I don't."

"You'll never admit it, but I know the truth." He sneered. "Go ahead, Dez. You want to be a social media whore? Do it, then. I don't give a damn."

A thin wail pierced the air: Ava. His daughter had a knack for bursting into tears whenever they were fighting, even if she wasn't in the room, as if she had a telepathic sense of their emotional states.

Dez wiped tears from her eyes, flashed him a *this-isn't-over* look, and hurried out of the bedroom.

Great job, Cam. You insulted your wife and woke up your kid at the same time.

He flung off his shoes and stormed into the bathroom. He turned on the shower as hot as it would go and got inside the stall, letting the water scald his skin until it wrung tears from his eyes.

55

Unable to sleep, Cam shuffled downstairs to watch television. Dez, for all he knew, went to bed. Their argument festered between them like a gangrenous wound. Cam hated leaving things on such a sour note, but he saw no peaceful resolution to their problems, didn't know what he could say to make it all better.

He could only hope that tomorrow he would have something helpful that he could tell her to smooth things over.

At first, he decided he would watch whatever looked interesting on Netflix. He spent a couple of hours streaming a true crime documentary about serial killers. But at some point, when he was watching one of those shows and heard a DVD player mentioned, he remembered the disc he had found.

Wait a minute. I still have that DVD, don't I?

He went to his desk drawer and dug out the disc he had taken from the Norcross property's bedroom closet. It felt heavy in his hand, but that was only his imagination.

They had a DVD player in the rental house, stashed away somewhere in a moving box. He went upstairs to the spare bedroom. In the closet, he found the cardboard box and the DVD unit buried underneath a stack of discs he hadn't watched in years: old favorites such as *Die Hard, Enemy of the State,* and *The Matrix.*

Bingo.

He took the player and its connection cables downstairs and hooked up the unit to the TV in the family room.

Let's see what we've got.

After he turned on the player and verified the link, he slid the disc inside. He hesitated before he pressed the PLAY button. The material on this disc might be unpleasant. Was he ready for that?

Can it be worse than the sorry state of my own life?

He wasn't sure what he hoped to accomplish by watching the disc. But he pressed PLAY and settled onto a chair.

Black-and-white images appeared on the screen; the narrow field of view reminded him of footage from a surveillance camera. A time stamp at the bottom of the screen marked the recording as coming from August of that year.

The camera capturing the video was positioned in the master bedroom suite of the house in Norcross. It picked up audio, too.

He saw a man and a woman arguing. Their faces matched the photographs of the people he had seen in the news article covering the murder-suicide.

The dead people.

A chill stepped down his spine.

As they argued, they seemed unaware of the camera, which led Cam to believe that the recording device was concealed.

"He's giving us work!" the man said. "What choice do we have?"

"This landlord of yours is destroying us," the woman said. "We never should've taken any of his goddamn money."

Cold sweat gathered on his brow. He might have been watching video of himself and Dez arguing about the same thing. The landlord. Money. Jesus.

The camera appeared to be motion-activated; it captured routine footage such as the people getting dressed in the morning, clipping their nails, combing their hair, and random comings and goings from the room. He used the remote control to fast-forward and discovered another incident. In this next segment, the husband and wife were fighting again, but this was an actual physical altercation.

Cam felt his insides recoil, and he almost skipped past the footage, but he forced himself to watch it. Cursing, the man slapped the woman. She reeled backward, grabbed the lamp off the night-stand, and tossed it at him. The lamp struck him in the head, and he put his hand to his temple and cursed.

"I'll kill you!" he shouted.

He lunged toward her and got his hands around her throat. They collapsed onto the bed, the man trying to choke her, and the woman gagging, struggling to throw him off.

Cam couldn't watch any more, especially knowing that these people were dead by the husband's hand. He fast-forwarded.

He watched a bit more footage, fast-forwarding through much of it, and confirmed that the contents of the disc had concluded prior to the murder-suicide. Thank God.

He switched it off.

He sat still for several minutes, sweat trickling down his face, the remote control resting in his clammy fingers.

Were he and Dez on the same track as this doomed couple?

No way, he thought. *Never. I've never raised my hand against Dez, and I never will.*

But one of the wife's remarks echoed in his mind like a bell of doom: *We never should've taken any of his goddamn money.*

Finally, a solution struck him.

56

He would give the landlord the money back.

Every penny that the landlord had paid him for the various tasks, Cam would return, and in doing so, he would gain his freedom from past and future obligations. He would wipe the slate clean. Clear his name, if only for his own sake.

This plan was so exciting to Cam, so simple, and logical, that he couldn't wait until the morning, and neither could he wait to discuss it with Dez. He was going to do it because he was certain that it would work. He would repay every dollar, and a reasonable person—he assumed the landlord was reasonable because he seemed to be a stone-cold businessman—would release him from their arrangement or whatever it was.

Adrenaline coursing through him, Cam logged onto his computer and accessed their bank accounts. He held some of the money that the landlord had paid him in a joint checking account; that checking account was linked to the payment app on his phone.

As he reviewed the balance, he recalled he'd used a small portion for certain items. For one, he'd paid Dez's father a thousand dollars to shut the man's mouth about the money Cam owed. He'd also spent a few hundred bucks eating out, and on other small items. He could make up the difference by dipping into his savings account, which was admittedly dwindling, but he had just enough to cover the gap.

Ordinarily, this idea would have repulsed him. He'd acquired a habit of hoarding every penny because money had been so tight. But the tide had turned in his favor; his agent, Ethan Knight, was excited about the new book and shopping around his proposal. More money, lots of it, was on the way.

He was sure of it.

Once he booted the landlord out of his personal business, all he had to do was wait for the book contract money to flood into his account.

With this new plan in mind, Cam picked up his phone. The clock read ten minutes past two o'clock in the morning. Nevertheless, he called the landlord's number. He assumed he would need to leave a message, but the landlord answered after the first ring.

"Yes, Mr. Woodson?"

Does this man ever sleep? His voice was crisp.

"I apologize for the late hour," Cam said, words pouring out of him. "But I've been thinking about everything, and I've decided that I don't want any part of this anymore. I want out. I'm going to give you back everything that you've paid me. Every dollar. I know I worked hard for some of that money, but I hope that by doing this, you understand how serious I am about ending our arrangement. I don't want to owe you anything."

The landlord didn't reply. Cam pressed on.

"All I ask is that when I give you back the money, you let me go," Cam said. "You forget about the place in Norcross. I want all of this to be over. I want to go back to my regular life with my wife and little girl." Cam swallowed, out of breath. "Do we have a deal? Can you agree that if I pay you back the money that we're good with each other? That it's done?"

The landlord waited so long to reply that Cam looked at the

phone, wondering if the man had ended the call. But the line was still open.

"I will consider your proposal, Mr. Woodson," the landlord said, and clicked off.

Relief washed over Cam. It felt like a victory, and that he had earned it without telling Dez a thing was even better. He didn't know how he would have explained any of this to his wife, so being able to slither out of it with no explanation offered to her seemed like the best possible outcome.

He yawned; a powerful urge to sleep came over him, and he didn't resist it. He shut off the lights, padded upstairs into the bedroom, and fell into a restful sleep.

57

That Thursday morning, Dez woke at her usual time, five thirty, to do her Pilates workout. Although she had suffered a fitful night of sleep, waking at that hour was hardwired into her body's internal clock. She didn't even need the alarm on her phone to wake her.

As she rose from the mattress and stretched, she noticed Cam had slid into their bed, too.

She didn't remember him coming back into the bedroom. When she had gone to sleep, he had remained downstairs, words from their nasty argument echoing like gunfire in her ears.

She hated they had gone to bed angry with each other. She hated having any arguments with Cam, though it was a natural part of marriage to work through disagreements.

But this felt like something different. His remark about how she seethed in envy whenever she looked at their friends cut deep.

Why would he say something so cruel? Her stomach tightened and she felt herself getting angry all over again.

As she dressed in her exercise gear, she wondered if she had made a mistake telling him about her decision to move forward with Lola.

Maybe all of it was a mistake, a dumb idea. If family strife was the cost of pursuing her ambitions, was it worth it? She told herself she wanted to set up the social media side hustle for the benefit of her family, but if she destroyed her marriage, what would she have when the dust settled?

Disturbed by her thoughts, she hurried out of the bedroom and went downstairs into the family room. She picked up the remote control, turned on the television.

Oddly, the TV was in DVD player mode. She looked around and spotted the disc player's remote lying on a nearby table.

She couldn't remember the last time she had played a disc and didn't even remember they had a player. Had Cam been up last night watching something?

Curious, she pressed PLAY, and the contents of the disc appeared on the screen.

It was a recording in black and white; it reminded her of material from a found footage film. The recording camera appeared to be positioned in a bedroom, and there were two people, a man and a woman, strangers to her, on the screen.

It sounded as if they were arguing.

What the heck is this? Is this a movie? Or something else?

Dez heard the woman mention a landlord. Her heart clutched.

Frowning, Dez kept watching. Where had this recording come from? Who were these people? What was going on with them? It felt as if she were a fly on the wall watching a dissolving marriage.

She fast-forwarded, saw more marital conflict, an actual fight, and decided she couldn't take it anymore. She didn't enjoy watching people hurt each other. But she would ask Cam about this disc when they got back on speaking terms.

Whenever that is, she thought, and felt anxiety pluck her nerves.

58

Without planning to do so, Cam slept in. When he woke a few minutes past ten o'clock in the morning, he found the voice mail indicator on his phone waiting for him.

He bolted upright in bed. He'd expected a call from the landlord with a decision about his proposal. But he had a message from his literary agent, Ethan Knight.

Cam held the phone to his ear and listened. His agent's voice crackled with excitement.

"A senior editor at St. Martin's is very interested, Cam," Ethan said. "I don't want to give you false hope, but she's a *big* fan of your prior work. Please shoot over the full manuscript ASAP. Ping me when've you sent it, so I can get it over to her right away."

Cam ripped aside the bedsheets and bounded out of the bed.

I knew it! Everything was going to work out. Now that he had volunteered to return the landlord's money, the universe had opened a better door. With a new publishing contract, he could be his own man again, not needing gigs and handouts from anybody.

He dressed in sweatpants and a T-shirt and rushed downstairs. Dez and Ava had left hours ago, leaving the house quiet.

He couldn't wait to tell his wife the good news. Perhaps it would make up for last night's train wreck.

Cam sat in front of his laptop and switched it on. Once the machine was ready, he checked for the folder in which he kept the new book manuscript and related files.

But the folder did not exist on the computer.

What's going on here? His pulse quickened. *There's no way that I changed that folder. I looked at it yesterday.*

Of course, he had heard stories over the years about writers who lost their material—manuscripts destroyed in house fires and marooned on malfunctioning hard drives. Like any prudent writer, he had a cloud storage account, a free one that provided limited space but met his purposes.

He saw the cloud account's folder in the files section on his laptop, as if it were a part of his machine's own hard drive. He always backed up his files to that folder.

But the cloud folder in which he stored his manuscript was empty.

"*No!*" Cam pounded his fists against the desk. "*What the hell happened?*"

There had to be something buggy with his computer. Reboot—that's what tech people always advised. *Reboot and it will sort itself out,* they said. *The machine's only having a hiccup.*

Gnawing his bottom lip, he restarted the computer. It seemed to take eons. When the reboot concluded, he looked again.

But the file was still gone. His stomach felt as if it had dropped onto the floor.

It can't be.

He searched on the computer for the file, and it yielded only the message: *No items match your search.*

The Recycle Bin was completely empty, too.

No.

He pushed out of the chair, paced the room.

How the hell had this happened? What was he going to tell Ethan? What was going to happen to that potential deal if he couldn't cough up the book?

You'll be done, Cam. That's what will happen. Back to driving for Uber and assembling furniture and hoping the landlord calls to offer you something better.

He wished he had sent the book to somebody. He could have emailed it to Dez or a writing partner, but he had hoarded it as if it were a secret manuscript and sent it to no one. It existed only on his computer and in the cloud, and now, incredibly, it was gone.

Desperate, looking around as if a printed manuscript would be sitting on the desk next to him, he grabbed his phone. He didn't call Ethan. He called Vic. Vic was good with technology, though his current job had nothing to do with tech; but in his prior role, before he was an administrator with the school district, he had taught computer science at the high school.

Because of the time of day and the fact that it was a Thursday, he figured Vic was working and might not answer, but his friend picked up on the second ring.

"Hey, Cam," Vic said.

Cam did not hear any enthusiasm in his friend's voice, and he remembered he hadn't patched things up between them since their beef at the poker game.

"Sort of weird getting a call from you right now," Vic said. "Is everything all right?"

"Vic, I'm desperate, man. Somehow, a file got deleted off my computer and it's not in my cloud folder, either. It's my book! I've gotta get it back."

"That's not good." Vic let out a low whistle. "I'm about to head into a meeting. Maybe I can call you back later with some ideas."

"How much later? I've got an editor who wants the book today."

"You could google some articles about recovering files. If that doesn't work, you can take it to a data recovery shop, and they can try to fish it out of the hard drive. That's all I can think of. Sorry, man, I've gotta go."

Cam slammed the phone onto the desk.

But he took Vic's advice and started searching online. His research took him to YouTube, and over the next hour, he watched a score of videos. None of them solved his issue.

A repair shop, he thought. *Data recovery place. That's what Vic suggested. That's my next step.*

His phone rang. It was Ethan.

Heart knocking, Cam kept his tone casual. "Hey, Ethan, how's it going?"

Cam heard horns honking, as if his agent was navigating Manhattan traffic. "Did you get my message, Cam? When can you get the manuscript over to me?"

"I'll get it over shortly." Cam forced out a gentle chuckle. "I'm running a final spell check. I'll call you as soon as I send it."

"Don't take too long." Ethan hung up.

Sighing, Cam put down the phone. He shouldn't have lied, but he didn't know what else he could say to buy more time without blowing up the opportunity.

Someone knocked on the front door.

59

A visitor had knocked, but Cam didn't intend to answer. He assumed someone was dropping off a package for Dez. He had more important business to attend to than dealing with a delivery driver.

But the person knocked several more times, harder, the sound echoing through the house. *What the hell?* Gritting his teeth, Cam turned away from his laptop and looked out the front window.

Oh shit. A black van stood in the driveway, the same sleek vehicle from last night.

It was Thor.

Cam could not have imagined a worse time for the handyman—or whatever he was called now, *part-time hit man?*—to visit. He didn't want to speak to him, but after last night he worried about what Thor might do if he ignored him. He had a vivid memory of watching Thor kick in a front door and use a stun gun on a man, and God knows what other violent acts he'd performed after Cam had left the scene. This was not the type of person Cam wanted to piss off.

Besides, as the handyman for the landlord's properties, Thor possessed the code to unlock the door via the keypad, anyway.

Whatever he wants, I need to deal with him quickly so I can solve this laptop issue.

Gathering his nerve, Cam opened the door.

"Hey," Cam said.

Thor entered without a greeting. Cam stepped aside to keep the man from knocking him over.

He wore the same clothing from last night, all-black attire. Cam didn't know what that meant, but he didn't think the man had visited to check the plumbing.

In the hallway, Thor turned and glowered at him.

"This is a bad time," Cam said. "I'm in the middle of an emergency."

Thor nodded. "Yes, you are in a crisis. Come with me."

"I've got to go get my laptop fixed. I *have* to do it now. I was actually getting ready to leave when I heard you knock."

"Do you say you are not coming with me?" Thor said.

"Whatever it is, it's gotta wait. I'll be back in a few hours. But I have to deal with this now, you don't understand—"

The punch came unexpectedly, Thor's fist smashing like a cannonball into Cam's stomach. Cam felt his knees wobble as agony exploded throughout his body. No one had hit him since he'd been bullied in the third grade. Gasping, he doubled over, and his sagging knees gave way and he found himself on the hardwood floor.

His head spun. He looked up. Through eyes full of tears, he saw Thor staring down at him as if he were studying a bug he might crush under his heel.

"I do not have patience for a stubborn person." Thor massaged his knuckles. "Do not test me again."

Cam struggled to breathe. His throbbing gut churned, and he thought he might vomit.

Fighting back was out of the question. Thor was huge, swollen with muscles, probably outweighed Cam by eighty pounds. Most importantly, Cam had no useful experience with combat. He was more inclined to send a sharply worded email than he was to come to blows with anyone.

But Thor was no stranger to violence.

Whistling, Thor marched past him and opened the hallway closet. He retrieved Cam's windbreaker jacket and tossed it onto the floor next to Cam.

"We will go," Thor said. "But first you will get your checkbook. Write out the check to the landlord as you offered."

"How . . . how . . . do you know about that?" Cam asked, the words barely making it past his trembling lips.

"I know whatever is required," Thor said. "Get up."

Sweating, Cam struggled to his feet, feeling as if the entire world tilted like a carnival ride around him. He put his hand against the wall to brace himself.

His stomach ached, and would hurt for a while. In another life, he might have accused Thor of assault, threatened to call the police. But in his sordid new life, all he did was drag himself toward the desk in the home office / living room. Thor followed him.

"If I give him the money, that means I'm good, right?" Cam asked.

"Good?"

"That I don't owe him anything. And where do you want me to go anyway?"

"Write the check, Cam."

Cam grabbed the checkbook out of a drawer. With a trembling hand he wrote a check in the full amount that he had promised to pay back the landlord, everything the man had paid him for his work. As he ripped it off and handed it to Thor, he wondered what Dez would say if she knew what he was doing.

But it was too late for that, wasn't it?

Thor snatched the check out of his fingers, glanced at it, tucked it into an inner pocket of his black jacket.

"Now you come with me," Thor said.

"Why? What do you need?"

"You owe me for leaving the job last night," Thor said.

"What're you talking about?"

"The landlord has a new job for you."

"But I wrote a check! I paid all the money back! I don't owe the landlord anything!"

A devious grin slid across Thor's face.

"The landlord is not done with you yet," Thor said.

60

"Go get in the van," Thor said.

He put his big, fat-knuckled hand on Cam's shoulder, the same hand he had balled into a fist and slammed into Cam's gut only a few minutes ago.

Cam had put on his jacket, but leaving the house was about as appealing as walking across a field of broken glass. He needed to recover the manuscript file and get it to his agent. From experience, he knew editorial interest in your book was fleeting, that something else could drop onto an editor's desk and they'd forget all about your manuscript.

"How much is the landlord paying you to harass me?" Cam asked. "How about you rip up that check for the landlord and I pay you directly to cut me loose?"

"What would I tell our landlord?" Thor asked.

"Whatever you want. Tell him I refused to go or threatened to call the police."

"I can see why you are a writer." Thor smiled, showing his crooked front tooth. "You have a vivid imagination." He clapped Cam's shoulder. "Now, go get in the van."

"I still don't understand why I have to do anything if he's taking the money back."

"My patience runs short." He literally steered Cam to the door.

It was worth a shot, Cam thought.

With Thor behind him, he went outside. He climbed into the van's passenger seat, his abdomen burning with every movement.

"Now I realize how you got that black eye a few weeks ago," Cam said to Thor as the man settled behind the wheel. "You're like a damn enforcer or something. Someone fought back, clocked you good."

Thor smiled. "You should see what the other guy looked like."

Thor removed a business-size envelope that was clipped to the sun visor and passed it to Cam. Cam saw his name inscribed on the front in blocky black letters.

"What is this?" Cam asked.

"A gift from our employer." Thor backed out of the driveway.

As Thor drove out of the neighborhood, Cam opened the envelope. He found three color photographs.

His pulse quickening, he examined the pictures. The first showed him arriving in his Jeep at the Norcross property on that fateful night last week, his license plate visible. Whoever had taken this photograph had been parked across the street.

In the second pic, Cam parked in the driveway, backing in so that the rear of the vehicle was parallel with the garage door. The third and final picture displayed Cam—his face plain thanks to a high-powered camera—taking the package out of the SUV, the garage door hanging open behind him.

"Who took these pictures?" Cam asked. His blood felt hot. "Did you?"

"Our landlord has many working on his behalf." Thor shrugged. "There are many like you, Cam. Everyone wants to earn an honest dollar."

An honest dollar, right. Cam thought about the man and woman he had watched on the DVD. Tenants manipulated into performing "assignments" for extra money. But when the gigs went south, what did you do?

He considered flinging the photos out the window, realized the pointlessness of it. Unquestionably, the landlord had copies of these pictures.

"I need to talk this out with the landlord directly," Cam said, raising his phone. "I need to understand why I 'owe' anything, as you say, when I wrote a check to repay him."

"Do you think I am lying to you?" Thor's eyebrows curved.

"I want to talk to him myself."

"You have his number."

Cam called the number, but there was no answer. Instead of leaving a voice mail, he sent a text message.

Thor says I owe you. Why do I owe you when I'm giving you the money back?

The landlord responded within a couple of minutes: *It's the principle of the matter, Mr. Woodson. You failed to complete last night's task. Your obstinance created a debt that you must repay in full.*

"This is garbage," Cam mumbled.

"What is garbage?" Thor glanced at Cam's phone, smirked. "You do not like our landlord's responses?"

Cam ignored him and sent another text: *After I do this thing, are we done?*

That depends on you, Mr. Woodson.

Cam's head pounded. If the phone hadn't belonged to him, he might have tossed it out the window.

"Listen, where are we going?" Cam asked Thor. "It won't be like last night, will it?"

"You will dispose of trash," Thor said.

"I'm not doing anything criminal. I don't care what you guys have got on me. I'm not doing anything shady again. If that's the plan, you might as well drop me off at the nearest police station and tell them to book me."

"You have much to say, eh? Relax. You will need your energy for the next job."

"*What* is the job?"

Instead of answering, Thor spun the volume knob of the radio, flooding the van with country western music. He gritted his teeth, wished he had earplugs to drown out the smothering sounds.

Thor merged into traffic on I-285. Cam kept himself busy looking up data recovery shops in the area and musing about what he would tell Ethan when his agent asked him again about the status of the manuscript.

Probably the truth, Cam thought. *Maybe Ethan could stall the editor, tell her I'm on vacation in the Australian outback without a computer and won't be back for two weeks.*

After about forty minutes of driving, they took an exit onto Memorial Drive, in DeKalb County. Soon, Thor veered into an older neighborhood, a community of ranch-style homes that had probably been built in the 1960s.

"What are we doing here?" Cam yelled to be heard over the music.

If Thor heard him, he gave no sign.

They parked in front of a ranch home with faded brown siding and black shutters. A gigantic trash dumpster occupied the driveway. The grass stood knee-high, rampant with tangled weeds. Slabs of plywood covered the front windows.

Thor switched off the engine and killed the music. Cam felt his eardrums contract.

"It doesn't look like anyone lives here," Cam said. Relief washed over him. No kicking in doors this time, he assumed.

"Here, you will clean." Thor clucked his tongue. "The job last night would have been easier."

"Only cleaning?" Cam asked. "That doesn't sound too bad."

"Open the glove compartment," Thor said. "You will need the gloves and the mask."

Cam opened the glove box and found a pair of brand-new work

gloves and a dust mask. Thor slipped on a mask and got out of the van. Cam grabbed the items and followed him.

Thor unlocked the front door and ushered Cam inside. Cam put on the mask and looked around. It looked as if a hoarder had lived there. Mountains of assorted junk—old furniture, trash, and anything else he could imagine—filled the hallway and rooms, piled up to the ceiling. Underneath it all, despite the mask, Cam detected the acrid stench of old cat urine and feces.

His stomach, already aching, churned. He held his breath, trying to keep himself from vomiting, and the urge passed.

"So, I'm supposed to clean out this place?" Cam asked, though he already knew the answer to the question.

"I told you last night would have been easier," Thor said, voice muffled by the mask.

"Are you helping?"

"I'm not in the landlord's debt."

Of course, he's not helping. Dumb question.

"I'm not being paid for this, either, am I?"

"Does a debt collector call you and say, 'Cam Woodson, I will pay you if you clear your debt'?"

Another dumb question.

"I can't finish all of this today," Cam said. "This is going to take days."

"You have plenty of time." Thor patted his shoulder. "We will return every day until you are done."

"When I'm done, do you think the landlord's going to let me go? We'll be square?"

Thor shrugged, as if to say, *Who can say? I only work for the man like you do.*

Cam sent Dez a text message, letting her know he was doing another of the infamous "landlord gigs" that she despised.

And despite his misgivings, he got to work.

61

After lunch, Cam sent Dez a text message. She read it between classes when she slipped into the teacher's lounge to brew a cup of ginger tea.

Busy working at a house in Stone Mountain. Be back later this evening.

He closed with a love emoji.

Her stomach clenched, as if she were drinking spoiled milk, not tea. She didn't bother asking what type of work he was doing, or for whom. She already knew the answer: household tasks for the landlord.

The DVD she watched that morning surfaced in her thoughts. The two strangers arguing, a "landlord" referenced.

She remembered what the woman had said: *This landlord of yours is destroying us . . .*

She hadn't a clue who those people were, but instinct told her that their landlords were the same. It made a twisted sort of sense.

Whatever task Cam was engaged in, she hoped the man compensated him this time. But that was questionable, too, wasn't it? Was it worth taking money from a party that triggered such strife in your household?

She wasn't blameless, either. As she'd told Cam last night, she intended to follow her own ambitions, too. That announcement had gone over as well as she'd expected.

I have the right to do what I please. Why is he the only one allowed to chase his goals?

Later, after she picked up Ava from her parents' house and arrived home, she decided she was going to chat with Lola again. Since Lola had cut off their last conversation with her vague comment about a family emergency, a sliver of anxiety had wormed into Dez. She felt an urgency to finalize their plans.

When she had settled Ava down with a snack at the kitchen table, Dez heard a knock at the basement door.

"Come in," Dez said.

Lola opened the door. "Hey, Dez. Do you have a minute?"

"You must've read my mind. I was going to come down to chat with you in a bit."

Lola gave her a wan smile and stepped into the kitchen, hands shoved deep into the pockets of her baggy jeans. She seemed reluctant to meet Dez's gaze.

"Is something wrong?" Dez asked.

"I'm so sorry," Lola said in a soft voice. "But there's been a change of plans."

62

Thor dropped Cam off at home around seven thirty that evening.

"You will do more cleanup at the property tomorrow," Thor said. "I will take you there."

"I have the address," Cam said. "I can drive there myself."

Thor shook his head. "Nine o'clock, I will be here. Be ready."

Cam felt like giving him a middle finger, but he settled for waving him away.

He had spent several hours disposing of trash in the house, tossing everything into the dumpster that stood in the driveway, but even though he had filled the dumpster, there was still plenty of garbage, rooms full of it, remaining in the house. Thor didn't help him at all; he spent his time wandering outdoors, and then at one point he drove off, leaving Cam there wondering when or if he would return. He returned perhaps an hour later and checked in on Cam's progress.

Cam didn't know what he could do to get out of it. Worse, his agent had called them once more, asking him about the status of the manuscript, and Cam finally confessed he couldn't locate the file.

"You *deleted* the book?" Ethan asked.

"Give me time, please. I'm going to a data recovery shop. I'm going to get the file back."

"This is terrible. You've got to find that file, Cam. We can't blow this opportunity."

Cam had felt like screaming.

When he entered the house that evening, he found Dez in the family room, Ava with her reading a book. Dez stood when he came into the room.

"I guess it was much ado about nothing," Dez said.

"What are you talking about?"

"The social media thing with Lola," Dez said. "It's dead in the water. She told me today that she's going in a new direction, and that she couldn't help me with it."

Although Cam was happy that Dez had given up on this ambition, he was too tired to ask her a follow-up question about it.

"I guess it is what it is," Cam said.

"Where have you been all day, anyway?" Her nose wrinkled. "You look filthy!"

Cam was tired of lying, but he didn't know how to tell her what he had been doing.

"And I wanted to ask you about this," Dez said. She picked up the DVD and handed it to him.

Cam felt a sinking feeling. Last night, he'd been so focused on escaping the landlord's trap that he'd forgotten to put away the disc.

"We need to have a serious talk," Cam said. "Let me grab a Red Bull. I'm totally wiped out—I need something to give me some energy."

Dez followed him into the kitchen. He grabbed an energy drink out of the refrigerator and guzzled half of it in a few gulps.

"Let's go out into the Jeep to have our chat," Cam said. "We can take a little drive."

It was time to tell Dez everything.

63

"Where we going, Daddy?" Ava asked as Dez buckled her into the Jeep's back seat.

"We're going for a ride, honey." Cam turned in the seat and tried to smile at his daughter. "Mommy and I are going to talk, and we'll cruise around, okay?"

"Okay." She wriggled her legs and clapped her hands, as if they were going on a road trip to Disney World. He envied her innocence.

Dez slid into the passenger seat, and he backed out of the garage. Despite his exhaustion, he was determined to unload everything with his wife. So much had happened that it required more effort for him to maintain secrets from her than it did for him to spill them out.

As he cruised around the neighborhood like a student driver practicing turns, he told Dez everything. He started with the package task: in his opinion, that was where his arrangement with the landlord had veered into criminal activity. He related last night's rendezvous with Thor to the "deadbeat tenant's" house and his fleeing the scene. He told her about the arson. The coercion. His gambit to pay the money back. His new "debt" and the landlord's unwillingness to release him.

He gave her the photographs Thor had given to him earlier. If they were not ironclad evidence of his participation in the Norcross property's destruction, they painted an incriminating profile, nonetheless.

Along the way, he mentioned his missing manuscript and the editor who wanted to read it.

Dez listened as he spoke and drove, not asking any questions, but her gaze alternated between his face and the photos in her hands. At certain points, she shook her head, gasped, or gave him a narrow look. But she didn't say a word.

"That's everything," he said. He had pulled into the rental's driveway as he concluded his tale. "I'm sorry I didn't tell you. I thought I could handle it on my own. I only wanted to keep you and Ava safe."

"There's nothing we can do about that now, Cam. Is there?"

Her gaze seared him. He lowered his head. Although relating everything had removed a tremendous weight from his shoulders, repairing his damaged relationship with his wife promised to be a new, perhaps more challenging task.

"I'm sorry," he said again. "I admit it, I've ruined everything. I don't even have the money anymore."

"The money?" Dez sneered. "I don't want this man's dirty money. That was probably the smartest thing you did, paying it back."

"But he still hasn't let me go. I've got nothing to show for what I've done."

"You've gained a clean conscience."

"A clean conscience doesn't pay the bills."

"Hmph." Dez dragged her fingers through her hair. "This is so much to process. I barely know where to start." She sucked in her bottom lip. "I want to know about the DVD I watched this morning. Where did you get it from?"

Cam had been so focused on the other details of his narrative that he hadn't discussed the disc.

"It's from the house in Norcross. A murder-suicide took place there."

"A what?"

"It's sad, really. Yeah, it was the couple in the recording. Later on, the husband killed the wife and then shot himself."

"My God." She shivered. "Is the . . . murder on the disc, too?"

"The disc I found was labeled for August, but the murder took place in September. Whoever cleaned out the place must've forgotten the disc that I found."

"It's evidence," she said.

"They're both dead. I don't think it matters anymore."

"So sad."

"Yeah." He glanced toward their rental home, the golden light glowing at the windows; it was a tableau of perfect domesticity, like a scene in a Norman Rockwell painting. "But I think I've figured out what's in that bedroom closet we haven't been able to crack."

"Recording equipment," Dez said with such certainty that he wondered if she had suspected the truth all along. "The landlord is recording us, like he recorded that other family. Is that what you think?"

"If we need to have a private chat, we can't do it in the house. That's why I wanted to get in the Jeep."

Closing her eyes, she leaned back in her seat, pressed her palm against her forehead. "I feel a migraine coming on."

"I'm sorry." He didn't know what else to say.

"The idea of someone seeing and hearing *everything*." She grimaced. "Isn't it illegal for him to film us? We have a right to privacy, surely."

"We have bigger issues to deal with right now, Dez."

"I don't want to live in a house where someone is watching me every second!"

"What are we going to do about it?" he asked.

"Call the police, obviously." She made an impatient gesture, as if he were slow to keep up. "Come on. That's what people do in situations like this."

"I don't think that's a good idea. At all."

"There are a million reasons why we need to call the police, Cam. A million sensible reasons. This isn't the time for your stubbornness."

Ignoring the jab, he swiveled in his seat, reached for her hands, held them. "Please, no police. The landlord set me up for this arson charge, but how can I prove that?"

"Do you have text messages from him?"

"I don't have any texts from him giving me instructions to do it. All of that was done verbally."

"Regardless, we get a criminal attorney," she said. "The attorney can deal with the police."

"What kind of lawyer could we afford without any money, Dez? I had to drain most of my other savings to pay the landlord back. We're running close to empty here."

"My parents—"

"*No.* Your dad already thinks you marrying me was a mistake."

Dez looked away from him. She knew he was right.

"Can you imagine how your father would respond to this?" Cam said. "No way. We keep your folks out of it."

"We're in over our heads. These people are criminals."

"I know." He rubbed his thumbs over her fingers. "But if we go to the police, trying to do the right thing, and I've got a felony charge hanging over me . . . I could be put in jail." He squeezed her hands. "Promise me. Work with me to find another way. Please."

"This is blackmail." But she clasped his hands.

"Coercion," he agreed. "He lured me in with money and I took the bait. I was desperate, then got greedy, didn't question it. Now I'm trapped."

"Why don't we move out?" She glanced toward the house, and he saw a tremor pass through her. "I can't imagine living here anymore."

"We're past moving out, breaking the lease. He's got me cold, no matter where I go." He turned away from her, wiped cold sweat away from his forehead with the back of his hand. "Thor's picking me up tomorrow to make me work in that shitty house again. I think they're going to keep forcing me to do things until . . ."

"Until they're done with you," Dez said with a note of finality. "Or he may never let you go. Why should he? You're free, skilled labor at this point. You'll do whatever he wants to stay out of trouble."

"I only wanted to earn some extra money." He pounded his fist against the steering wheel. "Dammit, how could I fall into this?"

"Are you okay, Daddy?" Ava asked, a quiver in her voice.

Cam turned. Tears hung in Ava's eyes.

"Sorry, honey. Daddy's okay. We're only having an important conversation."

"Are you sure, Daddy?" Her face was earnest.

"Positive, Pumpkin."

Ava returned her attention to the tablet Dez had given her, to distract her while they talked. Cam dragged his hand down his sweat-lined face and sighed.

"Have you ever met this landlord?" Dez asked. "Do you know his name?"

"I've talked to him on the phone, texted him. But I don't know his name." He laughed. "Silly, right?"

"How do you know it isn't Thor?" she asked.

"I've thought about that. But today, I was texting the landlord while Thor was driving. Thor wasn't holding a phone. It's not him." He touched his still-sore abdomen. "Thor is only muscle." He hadn't bothered telling her that Thor had punched him in the stomach. What good would it have done? He wasn't going to report an assault.

"We need a plan," Dez said. "You've said no police. I don't like that, but I'll respect it, for now. So what's your plan?"

"My best plan was paying him back." He laughed, a bitter sound. "That worked like a charm, huh?"

"How many other properties does the landlord own?" Dez asked.

"I dunno. Why?"

"There was the crime in Norcross. What if there are more crimes, at other properties?"

He sat up straighter in the seat, a memory flaring in his thoughts.

"Thor said something today, a remark about how there were other poor saps like me working for the landlord."

"People desperate for cash." Dez nodded. "Looking back, I think that's why they targeted us. They knew from the start that we had credit issues, money troubles. I think they were looking for people in dire straits."

"Beggars can't be choosers," Cam said, in sync with her. "If there have been others like us, or like the couple in Norcross—"

"There's a pattern of crimes," Dez said. "If we could link them all together, somehow, that could be evidence that the landlord is the guilty party here, that he's victimizing his tenants."

"You're onto something." He smiled at her, and she gave him a tense smile in return. "But how do we find the connection?"

"Property records are online," she said. "We know the name of the property management firm. We could search by company name, find out what other houses he owns, do a search on those houses to see what crimes are linked to them. We're bound to turn up something."

He snapped his fingers. "We could use that information to scare him away. Threaten to go to a lawyer if he doesn't back off. Hell, an ambitious lawyer might take on a case like that pro bono."

"Or we go to the media. You're a local writer. You've been in the newspaper. Remember the feature in the Atlanta newspaper last year?"

"How could I forget? It didn't do jack for sales."

"But you've got a contact there. You could call them and give them our story. It could make the news."

"The landlord would hate that kind of attention. Like you said— I don't know his name, what he looks like, anything. He likes his privacy. But if we threaten to blow him up in the media with all sorts of links to crimes at his properties, I think he'll cut me loose."

"And we can get on with our lives," Dez said. She rubbed her stomach, and he knew she was thinking about the new baby on the way. "Promise me, Cam, that you won't shut me out again. Promise me."

He lifted her hand to his lips, kissed her fingers.

"Promise," he said.

64

After they finalized their plan, they returned inside the house. Cam showered, changed into clean clothes, and came downstairs and popped open his laptop, telling Dez he was determined to do his best to retrieve the deleted file until he could get to a data recovery shop. Dez took Ava upstairs to give her a bath and put her down to bed. Cam offered to help, to read a book to Ava as he usually did, but Dez said she needed time alone, and going through the automatic motions of prepping their child for bedtime allowed her the space to think.

She was still processing what he had told her. Although they had put their heads together and formed a strategy, anger smoldered like acid in her chest.

How could he have gotten them into this situation and kept it hidden from her? Didn't he trust her? Why couldn't he understand that any decision he made was going to affect the rest of them?

If the landlord had trapped him, he had trapped *her*, too.

She believed he was genuinely sorry, but that didn't excuse his sorry behavior. He was on a losing streak of poor choices, and while she wanted to support him, give him the benefit of the doubt, he wasn't making it easy on her.

She wanted to call the police. She understood the reasons for his reluctance, but still. She was ready to let someone else take control of the situation.

But she would go along with their plan, such as it was. Try to dig into the landlord's dirt. She planned to take a sick day tomorrow so she could spend the day at the library, researching.

She certainly wasn't going to spend the day at the house.

Dez didn't want to spend another second in the rental. Had the landlord inserted cameras and listening devices in every room? What had they recorded so far? Did they have footage of her taking showers? Giving Ava baths? Having sex with her husband?

The idea repulsed her.

After she put down Ava, she stalked around the master bedroom suite, looking for likely hiding spots for a camera.

This is why the place was rented with furnishings provided, she realized. *So they could spy on us.*

There was a large circle-shaped clock hanging above the dresser, a likely place for a surveillance camera, she reasoned. She snatched it off the wall and tossed it onto the bed. Flipped it over and examined it.

It looked like a regular clock. She didn't see any evidence of a recording device hidden therein.

Go to the source, then.

She stomped into Ava's bedroom, the room illuminated by the bluish glow of the night-light beside Ava's toddler bed. Hands balled into fists on her hips, she stared at the keypad lock on the closet door as if she could break it open by sheer force of will.

He has no right to film us. He has no right!

Fuming, she charged into the hallway and pounded down the staircase. She went into the garage.

In the trunk of her car, she found a tire iron in a box of old tools her father had given her when she was a teenager with her first car, and she had kept boxed in every car she'd owned since. She lifted it, the cold metal feeling good in her hands, like a weapon of war.

It's a war, all right. Me against this damned landlord.

The iron swinging from her hand, she went upstairs. Cam pounded away on his keyboard in the living room, muttering to himself, oblivious to her. She wanted to keep it that way. He wouldn't approve of what she was about to do.

Back in the bedroom, she approached the closet. She looked from the curved end of the tire iron to the door, glanced behind her at her slumbering child.

The time is now. Let's do this, girl.

She fitted the tip of the iron between the door and the frame, and used all her weight to drive it in. Wood buckled and cracked, paint chips drifting to the carpet. When it felt as though she had gotten the tool inserted deep, a couple inches at least, she leaned back, trying to pry open the door as one would the lid on a can.

Snap!

The tire iron slipped out of her hands and thudded onto the carpet. She cursed to herself. She had broken off a small piece of the door, but it still held.

Do it again. Get in there. End this.

She picked up the tire iron. Suddenly, the overhead light switched on.

"Dez, what are you doing?"

She spun. Cam stood in the doorway, mouth hanging open.

Chest heaving, she said, "I'm getting in there and ripping out those cameras! That's what I'm doing! What are you doing, huh? Huh? What the hell are you doing?"

"You're destroying the door." He came into the room, hands raised as if to show he meant no harm. "Please, put down the tire iron, Dez."

"I wanna rip off the fucking door!" Tears stung her eyes. "I wanna see what they've got in there and get rid of it! I can't live like this!"

Behind them, Ava stirred on her bed, a thin cry escaping her.

"I know, babe. I know." Cam's voice was soft as velvet. He came to her, put his arms around her. "I know."

The tire iron slipped out of her hands. She wept against his chest. He pulled her closer, kissed her. She held him so tightly it was a wonder he didn't cry out in pain.

"I can't live like this," she said, choking on her sobs. "I'm sorry . . . I can't . . . I can't."

"We'll go to a hotel, babe," he said, kissed her again. "We'll take out the emergency credit card, okay? We'll book a hotel nearby. We don't have to stay. I don't want to make this any worse for you. I've screwed up enough."

She looked up at him, tears weaving down her face.

"We'll leave tonight?" she asked.

"Right now." He kissed her forehead. "Let's pack. I think we both need a break."

65

Cam slid their emergency credit card across the front desk at the Hampton Inn. The hotel clerk plucked the card off the counter.

"How many nights will you be staying?" she asked.

Cam looked over his shoulder at his family. Dez huddled on a chair in the lobby with Ava on her lap, surrounded by luggage. They looked like evacuees from a hurricane-ravaged city.

He hated using the credit card. It was an instrument of last resort. But when he'd seen Dez in the bedroom trying to pry open the closet with a tire iron, he realized he had no choice. He had pushed her over the edge with his reckless actions and he needed to do whatever was necessary to reel her back from the brink and restore some semblance of order in their household.

This was how they wound up at a hotel barely two miles away from the rental house at ten o'clock on a Thursday night. He yawned. It felt as if the day would never end.

"Sir?" the clerk asked. "How many nights?"

"What's the daily rate?" Cam asked.

When the clerk told him, he said, "Three nights, then."

He had no idea if three nights would be sufficient to get them back on track. They had a lot of work ahead of them. But it was a start. What was important was that they had fled ground zero, the rental house, and gone someplace where they could enjoy breathing space and privacy.

"Yaay!" Ava said, when Cam swiped the key card to open the hotel room door. She raced past him, into the room, clambered onto one of the queen-size beds.

"Can you bring in the luggage?" Dez said. Without waiting for his response, she left their suitcases in the hallway and brushed past him.

His wife had been chilly toward him since they had left the house, had thrown clothes into the luggage as if she were flinging them into a firepit. She was upset with him, and he didn't resent her for it. He deserved to be in the doghouse for a while.

He brought the luggage inside and closed the door behind him.

"Ava and I are taking this one." Dez pointed at the mattress on the far side of the room. She nodded toward the other bed. "That one's yours."

"We're sleeping in separate beds now?" he asked.

"Do you think your daughter can sleep alone in an unfamiliar bed in a strange hotel, Cam? Is that a reasonable expectation?"

He flinched; her tone was sharper than he expected. Turning away, he heaved his overnight bag onto the mattress.

Give her space, he thought. *You know how she is. She needs time.*

He fished his bedclothes and toiletries out of his bag and went to the bathroom, where he brushed his teeth and changed. He found Dez waiting impatiently for him when he opened the door.

"All yours," he said.

"Keep an eye on your child." She moved past him.

"One thing," he said. "We should probably talk about our plan for tomorrow."

"I'm taking Ava to my parents' and taking a sick day from work so I can go to the library and research your friend's properties."

"The landlord isn't my friend. What's with the sarcasm?"

"I'm exhausted and I've got a migraine. Is there anything else?"

"Tomorrow, I'm going to drop off my laptop at the data recovery place and then go work with Thor again."

"Right, your other buddy."

Cam ground his teeth.

"All right, then. Is that all?" she asked.

"Yeah," he muttered.

She shut the door in his face.

66

Despite staying in a hotel with a comfortable queen-size bed at his disposal, Cam spent most of the night staring at the dark ceiling, his thoughts racing, sleep eluding him. When he finally drifted off, it seemed only a few minutes later that sunlight peeked through the curtains. He groaned. He felt as if he hadn't slept at all.

Dez and Ava were awake, his wife getting their daughter ready, and she was already dressed.

Last night, Dez had followed him in her own car to the hotel so she wouldn't need to go back to the rental house to complete her errands for the day. After they exchanged a "good morning" greeting, they barely spoke. Leaving the room with Ava, she kissed him on the cheek and said, "I'll keep you posted on things."

He watched them go, wanting to say something to fix the situation, but not knowing the words. Saying he was sorry a thousand times wasn't going to magically correct their lives.

I've got to do better, he thought. She didn't want to stay in a hotel, and could he blame her? Being there was, at best, a temporary reprieve.

He needed to get back to the rental house before Thor returned to pick him up, but his first order of business was taking his laptop to the data recovery shop. He dressed and left the hotel. The shop opened at nine. Cam was waiting outside, the first customer, when an employee came to the front door and let him in. He hustled inside with his computer.

"I want the emergency rush service," Cam said. The technician asked him to explain what happened, taking notes as Cam spoke. Cam signed the release, provided his password credentials, and stressed the urgency of retrieving the file. He paid the service deposit with the same emergency credit card he'd used last night to secure the hotel room.

"We'll do our best," the tech said. She promised to call him with an update by the end of the day.

Fifteen minutes later, Cam arrived at the rental house. Thor's black van was already parked in the driveway; Miss Carver's Cadillac was there, too.

What the heck does she want? Cam wondered.

With the driveway occupied, he parked at the curb. As he got out of the Jeep, Thor and Miss Carver slipped out of their respective vehicles.

Miss Carver wore her usual funeral uniform. She strode toward him, hands clasped in front of her, her smile more severe than usual.

"To what do I owe the pleasure?" Cam said.

Thor came around the corner of the van, dressed in black like a cat burglar. Eyes simmering, his cheeks bulged, as if he were so furious he could spit a mouthful of fire at Cam.

"Property abandonment is against the terms of your lease agreement, Mr. Woodson," Miss Carver said.

"Where were you?" Thor asked. "Do not lie."

"Hang on a second, guys," Cam said. "No one abandoned the property. We needed to clear our heads, that's all. We're staying at a hotel for a little while. We're not moving out." *Not yet, assholes.*

"I certainly hope you're telling the truth," Miss Carver said. "Per the terms of your lease, the penalty for property abandonment is quite serious."

The woman nodded at Thor. Thor stepped forward and put his hand on Cam's shoulder. Cam reared back.

"Tell me to follow you, all right?" Cam said. "You don't need to put your hands on me, man."

"Get in the van," Thor said.

"I figured you were going to say that," Cam said. "Are we going back to clean up that house?"

Thor ignored him and marched to the driver's side of the van. Cam got in on the passenger side. Miss Carver watched this interaction with a smug smirk.

They got on I-285, but Thor didn't take the same route he had driven yesterday. Instead, they took an exit for Gwinnett County.

"Where are we going?" Cam asked. "Do you have a different job site this time?"

Ignoring him, Thor cranked up the volume of his country western music. Cam busied himself with his iPhone, checking obsessively for a message from the data recovery tech, reminding himself that he had dropped off his machine less than an hour ago.

A road sign announced a police department up ahead. Cam straightened. Thor turned into the parking lot of the Gwinnett County Police Department headquarters.

Coldness flashed down Cam's spine.

"What are we doing here?" Cam asked.

Thor parked in front of the large brick building, in the visitors section. He switched off the ignition and pivoted in his seat to face Cam.

"You took your family out of the house last night without permission," Thor said.

"Since when do I need permission to take my family somewhere?"

He pointed his thick index finger at Cam. "You are plotting something."

"I'm trying to keep my wife happy, man. She needed a break."

"You are a liar." Thor jabbed his finger against Cam's chest. Cam winced. The man's fingertip felt like a dull blade. "I do not like liars."

"I'm not lying!"

"Now, as a representative of Baron Properties, I am going to report a tip about an arson." Thor grabbed a manilla folder from the pocket of the door on his side.

"Hey, wait!" Cam said.

But Thor climbed out of the van with the folder. His heart leaping into his throat, Cam got out and raced around the van to intercept Thor as the big man thundered toward the building.

"Get out of my way," Thor said, brushing Cam aside.

A stout-bodied police officer leaving the headquarters saw the two of them and paused with a narrowed look.

"Hey, fellas," the officer said. "Is everything okay here?"

Thor nodded at Cam. "Answer the policeman, Cam. Is everything okay?"

"Yes, yes," Cam said. He raised his hands, backed up. He forced a laugh. "We're cool. No issues here, Officer."

The policeman frowned, seemed ready to ask more questions, and then his radio squawked. He cast them a final glance and then hurried to a police cruiser.

Grinning, Thor stepped closer to Cam. He tapped the folder against Cam's chest.

"No more hotel," Thor whispered. "Tell your wife. You stay home."

"She's not going to be happy about that."

"Then buy her flowers like a good husband." Thor motioned with his head. "Now get in the van so we can go to the job."

67

That Friday morning, Dez had called her school to inform them she was taking a sick day, and after she left the hotel, she took Ava to her parents' house. As she got Ava settled, fixing her a breakfast of strawberry yogurt and sliced banana, Dez made a remark to her mother that had been lingering in her mind.

"What would you think if we needed to move in with you and Daddy for a little bit? Purely hypothetical."

"Move in?" Perched on her usual stool near the kitchen counter, Mom set down her coffee mug and gave Dez a stern look over the rim of her glasses. "What's going on now with that rental house, Desiree?"

"It's a hypothetical question, like I said." As she organized the food on the place mat in front of Ava, Dez avoided her mother's probing gaze. "Would it be okay with you and Daddy?"

"Your family is always welcome here. But what's happening? Is there anything I can do?"

Dez clasped her hands, met her mother's gaze. She almost spilled the story. But she thought about Cam, and what he would say if he found out she'd gone to her parents without discussing it first with him. Hadn't they done enough of that lately, between the two of them? How could she expect him to come to her if she turned around and made plans behind his back with her folks?

"Please, forget I brought it up," Dez said.

"Come on, Desiree. I can't forget something like this."

"Please don't tell Daddy about this conversation, either. He'll have a fit."

"We only want to help. If you all are in trouble, we're here for you."

"It's going to be okay." Dez kissed Ava on the cheek and gave her mom a hug. "I'll see you later this afternoon."

Mom frowned at her as she left, and Dez regretted that she had broached the subject. When this nasty business with the landlord had concluded—in their favor, she hoped—she would sit down with her mother and give her the full scoop. But not before.

After leaving her parents' house, Dez drove to the nearest public library. It was time to dig into the landlord's business.

She set up her laptop and materials in a study carrel located next to a floor-to-ceiling window that overlooked a tranquil pond. Her first search: the Georgia Superior Court Clerk's Cooperative Authority website. The site offered a database that anyone could browse to gather information about properties registered in the state.

"Here we go," Dez said to herself.

She entered the address of their rental property. As expected, Baron Properties was listed as the owner of the residence, the same name as the company on their lease agreement.

Next, she searched the property in Norcross, where the murder-suicide had occurred. Surprisingly, a different firm owned the Norcross home: Midgard Management.

Dez tapped her finger against her chin, the pen in her hand poised above her notepad. What did this mean? Perhaps they had made incorrect assumptions about the landlord's ownership. Or maybe, their landlord had recently purchased the Norcross home and the database hadn't been updated yet.

I need the landlord's name, she thought. The man's name was a key piece of information. She suspected that Thor, the landlord's right-hand guy, knew a lot more than he was letting on with Cam. But Cam was convinced that Thor was *not* the landlord himself. If it wasn't Thor, who was it? Miss Carver? That seemed impossible. Cam said he had spoken to a man on the phone.

Next, Dez visited the Georgia Secretary of State web portal, seeking more information about the companies she had discovered thus far. The database contained listings of every business registered in the state, active and inactive. She looked up both Baron Properties and Midgard Management.

According to the company registration data, different officers were attached to each organization, names that she did not recognize. She noted the names but could not see a connection between the firms. They even had different office addresses, although, oddly, the Baron Properties address on the registration was not located in Midtown Atlanta. It looked like a mailbox address, in Marietta.

She returned to the Georgia real estate index and entered the company names. The search returned only the properties that she already knew about: their rental house, and the Norcross property.

Without more information to go on, she had reached a dead end. They would need a lot more data to connect reported crimes to the rental properties. A murder-suicide occurring at a home their landlord didn't even own wasn't going to build a case in their favor.

She took a restroom break. After she returned to the study carrel, she moved on to something that had been a new interest lately: real estate listings. Not rental homes, but homes for purchase. Perhaps it was only a blue-sky fantasy at this point, but her big ambition was for them to move into a house of their own. No more landlord, no more Miss Carver, no more ridiculous lease restrictions. A home of their own.

A girl could dream, right?

A couple of hours later, Dez left to grab lunch at a café. As she dipped her spoon in a steaming bowl of vegetable soup, her phone buzzed. Cam had sent her a text.

She read it, her fingers tightening on the phone until her knuckles were pale.

We can't stay in the hotel. We need to go home. They said they'll charge us with property abandonment.

Dez stifled a scream. She fired back a message: *I don't want to be there!*

After a minute, Cam responded.

Neither do I. But we don't have a choice.

68

Still fuming later in the day—being upset seemed like her default emotional state these days—Dez picked up Ava from her parents' house. She lingered there longer than she usually did on pickups, but neither her mother nor her father mentioned anything about the rental house. Her mother, bless her, had kept Dez's morning outburst confidential.

Finally, with a sense of crushing resignation, Dez returned to the rental. It was the last place on the planet that she wanted to go, but she believed Cam's warning about the repercussions that awaited them if they avoided staying in the damn place.

We've gotta get out of this ridiculous situation, she thought, driving. She was going to tell Cam about that, too. They needed a better plan. She could not live like this.

When she arrived at the rental, she saw a U-Haul truck parked in the driveway, the rear of the vehicle facing the garage. Miss Carver's Cadillac sedan was parked in front of the house, behind Cam's SUV. But she knew that Cam was out working with Thor. Another vehicle, an old Honda Odyssey, was parked in the cul-de-sac, too.

What was going on here?

Holding Ava's hand, she marched to the front door. Miss Carver opened the door as Dez reached for the knob.

The woman looked pleased with herself. Dez felt a sliver of heartburn. If Miss Carver was happy that wasn't good for them.

"Good evening, Mrs. Woodson. I'm happy you've returned."

"What's going on?" Dez asked. "What's the truck for?"

"A new family is moving in."

"Moving *in*? I don't understand. Are you kicking us out?"

She hoped the answer to that question would be "yes." How bad had things gotten that she would've been grateful to get evicted from a property?

Miss Carver chuckled. "We are decidedly not kicking you out. You will be sharing the house with new tenants." Her lips peeled back into a broad, wolfish grin. "This is a spacious residence. There's plenty of room for more of you."

"You can't do that," Dez said. "We have a lease!"

"I believe we had this discussion, Mrs. Woodson? When we discussed Lola's arrival, yes?" Miss Carver stepped aside and gestured for Dez to enter. "Local occupancy laws allow for many more residents to live in these fine rooms. Won't you come into your home and meet your new housemates?"

White hot rage came over Dez. Involuntarily, she squeezed her daughter's hand so hard that Ava cried out.

"Now you've upset the little brat," Miss Carver said.

Through a veil of stinging tears, Dez looked past Miss Carver. She saw people moving around in the house, moving around their things, their furniture. Would they rustle through their clothes, their most intimate possessions?

She needed to go in there and tell these people to get out, stay away from their stuff, but she couldn't do it. She just couldn't. She was so angry, she might actually hurt someone.

"Mrs. Woodson?" Miss Carver grinned. "Enter your home, dear."

"Kiss my black ass, bitch."

Dez scooped up Ava in her arms and hurried back to her car.

"You may not abandon the property!" Miss Carver called after her. Her laughter rang out like a bell. "I expect to see you back here tonight, Mrs. Woodson!"

69

Cam spent another grueling day cleaning trash out of the property in Stone Mountain, and as before, Thor did not assist. But Cam saw the end nearing for this onerous task. Based on the amount of junk remaining, he estimated one more day there would do it.

But would the landlord release him afterward? Neither Thor nor the landlord would answer that question.

How long will I allow them to push me around? Cam asked himself. He and Dez had their plan, but what if that didn't yield anything? Was he fated to be the landlord's lackey for the indefinite future?

Later, as Thor drove them back to the rental in silence, Dez called. For her to be calling him and not texting, Cam realized it had to be critical.

He pressed the phone to his ear and turned away from Thor, trying to keep the man from overhearing.

"I'm in the van with Thor," Cam whispered. "What is it?"

"There're strangers in the house!" Dez said. He heard the emotion thick in her voice. She sounded on the edge of tears.

"Strangers in the house?" he asked.

"Miss Carver, that bitch, said they have the right to put new tenants in the house while we're still there!"

No, they didn't, Cam thought. He slumped in his seat. The landlord continued to tighten the screws, didn't he?

"They'll charge us with property abandonment if we leave," Cam said. "We'll be on the hook for thousands of dollars we don't have."

"Is everything okay, friend?" Thor asked. "Do you want me to take you to get flowers for your wife?"

Cam ignored him.

"Meet me somewhere, please," Dez said. "I can't be here while these people are in the house moving in their shit."

They agreed upon a bar-and-grill within a couple of miles of the rental. When Thor dropped him off, Cam saw the U-Haul parked in the driveway and a minivan parked nearby, and he didn't bother going inside to see what was happening. He drove to meet Dez.

She had already arrived at the restaurant with Ava, sitting at a booth in the corner. Her eyes were puffy, her hair in disarray. Ava, however, was happy to see him, dropping the crayons she had been using to scribble on a kiddie menu. He held his daughter in his lap and asked the server to bring him a beer, and then he remembered that he didn't have any money.

Emergency credit card to the rescue, he thought.

"I can't go back there," Dez said, elbows on the table, fingers dug deep into her hair. "I can't, Cam. I want to stay with my parents."

Cam winced at the suggestion. "Let's focus on what we've got to do to get out of there. What did you find out today?"

Dez pulled out her notepad, flipped it open. She sipped from a glass of iced tea and appeared to settle her nerves.

"All right," she said. "Both the rental house and the place in Norcross are held under two different property management companies. Those companies have different officers, different addresses. I don't see any connection at all between them."

"But I know the landlord owns the Norcross house," Cam said. "Maybe these other companies are shells or something?"

"Until you can give me his name or some other piece of information, we have no way to tie anything together. So much for the master plan." She glanced at the beer he had ordered. "God, I could use a drink."

"The baby . . ."

"I know that, Cam. I didn't say I was going to order a drink. I said it would taste good."

"It's going to be okay." Cam folded his hands on the table. "We'll figure out something."

"What's going on with your laptop?" Dez asked in a sharp tone.

"The data recovery tech still hasn't recovered the file. It's in progress."

"When it rains, it pours." She covered her face with her hands.

Cam felt sick, but he didn't know what to say, what to do to make things better. He drained his beer and ordered another one.

They lingered over their food, delayed leaving the restaurant as long as possible, but with bedtime nearing for Ava, they had to go back.

At the rental, they met the new family. They looked European, and there were four of them: a man and woman who appeared to be in their late twenties, an older man who looked to be the father perhaps, and an older woman as well who may have been the older man's wife. None of them spoke any comprehensible English. Cam tried to communicate through gestures and his attempts didn't seem to register, but at least the family had moved into the spare bedrooms as they recognized that Cam's family had already settled in.

Cam assumed these people were obligated to the landlord, too.

"Unbelievable," Dez muttered to herself. They holed up in their master suite. That night, Ava would sleep in their bed. Dez didn't feel comfortable leaving Ava in her bedroom with these new people in the house (*they could be child abductors for all we know*, she said) and Cam didn't fight her on it.

That night, with Ava lying between them, Dez fell asleep crying, and Cam didn't know how to console her. He lay there in the darkness feeling powerless, the landlord's taunt echoing through his mind.

I own your home.

I own your family.

I own you . . .

70

"Peek-a-boo, Daddy."

Cam awoke the next morning to find Ava's hand pressed against his forehead. His daughter stood beside the bed, already dressed, giggling at him as if he'd been cracking jokes in his sleep.

"Hey, Pumpkin." Cam yawned and rubbed his eyes. His clock read a quarter past eight, and his head felt as if it were stuffed full of down feathers.

He didn't recall getting much sleep. Disturbed over what was going on, upset because Dez was upset . . . To top things off, one of their new housemates had been awake late into the night, ranting, and Cam could not understand anything the person was saying.

Probably he was cursing the landlord, he thought.

Dez had already gotten out of bed. He heard water running in the bathroom, the door open. He sat up and found a smile for Ava.

"Mommy's sad," Ava said, her lips turned down in a frown. "Mommy's been crying."

Cam's heart kicked. Of course, Ava sensed the emotional temperature in their family. She was three years old, not an infant. It couldn't be good for her to see them at odds, embroiled in strife. Was this the life he wanted for his children?

"It's going to get better soon, sweetheart," Cam said. He lifted her onto his lap and kissed her cheek. "I promise, okay?"

"Okay."

The running water shut off. Dez emerged dressed in a blouse and jeans, her hair done, makeup applied.

She looked beautiful as ever, but he could see the puffiness in her eyes, the stress lines bracketing her face.

"Morning," he said. "Where are you going?"

"Out of here. I'm not hanging out here with a group of strangers." She drew in a breath, seemed to stabilize herself. "I barely slept."

"You're coming back, aren't you?"

Her gaze torched him. "Do I have a choice?"

"We're going to figure a way out of this, Dez. Trust me."

"Hmph." Lips pressed together, Dez plucked Ava off his lap. "Say bye to Daddy."

Ava waved. "Bye-bye, Daddy."

But Dez didn't say goodbye. He stood and tried to kiss her, and she gave him her shoulder.

A fine start to a Saturday morning, Cam thought.

Thor would pick him up soon. He showered and dressed in clothes he didn't mind ruining and went downstairs.

He found one of their new housemates in the kitchen, the younger man. Several grocery bags stood on the counter. The man sorted through the refrigerator, trying to find space for his items.

I feel as if I'm back in college again, sharing a communal fridge, Cam thought.

"Good morning," Cam said.

The man turned, smiled, nodded.

"I'm Cam." Cam tapped his chest, extended his hand.

The stranger said, "Andrei," and shook Cam's hand.

It was progress compared to their last awkward interaction. Cam thought he needed to make small talk, but he didn't know quite what to say. It was such a surreal situation, these people tossed into the rental at a moment's notice, that this man and his family were likely disoriented, too.

Cam prepared to brew a cup of coffee with his machine. Andrei noted this with interest.

"You can have some, too," Cam said. *Might as well be sociable if we're all here.*

He demonstrated how to use the brewer. Andrei studied him and, when Cam was done, gave him the thumbs-up sign.

A knock came at the door. Thor stood outside, freshly shaven, eyes hooded like a cobra's.

"Time to work," Thor said. "We leave now."

"I thought you'd never get here," Cam said.

Thor frowned at his attempt at humor. Cam followed him, got in the van. He looked at the U-Haul and the minivan parked in front of the house.

"Did you know the landlord was going to move new tenants into the house?" Cam asked.

"It is a large home," Thor said. "I lived in a tiny house as a boy." Thor made a small shape with his big fingers. "You are fortunate to have so much space."

"My wife doesn't see it that way."

"Did you buy her flowers?" Thor grinned.

Cam couldn't tell if the man was kidding with him or not, but sometimes, he got the sense that Thor knew a lot more than he disclosed, that he was humoring Cam, at Cam's expense.

As Thor drove, Cam called the data recovery shop to check on his laptop.

Still working on your case, the tech said. *We'll provide an update on Monday.*

This doesn't seem like the emergency service that I paid for, Cam wanted to say, but he let it ride. He didn't have the energy to argue.

When they arrived at the Stone Mountain property, Cam pulled on the work gloves. Thor opened the garage door.

"Today, you should finish cleaning," Thor said.

"And then we're done?" Cam asked. He tossed a moldy phone book into the trash dumpster standing at the edge of the garage. The bin was empty, which meant the company that owned the dumpster had visited to clear it out.

"There will be more work tomorrow," Thor said.

"More work? I thought I had to do only this last thing?"

"There is always more work. We have many, many properties. The landlord is not done with you yet."

"This is bullshit, Thor. Do you know that?"

"Bullshit?" Thor's lips twisted into a snarl. He charged toward Cam.

Cam spun around and crashed into the metal dumpster. Thor grabbed him by the waist of his jeans and lifted him into the air as easily as Cam might have lifted his little girl.

"Hey!" Cam said.

"You want to see shit?" Thor laughed. "Here!"

He tossed Cam into the dumpster. Cam landed on the hard metal bottom, the impact snapping through his bones. The receptacle was empty, but it reeked of foul odors that made Cam's stomach turn. He gagged.

"*We* say when you are done," Thor said. He dusted off his hands and strode into the house.

Dizzy, coughing, Cam struggled to climb out of the dumpster. He threw his leg over the lip, straining, and heaved himself over the edge, onto the driveway.

He wiped his eyes, rested his head against the bin's cold exterior wall.

His body ached. But his pride, his sense of control over his own life, had been more damaged than anything else. All his life, he had been his own man, resolute about doing things his way, forging his own path. How had he been reduced to cleaning trash out of a house he didn't even own, with the promise of more grunt work in the fore-seeable future?

I'm never going to get away from these guys.

He struggled to his feet, one hand braced against the dumpster for support. His gloved fingers rested against the label of the waste management company that owned the trash receptacle: *Peachtree Disposal.* It listed the company's phone number, too.

Cam studied the telephone number.

And finally, a new idea struck him.

71

Dez met Ebony for breakfast at IHOP. They brought their children along, an ambitious undertaking, but Dez had so many other troubles weighing on her that the kids' antics barely registered.

She could not believe that new tenants had moved into the rental, and that the landlord and his minion, Miss Carver, expected them to live there still. Dez yearned to break the lease, or abandon the place altogether, but the financial penalties for either course were onerous.

They were trapped, unless they could find a way out. But she needed to get her mind in order. She had slept so poorly that she wanted to cry, and if she wasn't pregnant, she would have downed a gallon of coffee. Since she was, she settled for one cup of green tea.

The host had seated them at a table in the corner of the dining room that appeared to be the kiddie section, because Dez noticed other families with young children had been cast away over there, too. She didn't mind. For the time being, anywhere was better than inhabiting the rental house.

"You look exhausted, girl," Ebony said. She sipped her coffee, leaned closer across the table. "Is everything okay? Vic said Cam's been kind of erratic lately."

Dez had confided nothing about her predicament to Ebony. At her friend's comment, she dropped the spoon she had been using to stir honey into her tea. What had Cam said to Vic?

Ebony nodded as if pleased by her insight. "Is it money trouble?"

Money trouble. Dez could have laughed. Compared to what confronted them, simple money trouble would have been easy to solve. Whatever Cam had told Vic, it wasn't the full scoop.

"We've got a difficult situation with our landlord," Dez said. Although Ebony was her best girlfriend, that didn't mean she could confide everything to her. Cam's misguided actions infuriated her, but there was no way she would divulge the entire story to Ebony. *Yes, Cam burned down a house, and the landlord is blackmailing us and putting us through sheer hell. We're trying to dig up dirt on him so we can fight back.* It sounded insane.

"Wow, a shitty landlord can be the *worst*," Ebony said. "Is there some kind of trouble with the house? Are they refusing to do repairs? You know, I'm so glad that Vic and I are homeowners."

That tone-deaf comment kindled a spark of annoyance in Dez's chest. *I can't discuss this with her or I'm going to scream.* She picked up her teacup and took a long sip.

"I'd rather not talk about it," Dez said. "It puts me in a pissy mood."

"Okay." Ebony's face froze, and Dez saw the hurt in her eyes. "I understand."

"I think I'm going to go house-hunting today, though. Wanna join me?"

"House-hunting? That sounds like fun."

"Come along, then. We'll make it a party."

An hour later, they were touring newly constructed homes in a high-priced subdivision in John's Creek. The houses were fabulous and well beyond Dez and Cam's budget, but it was a pleasure to dream about a life free of their current worries. Like any concerned friend, Ebony tried to pry a couple of times into Dez's "landlord situation," but Dez redirected her into neutral territory.

"This is so much fun," Ebony said, at one point. She spun around in the kitchen of a model home. "We used to tour these homes all the time—remember that?"

"I do," Dez said. When they were single, which felt like decades ago, she and Ebony would often drop into newly constructed subdivisions—they were everywhere in metro Atlanta—to gawk and fantasize about one day living in such places. "The good old days, huh?"

"A place like this is in the future for you guys," Ebony said. "I can feel it right here." She tapped her chest.

"I'd settle for only a place that's ours," Dez said. She gestured to the kitchen. "It doesn't have to be a showstopper like this."

Ebony's eyes were kind. Dez almost told her more about what was going on, but then her phone buzzed.

It was Cam. He was calling, not texting.

"Let me take this." Dez hurried out of the kitchen, pulling Ava with her.

"Hey," Cam said. He sounded out of breath. "I've got something that might help us."

Five minutes later, Dez went back to Ebony. Her friend had entered the magnificent dining room, her twins racing like hamsters around the table.

"Is everything okay?" Ebony asked.

"I've gotta go," Dez said.

72

After parting ways with Ebony, Dez drove to the public library. Her phone conversation with Cam replayed through her thoughts.

"I've got to be quick," Cam had said. "Thor's gone, but he'll be back any minute. I called the waste management company at the house we've been working at and asked them who rented the dumpster we've been using at this address."

Smart, Dez thought. She had been so down on her husband lately that she had forgotten what had attracted her to him in the first place. He was an insightful thinker, observant, quick-witted. Probably the most headstrong man she knew, too, but no one was perfect.

"What's the name of the company?" Dez asked.

"Here's the thing," Cam said. "I thought they'd give me a company name, but they gave me a man's name."

Dez's heart stuttered. "The landlord?"

"Edward Masters," Cam said, his voice crackling with excitement. "Babe, I think it's him. Can you please look into it?"

"I'm on it," Dez said. With something useful to do, she already felt better.

She had planned to be out of the house all day and had brought her laptop and Ava's tablet, along with three of her daughter's favorite picture books. Inside the library, she found a cozy spot in a quiet corner, and they settled in.

She resumed her search on the Georgia Secretary of State web portal, to look up business registration data. She entered *Edward Masters* into the "Officer Name" field.

The search returned over two dozen business listings.

"Oh, wow," Dez said.

She scanned the list. All the enterprises appeared to be property management firms, based on the names. Surprisingly, she saw the two companies she had looked at previously that were linked to their rental and the destroyed Norcross home. How could that be?

She clicked on the Baron Properties entry. She didn't see "Edward Masters" listed on the Business Information profile as a company officer.

Filing history, she thought, noticing the button at the bottom of the page. *I didn't check that yesterday, did I?*

She clicked it this time.

The top result in the filing history was "Business Formation." She selected it, and the browser popped open a .pdf. It was the original "Certificate of Incorporation" document filed with the state of Georgia several years ago.

Edward Masters was named on that document as an "Incorporator." Beside his name, there was an address in Atlanta—the Baron Properties headquarters.

I bet he's the incorporator of all these companies. Dez tapped her pen against her bottom lip.

My God, I think we've found the landlord.

Invigorated by this discovery, she copied the company names into a file on her computer. Then she returned to the real estate index database she had perused yesterday. Using the company names, she ran a search on each one.

"You're quite the real estate investor, aren't you, Ed Masters?" Dez said to herself.

She unearthed an impressive list of properties: approximately two hundred and eighty throughout the state. She copied those addresses. Next, she began inputting those addresses into databases she had found on Google to pull Georgia crime data.

Results flooded her screen.

"Jackpot." Her heart knocked. "We've got him."

73

Cam swung his SUV into an open spot in the parking garage at the skyscraper in Midtown. Dez sat beside him in the passenger seat.

It was Monday morning, Halloween, and he had a trick or treat up his sleeve for the landlord, Miss Carver, and whoever else showed up in the office.

He shut off the engine and turned to Dez.

"You look fantastic, babe. I'd listen to anything you've got to say."

"Thanks." She wore a beige business suit and a full face of makeup, and she had taken the day off from school. Clasping her hands, she said, "Are you sure about this? Do you think that if you call your newspaper contact and go public, that might be better?"

They had spent the weekend poring over the results of Dez's research, and ironically, the activity had restored some measure of marital bliss, despite everything. Having a common goal had erased the conflict, reminded them of why they had married in the first place: together, they were stronger than either of them were individually.

"Let's follow the original plan," Cam said. "We go in there and show them a few of our cards and threaten them to fall back, release us from the lease and sever all ties. If they don't, we blow them up."

"I hope you're right about this," Dez said.

"Eddie Masters doesn't want public scrutiny," Cam said. He had taken to calling the man he was convinced was the landlord "Eddie." "He'll want to keep this under wraps. They've been blackmailing me —now we can blackmail *him*."

"All right." She touched his arm. "Let's do it, then."

They got out of the SUV, Cam grabbing his backpack containing their research documents from the back seat. Hand in hand, they strolled across the garage to the bank of elevators.

The last time he had visited the office, he had found Thor's white van in the parking garage, but he saw no sign of the vehicle this time. Probably, Thor was coming to the rental that morning to pick him up for another "job" that he thought Cam wouldn't refuse.

Screw him, Cam thought. He hoped never to see Thor again after they finished here.

From the lobby, they took the elevator to the fourteenth floor.

"It's down this hallway." Cam led the way along the quiet, carpeted corridor.

He opened the door to enter the office's waiting area. There was no one sitting in the reception section, but Miss Carver stood behind the front desk, her gaze focused on an iPad.

"Happy Halloween," Cam said. "Trick or treat."

Miss Carver looked up. Her thin lips twitched, crow's-feet around her eyes tightening.

"Good morning," Dez said. "You look ready to attend a funeral, as usual."

Cam wanted to give Dez a high five.

"Woodson family," Miss Carver said, her voice nearly a growl. "What do you want?"

"Is Edward Masters in the office today?" Cam asked.

Miss Carver took a step back, as if Cam had tossed cold water into her face. She touched her long neck.

"I don't know who you're talking about," Miss Carver said.

"No?" Cam unzipped his bag and withdrew a manilla folder bulging with documents. "I've got a shitload of official documentation here that says otherwise. He's incorporated twenty-four property management companies over the past twenty years, and his address is right here, in this office." Cam tapped the desk with his palm.

"We want to speak to him," Dez said.

"I am the landlord's *authorized* agent." Miss Carver adjusted her dress collar, regaining her composure as she fell back on familiar responses. "Any business discussions intended for him can go through me."

Cam glanced at Dez, a thought passing between them like an electric current. *We were right. Edward Masters is the landlord.*

"If you want to play it that way, fine," Cam said. He hauled another folder out of his bag. "Let's go back into the inner office there and talk about the shady incidents at the landlord's properties. Certain *criminal* incidents."

Miss Carver gave him an appraising look, swiveled to scrutinize Dez. As if deciding whether to believe them.

"We mean it," Dez said.

Miss Carver sighed.

"If you insist, Woodson family." Miss Carver stepped away from the desk and opened the door behind her. "Come on, then. I haven't got all day."

Cam gestured for Dez to walk ahead of him. He followed her into the next area, Miss Carver shutting the door behind them.

They found themselves in a spacious, well-lit office with floor-to-ceiling windows offering panoramic views of the city. A gigantic oak desk stood in the middle of the space. Aside from the desk, Cam saw a conference table flanked by several padded chairs and a large flat-screen television hanging on the wall. Another door lay on the other side of the room.

"Be seated." Miss Carver indicated the table.

"Where's Eddie Masters?" Cam asked.

Miss Carver scowled. "*Mister* Masters is not needed for this discussion. As I stated many times, I am the—"

"—landlord's authorized agent," Dez finished. "We get it. Babe, let's do this, all right?"

Cam and Dez sat side by side at the conference table. Cam arranged his folders on the table in front of him. Miss Carver stood on the other side of the table, her spider leg fingers resting on the back of a chair.

"You might want to sit down for this," Cam said.

"I highly doubt that, Mr. Woodson. But I suggest you remain in your chair."

Why is she so confident? Cam felt a quiver in his stomach, but decided to ignore it. *Wait until I blow her mind.*

He opened the folder, which he had labeled "*Crimes.*"

Cam cleared his throat and said, "Under various company names, the landlord owns, at last count, almost two hundred and eighty residential properties."

"And you assume this is a revelation to us?" Miss Carver asked.

"Be quiet, let him talk," Dez fired back, and redness touched Miss Carver's cheeks.

"According to the data we've uncovered," Cam said, "crimes have been reported at approximately *nine* percent of these properties."

Miss Carver's gaze narrowed, but she remained silent.

"In 2019, there was a murder at one of your homes in Fulton County," Dez said, reading from one of the sheets. "A thirty-three-year-old woman stabbed her boyfriend to death."

"I wonder why?" Cam said. "I wonder if you guys have video from that night?"

Miss Carver's face was a granite slab.

"In 2018, there was an arson at a property in Forsyth County," Dez said. "The home was destroyed, and the tenant was charged."

"You are quite familiar with arson, eh?" Miss Carver glanced at Cam.

Cam ignored her, focused on the documents spread in front of him.

"In 2016, there was an attempted murder at one of the landlord's homes in DeKalb County," Cam said. "A twenty-five-year-old man shot his grandmother with a shotgun. Fortunately, she lived."

"Good for her," Miss Carver said.

"A drug bust in 2021 at a house in Cobb County," Dez said. "The man charged had never committed a crime in his life, but when he rents the house, suddenly he's a drug kingpin."

"Funny how that works, isn't it?" Cam asked. "Crime seems to follow your tenants. I wonder if you guys set him up because he wouldn't play ball, planted drugs in the house and tipped off the police."

Miss Carver's gaze drilled him.

Cam turned to another page. "In Clayton County earlier this year, a man beat his elderly mother to a pulp. He was charged with aggravated battery, among other things."

Miss Carver tented her hands atop the chair.

"There's more," Dez said, thumbing through the pages. "We've brought these cases only as a sample of what we uncovered in our research."

"I fail to see the purpose of this alleged research," Miss Carver said. "What are you seeking to accomplish, Woodson family?"

"You guys set me up, got to me," Cam said. "Now, you and your crew know that we can get to *you*. I have contacts in the media. If I go to them, and they start digging deeper into Fast Eddie's tenants and properties, who knows what they'll find?"

"We've figured out your business model," Dez said. "You look for tenants with bad credit, folks under financial duress. You manipulate them into signing these ridiculous leases, knowing the laws in

Georgia support the landlords. You keep recording equipment in the houses so you can see and hear everything."

"And then you start offering gigs to the tenants so they can earn a little extra money, to lure them in deeper," Cam said. "They take it because they're desperate and you pay so well. But soon enough, they're hooked like drug addicts, and you push them into illegal activities without their knowledge. Now, you can blackmail them— and get them to do even more work, for free, because they're afraid to go to jail. They're enslaved."

"But many of them crack under the pressure," Dez said. She tapped the pages gathered around them. "These crimes are the final outcome."

"It's amazing that no one has blown up the landlord's business yet," Cam said. He grinned at Miss Carver. "There's a first time for everything. We're warning you: release us from the lease; cut all ties."

"Or we go public," Dez said.

"I see." Miss Carver absorbed their words, smoothed the front of her dress. "Perhaps we underestimated you, Woodson family."

Cam smiled at Dez. *I knew it.*

"Or perhaps you overplayed your hand," Miss Carver said.

"I'm not bluffing." Cam tapped the stack of documents. "I *will* go to the media with this information. It's over."

"I have something I'd like you to see." Miss Carver whirled away from the conference table and strode to the desk. She typed on the computer.

Dez leaned closer to Cam, whispered, "What is she talking about?"

Cam didn't answer. He noticed images flickering on the flat-screen TV hanging on the wall.

"There you go," Miss Carver said.

The picture on the display clarified. On the screen, a video showed Cam and Lola in the basement at the rental; the camera was mounted on the side of the room, clearly showing both their faces in full color.

The camera also revealed that Lola was topless. She brought Cam's hand to her breast. The recording paused with Cam frozen in that compromising position.

Oh fuck, Cam thought. They had footage of this, too?

Dez gasped.

"I apologize," Miss Carver said. "Did you forget all about your affair with our lovely Miss Lola?"

Dez swung to Cam. "Did you . . ."

"Nothing happened, I swear!" Cam said.

Dez shot out of her chair so quickly that the chair tipped back, teetered, and crashed against the floor.

"Dez, wait!" he said.

Snarling, Dez slapped him across the face. He reeled back in the chair from the force of the blow. The momentum sent him and the chair tilting backward, and he lost his balance, tumbled farther back, and fell off the seat, spilling onto the floor.

"You bastard!" Dez screamed.

She charged out of the room, the clicking of her heels like echoing gunshots. Face burning with pain and shame, Cam grabbed the edge of the table and hauled himself to his feet.

"Dez, please!" He raced after her, catching up to her in the outer office. "Let me explain, please!"

She whirled around to face him, tears streaming down her face.

"Was that you in the video?" she asked.

"Nothing happened, I swear!"

"*Yes or no?* Was that you?"

Cam lowered his head.

"Now I know why you don't want me working with her," Dez said. "Now I know why she backed out. It all makes sense."

"They set me up, Dez. Lola's working for them—I see it now. Don't you? It was a setup."

"It's never your fault, is it, Cam?" Dez looked as if she wanted to spit on him. "Always have to do everything your way, but when it goes to hell, it's never your fault."

"Babe, please." He stepped forward.

Dez stepped back. "Stay away from me."

"Can't you see? This is what they want. They want to ruin us."

"*You* ruined us." She shook her finger at him, fresh tears crawling down her face. "It was all you."

"I'm sorry," he said.

But she turned around and walked away, leaving him there, alone.

74

Cam shuffled across the parking garage, backpack swinging from his shoulder. A few minutes prior, Miss Carver had dropped his bag onto the desk in the waiting area, papers spilling out of it.

"This isn't over," Cam had said.

"Leave this office at once, Mr. Woodson," Miss Carver said. "Go home and await further instructions. Run along now." She made a shooing gesture, as if he were a bothersome child.

In the parking garage, Cam neared the Jeep. He expected—hoped in vain, perhaps—to find Dez waiting nearby.

But she was gone. Probably, she planned to take an Uber.

He slipped out his phone, thinking he could call her. Punched the button to call her.

She didn't answer.

He sent her a text: *Please, talk to me, babe. I love you.*

She didn't respond.

Then his phone vibrated. It was the data recovery shop.

"Mr. Woodson?" the tech said.

"Yeah," he said. "Do you have some good news for me? It's been a helluva day so far."

"Umm, we've finished our investigation, and unfortunately, we are unable to recover the file. We can provide a partial refund—"

Cam lowered the phone to his side, the tech's tinny voice coming from the speaker.

No manuscript.

No wife.

No family.

He dragged himself into the Jeep and wept.

75

That morning before they had traveled to the city, they had dropped off Ava at his in-laws' house. Cam drove there, hopeful that Dez would be there, too. She certainly wouldn't return to the rental, the bane of their existence.

Along the way, he tried calling her, and she refused to answer.

William answered the front door. He looked less pleased to see Cam than usual, and that was saying something.

He knows, too, doesn't he?

William didn't step aside to let Cam in. He crossed his beefy arms over his chest and blocked the doorway.

"What do you want, Woodson?" William asked.

"Is Dez here?" Cam asked. "Is my daughter here?"

"They are." William didn't budge.

"Can I come in?"

"My daughter doesn't want to see you."

Cam tried to look past William, but the older man shifted, blocking Cam's line of sight into the house.

"Come on, William," Cam said. "I need to speak to my wife."

"You need to leave."

Cam sucked in a breath, his head pounding. "Then let me see my daughter."

"Leave, Woodson." William's lips formed a tight, unyielding line. "You know, I never liked you. I've always told my baby girl she could do better. She settled, marrying you."

"I don't care what you think about me." Cam stepped forward. "I want to see Ava."

"I told you to leave." William lowered his right hand to his hip, where something bulged underneath the edges of his button-down shirt. "Don't push me, son. Have some dignity, for God's sake."

"Or you'll do what? Shoot me with your Glock?" Shaking his head, Cam took a step back. He felt tears pushing at his eyes, but he didn't dare shed them in front of this man.

He saw a curtain stir at one of the front windows, a small shape part the folds. Ava. She stood at the glass, waving at him, crying.

His heart felt as if it were going to rupture.

He waved back at his child.

"I'll see you soon, Pumpkin," he whispered.

William slammed the door in his face.

76

Cam picked up his laptop from the data recovery shop, absorbing their apologies with a shrug, and then, alone, he drove back to the rental house.

Rain poured from the sky, thunder booming in the distance. Although it was only noon, the storm clouds had plunged the day into a premature twilight.

He parked in the driveway. The minivan that belonged to the new tenants was gone.

I can't live here anymore, he thought.

But where else could he go? A hotel? That hadn't worked out well before.

He tried to call Dez again and again she didn't answer. He decided he would back off for a while, give her space and time. This wasn't over.

But it sure felt as if it were. Never at any point in their relationship had he done anything that could be remotely interpreted as cheating. He was nearly as shocked as she was at what he had done.

What was I thinking?

He shuffled inside the house. Humming to a song, earbuds

nestled in her ears, Lola flitted around the kitchen using his coffee machine like a barista-in-training. She wore a tight-fitting orange tank top and high-cut white shorts, but he would have found a lizard more attractive.

He didn't hear or see any of the new tenants. Perhaps all of them were gone for the day, working for the landlord.

"You." He pointed at Lola. "You work for them, too, don't you?"

"Huh?" She popped out her earbuds.

"You're working for them."

He noticed she held one of his coffee mugs, too. But she only shrugged at his remark, and the weariness in her eyes made her appear much older than her age.

"It's a job, Cam," she said. "Same as you got. We do what we've gotta do."

"You destroyed my family. Was that your job, too?"

"You did that to yourself." Her beautiful face was so hard it might have been cast in marble. "Don't take it out on me. I only work here."

"You only work here?" Cam laughed, brushed past her, and collapsed onto a chair at the kitchen table. "You screwed up my life, but hey, so what? It was only a gig."

"I didn't force you to do anything."

"I don't give a damn about money, tasks, book deals, Lola. Can you understand that? If I don't have my family together . . . none of it matters." He lowered his head, his chest tightening as if iron pincers squeezed him. At loose ends, he looked at his phone, hoping for a message from his wife, but of course, there was nothing.

"Was Dez really angry?" Lola asked.

He looked up. "What do you think? And what the hell do you care?" As he glared at her, a realization hit him. "You deleted my manuscript file, too. It's obvious now. It had to be you."

Lola sipped coffee and didn't respond, but the awareness in her gaze told him everything.

"That day at Starbucks, spilling your coffee on me—that's when you got my password." He laughed bitterly. "Another setup. Wow."

"You and Dez had a bad fight? You know, I was living here before y'all moved in, with two other families—those guys had a flat-out *brawl* in the basement, blood everywhere." She grimaced. "I feel kinda bad about that now."

Cam remembered the blood stain he had spotted on the basement wall the day they toured the house. It had been literally a red flag, and like a fool, he had ignored it.

"You were behind that, too?" he said. "You're nothing but a homewrecker, you know that?"

Lola winced. As if deciding on something, she put the coffee cup on the counter and approached the table, getting so close to him that he leaned back in the chair.

"Hey," he said. "What gives?"

Putting her hand on his shoulder, she bent close to him.

"Look," he said, "this isn't—"

Lola put her finger to her lips.

"Speak softly," she whispered. "They're listening."

He locked gazes with her, but he dropped his voice. "I know. What is it?"

"I'm sorry. Really. I feel bad, okay? I do whatever they ask. They've got leverage on me. Really awful pics of me." Her lips curved in a sad line. "It would be terrible if those photos got out. My folks would disown me."

"But you're a social media influencer."

"They're mostly fake followers on my account, Cam. Bot accounts. You can buy packages to boost your numbers."

"Fake?" Cam chuckled. "Damn. Don't believe everything you see on the internet, huh?"

"Can I sit on your lap?" she asked.

"What? I'm not interested."

"We need to make this look legit for the cameras. Or else they'll get suspicious. It needs to look like we're gonna go for it."

"I guess it doesn't matter at this point if Dez sees more video." He scooted his chair backward.

Lola slung her leg across him and eased down onto his lap, straddling him. She put her arms around his neck, leaned closer, but anxiety flickered in her gaze. Still, if the circumstances had been different, Cam would have been aroused beyond belief.

"Try to act like you're enjoying this, okay?" she said. "Put your hands on my hips, pull me closer to you."

Awkwardly, he did as she asked. She put her lips against his ear.

"I wanna try to help," she whispered. "You and Dez, you guys seem like nice people. It'd be a shame for your family to get busted up over this. I've gotta make this right."

"You want to help? Tell Dez it was all a setup. Entrapment."

"I will." She leaned in closer. "But I need you to help me out, too. Win-win."

"How do I know you're not setting me up right now? Again?"

"I know you don't trust me. But I have something I think you want. If you help me out—if we help each other out—I'll give it to you."

"What is it?"

"Help me out and you'll get it and see for yourself."

He considered her words. "What kind of help are you talking about?"

"I wanna be free from them. From *him*."

His heart thundered. "Edward Masters."

Her eyes widened. "How'd you figure out his name? I know they didn't tell you."

"Dez and I, we did research. That's what scared them. That's why they showed her the video of me and you. We scared them, and they punched back."

"I've never seen the guy. Have you?"

Cam shook his head. "If you're talking about finding him, then we both want the same thing. I want to find him and strangle him."

"I don't wanna kill him. But I want him to cut me loose." She rested her head against his, and he thought it was a genuine display of emotion, not acting for the camera. "I wanna get my life back."

"Were you really going to help Dez start a social media thing of her own?"

A cloud darkened her gaze. "That was only bait. They wanted to trap her, like they got me. They gave me money to pass along to her, to reel her in."

"All so they could get some incriminating photos." Cam's stomach churned.

"But when you pissed him off the other night, Miss Carver said to drop it," Lola said. "He wanted to squeeze y'all, I heard."

"Where is he?"

"Not sure." She sucked in her bottom lip. "I don't think he lives around here, though."

"Why do you say that?"

"When I first got hooked up with them, he called me from a different area code."

"What area code?"

"I looked it up." She squeezed her eyes shut, as if trying to remember. "Gray, I think my phone said?"

"Gray? Down near Macon?"

"Is that where it is? It's been a while since I checked. I had this fancy notion of tracking him down, but that never went anywhere."

"That's where it is." His mouth was dry. He remembered his trip to Gray the night he had picked up the fateful package of fertilizer. "Damn."

"What's wrong?"

"I think I actually *met* him." Cam tried to get out of the chair. Alarmed, she rose, freeing him. "Lola, I've gotta go. Right now."

She grabbed his arm. "Are you gonna help me or not?"

"Call my wife and tell her the truth," he said. "You do that, and we're good."

He rushed out of the house.

Next stop: Gray, Georgia.
He had a meeting with the landlord.

77

The rain accompanied Cam for the entire duration of his drive to Gray, extending a journey that should have required less than a couple hours to a full two-and-a-half hours.

The lengthy trip afforded him plenty of time to think, mostly about Dez and the mess he had made of things. Could she find it in her heart to forgive him? If Lola followed through, called Dez and explained her machinations, maybe they had a chance at reconciliation, though nothing excused what he had allowed to happen.

He was tempted to dictate a text message to her while he drove: *I know where Masters lives—going to see him now.* As if that could nudge him back into her good graces, but he nixed the idea. What if he was wrong about Masters' identity? What if he were right, but confronting the man, face-to-face, led only to more problems?

Throughout the past few weeks, he had committed the sin of overconfidence. Hubris. It had driven them into this debacle. He needed to report only a true win to his wife and pray that she cared enough to respond.

The clock had ticked past three o'clock in the afternoon when

Cam arrived in the town. Ahead, he spotted the sign for the mobile home community: *Asgard Gardens.* In the driving rain, the faded gold lettering was blurry, like signage in a dream.

He made the right turn to enter the trailer park. During the daytime, the community looked even worse for wear.

How could the landlord, with his vast real estate portfolio, live in such a place? Doubt gnawed at the edges of Cam's mind.

I'm here to get answers, he told himself. *The man here will have them.*

He closed on the double-wide trailer near the end of the road. The last time he visited, an F-150 had occupied the parking space. But this time, the truck was gone.

Cam drummed the steering wheel. Should he await the man's return? Or see what he could find out?

I came all this way. I'm not waiting any longer.

He cruised past the trailer and parked on the side of the road, at the gravel lane's dead end. No need to make his arrival obvious if someone showed up later.

He switched off the engine. Rain pattered against the windshield.

He pinched the bridge of his nose. He wasn't certain exactly what he hoped to gain from this trip. Answers? Absolution? Freedom?

All the above?

He got out.

78

Walking in the rain, icy water trickling over the edges of his jacket's hood, Cam ascended the short wooden staircase and knocked on the trailer's main door.

He waited. As he expected, no one answered. He tried the knob. Locked.

He swept his gaze back and forth along the home's exterior wall. It had several windows, the curtains drawn on each, giving no indication of what lay inside.

He pounded down the steps and walked to the opposite side of the mobile home, sloshing through muddy puddles. He discovered more windows on the other side. A small wooden deck was attached, too, furnished with a couple of lawn chairs, a patio umbrella, and a miniature Big Green Egg smoker so bright green it looked brand new.

There weren't any neighbors facing that side of the house. A thick wall of hedges bordered the area.

He climbed the steps onto the deck. It led to a screened door. He tried the exterior door, and it opened for him, but the interior entry was locked.

Had he driven this far to be sent away by locks?

In the Jeep's cargo area, he found a crowbar wedged next to the spare tire. When he went back to the house, he focused his attention on the window beside the door that opened onto the deck. It was less likely that a security alarm was linked to the window.

Here goes nothing.

With a swing of the crowbar, he shattered the glass. The rain muffled the noise. Shards tinkled out of the frame and onto the deck's floorboards. Using the crowbar, he cleared out a few jagged edges, and used the end of the tool to force the screen out of the frame. It dropped away into the room beyond.

He looked around, ensuring no one had observed him.

Next, he climbed inside.

79

Deep shadows lurked inside the trailer. The thick, dark curtains absorbed the daylight. The only brightness streamed from the window Cam had broken, cold, damp air gusting inside, ruffling the drapes.

He activated the flashlight app on his iPhone. While holding the crowbar in his other hand, he swept the thin beam around.

It looked like a model home. Laminate flooring. Contemporary furniture: sofas with throw pillows, chairs, tables. Generic landscape paintings hanging on the beige walls.

It smelled of lemon-scented disinfectant, as if recently cleaned.

There was no evidence that anyone lived there. He found not a single glass or dish in the sink. No junk mail lying on the countertop. No magnets affixed to the stainless-steel refrigerator.

He opened the refrigerator and found it barren.

What the heck is going on here?

He checked the bathroom. Towels hung from the bar near the sink, and a roll of toilet paper occupied a holder, but none of it had ever been used. He checked the cabinet below the sink. Empty.

He looked inside both bedrooms. The beds were made but looked new, and the closets were empty.

This wasn't what he had expected to find. He stood in the middle of the trailer, deliberating his next move.

Somewhere nearby, doors slammed.

His heart lurched. He quick-stepped to a window and looked outside.

Two vehicles had parked next to the trailer: the silver Ford F-150, and a familiar black van.

Cam hurried to the broken window on the other side. Glass shards crackled beneath his shoes. As he was about to climb through, he heard footsteps thudding across the wooden deck, and the door next to the window burst open.

Thor entered the trailer.

Shit.

Cam backed away. He raised the crowbar, held it like a baseball bat.

"Stay back," Cam said.

Thor grinned at him. He wore his all-black ensemble. He spread his hands, as if to show he was defenseless.

The door on the other end of the trailer opened. The man Cam had met during his last visit, the Willie Nelson clone, stepped inside. He flipped a switch, flooding the trailer with light.

Cam blinked, blinded by the sudden brightness.

"Look what the cat drug in, bro," the Willie Nelson look-alike said.

"You're a good piece away from home, buddy." Thor smiled. "I followed you, you know. Didn't take too long to figure out where you were headed. We decided to drop in and see what you were doing here."

Cam shifted to Thor. "Wait. What happened to your accent?"

Thor turned to the other man, still grinning. The other man chuckled, as if at some private joke between them.

"What the hell is going on here?" Cam said. He pointed at the Willie Nelson clone. "*He's* Edward Masters, the landlord. I know it. We figured it out!"

Thor's partner sauntered toward them. He plucked a cigarette from behind his ear, lit it with a silver Zippo lighter.

"Do you hear that, bro?" he said. "They figured it out." He took a drag on the cigarette, paused to exhale smoke, and placed a tiny black gadget to his lips. In a crisp, baritone voice that matched the landlord's, he said, "I am impressed, Mr. Woodson! You've earned yourself a cash reward."

Cam felt as if the room were spinning. He backed up to a chair, leaned against it. The crowbar sagged in his grip; he was suddenly so weak it felt as if it weighed a hundred pounds.

"We've got this fella confused, bro," Thor said. "Why don't we run it down for him?"

"You're Edward Masters." Cam pointed at Thor's partner. "Right?"

"Name's Luke, actually." Without the voice changer, he sounded again like the guy Cam had met who'd given him the package of fertilizer. He cracked a gap-toothed grin. "Edward Masters was our daddy."

"May he rest in peace." Thor touched his chest. "We often use Daddy's name for business. It still holds weight."

"You're brothers?" Cam asked.

"It's a family business, Cam," Luke said. "Sandra Carver? First cousin."

"Then who is the landlord?" Cam said.

"There's no official landlord at the moment, Cam," Thor said. "Luke and I share the duties. He makes the calls; sometimes I do the text messages. We're twins, believe it or not. Tight like this." He lifted his hand, two fingers intertwined.

"Yup," Luke said. "Fraternal, obviously."

"And you're not Swedish?" Cam asked.

Thor laughed. "Born and bred right here in Gray, Georgia." He gestured to the trailer. "We grew up in this double-wide. Don't live here anymore but we keep it looking nice."

"Sentimental value," Luke said. "It all started here 'fore our daddy bought his first property."

"Daddy was the original landlord," Thor said. "Taught us everything we know."

"Wise, wise man." Luke grinned. "Bet we've made him proud, bro."

"I think about that every day," Thor said. "Am I making Daddy proud?"

"Daddy *really* knew how to put the screws to the tenants." Luke whistled. "The shit he did. Damn!"

"The things he taught us." Thor grinned. "Priceless, Cam."

Cam swiveled back and forth between the two men.

"This is nothing but a game to you guys," Cam said. "Some sick motherfuckin' game you're playing with people's lives."

"And you're the grand prize winner, Mr. Woodson!" Luke said, using the voice changer once more. He pointed his glowing cigarette at Cam like a magic wand. "Would you like to discover your reward for your loyal service?"

"You're going to kill me," Cam said.

"Kill you?" Thor scoffed. "You're the cleverest tenant we've ever had. Nah, buddy, we want to invite you to join the inner circle."

"The inner what?"

"We want *you* to be the new landlord," Luke said. "It's a symbolic role, sort of, but fun, huh?"

"You get to make the calls, send the texts, and in general, make life hell for our pathetic tenants," Thor said. "With direction from us, of course."

"You aren't going to be a free agent, exactly," Luke said. "Like my bro said, you gotta take some input from us. But, dude, you would get some amazing perks."

"Live in a property of your choosing, rent free," Thor said.

"Get paid," Luke said. He brought the voice modulator to his mouth. "You shall earn a respectable wage, Mr. Woodson!"

"Let's not forget about Miss Lola." Thor winked at Cam. "You get her whenever you want. Exercise a little bit of leverage, that's all, and she'll fall in line. She wouldn't even have to know that *you're* the landlord. That young lady has some serious skills in the sack, let me tell you, buddy."

"He ain't never lied." Luke snickered. "Good Lord, that girl. Yummy."

Cam felt ill. "You're insane. Both of you. Why would I want anything to do with this shit after you've destroyed my life?"

"It's business, Cam," Thor said. "The American way. You're moving on up. You've proven yourself."

"But you're criminals!" Cam said.

"Like my bro said." Luke winked. "It's the American way. How's that saying go? Behind every great fortune there's a crime."

"From *The Godfather*," Thor said. "The book, not the movie. You've probably read it, Mr. Writer."

"I don't want anything to do with this, with you," Cam said. "I want my life back. And I've got dirt on you guys."

"Everybody important has got a little dirt on 'em," Thor said.

"I could ruin your business," Cam said. "You know I can."

Thor's face hardened. He glanced at his brother.

"We can ruin you," Luke said. "Remember what you did? We got the evidence."

"I don't care anymore," Cam said. "I'm done. You can threaten me all you want, but I'm done."

"Stubborn as a goddamn mule," Thor said. "You've ruined your career, your family. All we've gotta do is drop a tip to the police and you'll lose your freedom, too, my little arsonist buddy."

"Then do it," Cam said.

He walked between the two men, to the door on the other side of the mobile home.

"We'll give you a little time to think it over," Luke said.

"Get your mind right, Cam." Thor tapped his own skull. "Or the hammer comes down. I'll be watching."

Cam flipped them the middle finger and got out of there.

80

Cam drove back to metro Atlanta. His brain felt as if it were about to explode from everything he had learned.

Thor and his brother, Luke, working together all along—co-landlords. Their corrupt family business. Offering the landlord responsibility to *him*.

It was overwhelming. He needed to talk to someone who would understand, and only one person fit that requirement.

But she didn't want to talk to him.

Still, he found himself driving to his in-laws' house, drawn to his wife like a compass needle to true north. She probably wouldn't want to see his face. She hadn't returned his calls or texts. Going over there again would no doubt prove a waste of time.

But he would say whatever he needed to say to convince her to give him another chance, and he would mean every word of it.

A few minutes past six that evening, he nosed his SUV into the driveway, parked behind William's Lexus sedan.

The rain had ceased, but storm clouds covered the evening like an iron dome. The forecast predicted a new thunderstorm entering the area soon.

Cam expected William to open the front door again, and he was not disappointed.

His father-in-law scowled at him. He had a napkin tucked inside his shirt collar, a sure sign that he had sat down to dinner.

"Why are you back, Woodson? I told you my daughter isn't interested in talking to you."

"It's important."

The furrows in William's face deepened. He squared his shoulders, stepped forward as if he intended to physically remove Cam from his property. But Dez sidled up to her father, rested her hand on his arm.

Grateful that she had at least shown her face, Cam exhaled. "Please, Dez. We need to talk."

"I know." Her eyes looked bloodshot, but she nudged her father aside. "It's okay, Daddy."

"Are you sure?" William gave Cam a skeptical look.

"Positive," Dez said. "Thank you."

Grumbling, William retreated into the house. Dez stepped outside and shut the door behind her. Cam craved her touch, wanted to hug her, but he restrained himself.

"Let's go talk in the car," she said.

They got in the SUV, Cam behind the steering wheel, Dez in the passenger seat. He turned to her. Now that she was with him, he wasn't sure how to begin.

"Dez, a lot has happened—" he started.

She silenced him with a stop gesture.

"Lola called me," Dez said. "She told me everything."

"Everything?"

Dez nodded.

"When I saw that video of the two of you, I lost it, Cam. I felt so betrayed. You'd promised you'd given me the full story, and then, when I saw that . . . I snapped." She grimaced at the memory.

"It was a snap-worthy moment."

"But I shouldn't have slapped you. I lost control of myself. I'm sorry."

"I deserved it."

"Lola said Miss Carver put her in the house with us to disrupt our family. They told her to dangle a social media opportunity in front of me, to bait me. And they ordered her to manipulate you, lure you into a compromising position."

"Yeah. I fell for that."

"Now, I don't like that *touch* I saw." She said the word as if it tasted acidic. "But she promised me nothing happened between the two of you. She said that she came on to you and you turned her down flat."

"You're the only woman I want, Dez. You always have been." Her face thawed a few degrees, and he continued: "But they've got leverage over Lola, too. Incriminating photos. It's how they operate."

"She told me all about it. I think the confession helped her feel better." Dez touched her forehead as if she felt a headache coming on. "As upsetting as it was for me to hear, I'm thankful she came clean with me. It was all a sham." Anger sparked in her eyes. "I'm still upset with you, Cam. It's going to take time for me to get over this."

He listened, clammy hands knotted in his lap.

Dez pulled in a deep breath, released it, her face softening.

"But I forgive you." She reached across the seat and grasped one of his hands. "You aren't perfect; neither of us are. But I know your heart. I know you've always wanted the best for us."

Cam felt as if a stone had been removed from his chest.

"I never wanted to hurt you," he said. "I've made some terrible mistakes. I'm going to do better, Dez. My stubbornness has led me to some bad decisions. I admit it."

"Yes, it has." Her gaze was direct.

He didn't look away. "The first thing tomorrow, I'm calling Vic and asking him to put in a word for that teaching position he offered."

"You are?"

"It's the best decision for our family," he said. "With a new baby on the way, I can't risk instability. It's time for me to grow up and put my family's needs above my own ambitions."

"That makes two of us," she said.

He squeezed her hand. "I need to tell you what I learned about the landlords."

"Wait—*landlords*? Plural?"

He narrated what he had discussed earlier with Lola and his epiphany about Edward Masters, how he had driven back to Gray, the surreal, revealing discussion with Thor and Luke, their absurd offer. Putting the story into words for Dez made him feel as if he were describing something that had happened to him in a dream.

There's gotta be a book in here, somewhere, he thought in the back of his mind. But he'd be damned if he knew what it might be.

"They offered you an inside position and you walked out." Dez gave him a real smile for the first time that evening. "I'm proud of you."

"Hell, it was easy. But they've packaged it as an offer I can't refuse. They say they're giving me time to consider." He paused. "I don't think Thor is happy about that, and I don't trust him. He's the bully in the pair."

"What do you want to do?" she said.

"They're not pushing me around anymore. They can tip off the cops about the arson thing. I don't care. We're going to get a lawyer. Tomorrow."

"I can help with that."

"Another thing: tomorrow I'm also calling my contact at the newspaper. It's time to blow up this whole sordid enterprise of theirs."

"No more negotiation," she said.

"No more nights at the rental." He hesitated: "Will you be okay if I stay here with you and Ava?"

"I said I'm still upset with you. I didn't say I want you to stay away. We need to be together."

"Will your parents mind?"

"They're upset, but they'll get over it."

"Thanks for giving me another chance, babe." He leaned across the seat, kissed her. She put an arm around him, held him close.

I'm never letting her down again, Cam vowed to himself. *Ever.*

"Can you take me by the rental?" Dez asked. "The Uber brought me straight here from the office this morning. I need to get my car, collect some things for me and Ava. It won't take long."

"We'll do that, then come right back. I want to see my little girl."

As he pulled out of the driveway, Dez called her parents and assured them everything was fine, that she and Cam were working things out, and they were making a quick stop at the rental property and would return shortly. Dez asked her mother to put Ava on the phone, and she switched to speakerphone mode.

"Hey, Pumpkin," Cam said.

"Daddy! Where are you? I was sad."

Cam struggled to hold back tears. "It's going to be okay, sweetheart. I'll be back soon with your mother, okay?"

"Okay. Bye-bye."

"I need to fill in Lola on the latest," Cam said. "She's got a stake in this, too."

"Agreed. We can chat with her at the rental or call her if she's not there. I've got her number."

Thunder rumbled through the evening as Cam pulled into the rental property's neighborhood. Fresh rain spattered the windshield.

"Another storm passing through," Dez said.

"And look who we've got here." Cam nodded toward the house.

Miss Carver's Cadillac sedan was parked in the driveway next to Dez's Honda. Dez's jaw tightened.

"She's not going to intimidate me anymore," Dez said. "She's harmless."

"All talk." Cam parked behind Dez's car. "Let's make this quick, then."

81

Dez had been honest with Cam when she told him she was still upset over what he had done. Processing her emotions would take time; she wasn't a machine, capable of switching off her feelings with the push of a button. It might take days, or weeks, for them to restore the harmony in their marriage.

But as she gazed at the rental house through the Jeep's windshield, she believed they were finally on the same page.

We're getting out of this damn place and moving on with our lives.

"Ready?" Cam asked, his hand on the door lever.

"Yeah, but what happened to the new tenants? They had a minivan."

"They're out slaving for the overlords most likely. They've been gone all day."

Disgust reeled through her stomach. "The sooner we take down these guys, the sooner everyone gets relief. It's bigger than you, me, Lola."

Cold rain peppered them as they hurried to the front door. Cam entered the keycode, and she followed him inside.

Dez didn't intend to look for Miss Carver, or even to speak to her. She was going to go upstairs and pack a few things. But when she and Cam entered, Miss Carver emerged from the kitchen.

Miss Carver wore a pair of blue latex gloves, like a surgeon.

"Woodson family," she said, "I suggest you leave until further notice. I've business at hand."

Something was wrong, Dez realized. The gloves she wore, her odd comment. Dez's intuition buzzed.

Cam seemed to pick up on it, too. He frowned at Miss Carver.

"What are you doing in here?" Dez asked. She stepped down the hallway, toward the kitchen.

She gasped.

Lola lay on the floor beside the table in a puddle of blood, and the young woman wasn't moving.

"I warned you to leave," Miss Carver said.

Behind her, Cam shouted.

Someone emerged cat-quick from the shadows and grabbed her.

82

Thor materialized from the shadowed dining room and seized Dez by the throat. Cam saw it about to happen, shouted to warn Dez, but the big man moved so fast that by the time Dez turned, he already had his rough hands on her.

Cam ran forward. Thor spun around with Dez as if she weighed no more than a Barbie doll. His hand clamped over her throat, stifling her scream, her eyes bulging with terror. She struggled, but he was so much larger than her that he had no trouble restraining her.

In his peripheral vision, Cam saw a figure lying on the floor in the kitchen, and with horror realized it was Lola, surrounded by blood.

Oh no.

"You should have taken our offer down in Gray, Cam," Thor said. "We could have all been colleagues, buddy."

"Let her go!" Cam said.

Thor tossed a look at Miss Carver. "We're doing this now, Cousin. To hell with giving this prick more time. The Woodsons are signing a new lease tonight."

Miss Carver gestured to the dining room. He noticed she gripped a small stun gun. "Go."

"No!" Cam shouted.

"Go sit down, or I'll bludgeon your wife's pretty face like I did Lola's." Thor tightened his grip on Dez. "Or maybe I'll settle for snapping her neck."

Cam had his phone in his pocket, but if he made one move to use it to call for help, he had no doubt Thor would follow through on his threat. He had proven himself a man of violence on many occasions.

Cam shuffled into the dining room.

"I knew you and the whore were conspiring," Miss Carver said, following him. She sneered: "She was ripe to be taught a lesson, the little strumpet."

Cam didn't know if Lola was alive or dead, but hoped if she was alive, she could hang on a little longer.

"Sit." Thor forced Dez into a chair.

"Get off me!" Dez screamed. "Oh, Jesus."

Thor clamped his hand on the back of her neck like a hook. "Knock it off, lady. No one's coming to save you. We're in my world. I'm your god."

Tears glistened in Dez's eyes. Cam felt powerless, prayed that if they went along with this they would come up with a plan.

Thor pointed at Cam. "You. Sit next to her. Like a good husband."

Cam obeyed. Dez shuddered with sobs. He put his arm around her.

Thor dropped his hand onto Cam's shoulder. The man's thick fingers dug into his flesh, making Cam wince.

Miss Carver came next to Dez and slid a folder onto the table.

"This contains the new lease amendment," Miss Carver said. "It's used in certain, special circumstances."

"This will be your forever home," Thor said. "Forever renting. No privileges. Twenty percent annual rent increases."

"No credit check required." Miss Carver grinned. She placed a ballpoint pen onto the table. "Sign."

"You're crazy," Dez sobbed. "Oh God. Please."

"*Sign.*" Thor squeezed Cam's shoulder. Pain leaped down his arm.

Slowly, Cam reached forward and grabbed the ballpoint pen. He noted the pen's pointed tip.

Thor leaned across the table and flipped open the folder.

Seizing the opportunity, Cam swung his arm and jammed the pen into Thor's liver.

83

For Dez, a situation that should have triggered only minor annoyance—seeing Miss Carver there at the rental—had descended into a nightmare with head-spinning quickness. Seeing Lola dead (or near dead) in the kitchen. Feeling big hands close around her throat, cutting off her breath. The sheer madness of what these evil people wanted them to do, signing a lease or an amendment, signing their lives away to devils.

She couldn't stop crying, couldn't get a handle on her fear, but a voice in the back of her head, the voice that knew she had to look out for her family no matter what, told her, *take any opportunity you get to get free.*

It happened when Cam stabbed Thor in the stomach with a ball-point pen.

The big man gasped and reeled away from the table, the pen jutting out of his side. Cam shot out of his chair, the chair tipping back and crashing against the carpet.

Beside Dez, Miss Carver snarled. The woman had a stun gun, Dez had remembered seeing. She was going to use it on them to regain control of the situation.

Dez grabbed the woman's bony arm.

"Get off me, you heathen!" Miss Carver cried.

Screaming, Dez launched out of the chair and onto the woman. They fell onto the floor together, the older lady cushioning Dez's fall. She squirmed beneath Dez, got her fists deep in Dez's hair and tugged, her face a red mask of rage.

It felt as if she were ripping out Dez's hair by the roots. Dez howled.

But Miss Carver had dropped the stun weapon. It had fallen beneath the table, within Dez's reach.

Gritting her teeth, tears streaming down her cheeks, Dez seized the weapon, mashed the button, and pressed the business end against Miss Carver's long neck.

Miss Carver went rigid as a log as electricity surged into her, her lips frozen in a rictus of agony, her fingers twitching uselessly around Dez's head.

Weeping, Dez rolled away from the incapacitated woman. She looked over her shoulder.

Thor staggered out of the dining room, leaving a trail of blood. Cam swung to Dez.

"Call 911," he said. "Check on Lola."

"Okay." She swallowed. "Here."

She tossed the stun gun to her husband.

He caught it, looked from the weapon to the darkened hallway, where their tormentor had fled.

"I'm finishing this," Cam said.

84

As thunder boomed and echoed through the night, Cam pursued Thor through the house.

The pen he had driven into Thor's liver had wounded the man, forcing a temporary retreat, but Cam understood Thor's true nature: he would never relent. He was, in his way, as stubborn as Cam.

I'm not backing down. We finish this.

He didn't plan to kill Thor, didn't arm himself with anything except the stun gun, but he needed to stop Thor from coming back while they waited for help to arrive. A man like Thor, when he saw the walls closing in, would take hostages. Cam had allowed this man to bully him and his family for long enough.

He only prayed the ambulance arrived in time to save Lola's life.

As the storm raged, the lights stuttered erratically. Cam tracked Thor to the main hallway, couldn't see any more blood on the dark hardwood floors.

But he thought he heard Thor rambling upstairs.

Cam climbed the staircase, too. It was dark up there, but a few drops of crimson on the carpeted steps confirmed his suspicion.

At the top of the staircase, Cam flipped the switch to turn on the hallway lights.

More blood droplets glistened on the carpet, like a trail of breadcrumbs. It led to the master bedroom suite.

The bedroom door hung open, but the room beyond was dark.

"Dez called the police," Cam said. He stalked along the corridor. "It's over, Thor. All of it. Those cameras you guys keep running will be evidence of what you did. You're done."

Thunder rocked the night. The lights flickered—and went out.

No.

Thunder rumbled again, so loud it seemed to originate from directly above the house. Holding the stun weapon in one hand, Cam dug inside his pocket, grabbed his phone.

As the screen brightened, he saw a shadowed, hulking figure bearing down on him.

Thor, coming fast.

Cam raised the stun gun and mashed the trigger.

Blue electricity crackled, but unlike a Taser, which fired projectiles, a stun gun had to be pressed against your attacker's body, but in the darkness, he couldn't get a handle on Thor's exact location.

Pain erupted in Cam's shoulder.

Cam yelped, dropped the stun gun.

The lights flickered back on.

Thor was upon him, a club in his hand, a maniacal grin on his face.

"I'll tell *you* when it's over," Thor said. "Pawn."

Cam spun to flee into a nearby bedroom.

The lights stuttered again, dropping him into darkness.

He banged against a doorway with his wounded shoulder, sending a fresh spike of pain down his arm.

He heard Thor behind him, grunting.

The lights flickered on.

Thor swung the club. It shattered the drywall, chips flying.

He had missed Cam, barely. He charged into the room.

Cam saw the stun weapon lying on the floor, inches outside the doorway.

The lights went out as Thor wound up for another swing.

Cam dropped to his knees. He scurried like a crab across the room to the doorway, Thor's legs brushing past him.

Crawling worsened the agonizing pain in his shoulder, but he ignored it.

He tried to recall exactly where the stun gun had landed, groping ahead of him like a blind man.

"Gonna smash you," Thor said.

Cam's hand closed over something that felt like a weapon. He got his finger on the trigger.

The lights flared on again.

Thor loomed above him. Cam jammed the business end against Thor's stomach and pressed the trigger.

Thor roared like a speared lion.

Using both hands despite his own pain, Cam kept the stun gun mashed against him.

Gasping, twitching, Thor lurched past him, to the catwalk railing. Unable to stop himself, his limbs moving with a mind of their own, he tipped over the edge and flipped over, plummeted to the hard floor below, the impact of his body striking the floor sounding like another crash of thunder, the house settling briefly into a silence . . . a stillness broken shortly thereafter by the wail of an approaching ambulance.

AFTER

Eleven months later

"It's too good to be true," Cam said.

He drove their Honda Odyssey toward the two-story brick home standing in the cul-de-sac. A "Sold" sign stood in the front yard.

"Too good to be true?" Dez said. "How about well earned and well deserved?"

In the back seat, Ava played with a teddy bear. Next to her, their newborn son, Cameron Junior, lay in a rear-facing car seat, a mirror attached to the headrest allowing Cam and Dez to see his bright, innocent face.

Cam had long worried about achieving a credit score high enough for him to qualify for a mortgage on an eventual home purchase. Those concerns proved baseless. They had paid cash for the house, and for the new minivan, too.

Lola had survived that fateful night; reconstructive surgery repaired the damage to her face. She had kept her word and given Cam the "something I think you want"; before deleting the file of his new book from his computer and his cloud account, she had secretly saved it to a memory stick, intending to one day read the novel herself.

Cam's agent sold the novel to a publisher as the first title in a new, three-book contract for a high-six-figure sum. Foreign rights sales to fourteen countries brought in another mid-six-figure haul. A popular streaming company also got a piece of the action, purchasing the TV/film rights for almost one million.

The book had been published two weeks ago and debuted at the number five spot on the *New York Times* bestseller list.

Sometimes, Cam still couldn't believe the turn of events.

He parked in the driveway. They had closed on the house that morning, a fresh set of keys in his pocket.

"I still feel as if I'm dreaming," Cam said. "What a ride, huh?"

Thor had survived that night, too. Thor, Luke, and Sandra Carver had earned lengthy prison sentences for running their criminal rental-property ring for decades. Dozens of tenants, old and new, came forward as witnesses to testify about the long history of coercion, blackmail, and violence. Recorded evidence from the house Cam and Dez had rented (the bedroom closet indeed held high-tech recording equipment), as well as video from their other homes, sealed their fates.

"Quite a ride," Dez said.

After giving birth to their son, Dez took a leave from teaching. Although Cam assured her that she could stay on leave indefinitely, she planned to return to the classroom when their children were school-aged. *It's not a perfect career, but I can make a difference,* she said.

"All right, gang." Cam unbuckled his seat belt. "Are you ready to go inside?"

"Are we going to stay this time, Daddy?" Ava asked.

Since leaving "the bad place," as Ava called it, they had stayed with Dez's parents, and then in an apartment.

"We're staying this time," he said. "It's not a rental. It's all ours."

"Good." Ava clapped, as if this news met with her approval. "No more renting!"

Cam and Dez laughed.

The family went inside their new home together.

HEAR MORE FROM BRANDON

Did you enjoy this novel? Visit www.brandonmassey.com now to sign up for Brandon Massey's free mailing list. Mailing list members get advance news on the latest releases, the chance to win autographed copies in exclusive contests, and much more. Your email address will never be shared and you can unsubscribe at any time.

ABOUT BRANDON MASSEY

Brandon Massey was born June 9, 1973, and grew up in Zion, Illinois. He lives with his family near Atlanta, Georgia, where he is at work on his next novel. Visit his web site at www.brandon-massey.com for the latest news on his upcoming books.

Printed in Great Britain
by Amazon

42626659R00179